ACKNOWLEDGMENTS

ONCE AGAIN, Julie Schonhoff of J & M Printing has done a great job on the cover. Thanks, Julie. Thank you Bruce Johnson and Dennie Iverson for your expertise regarding fishing in the winter. Greetings to my friend Ardith Hoehn who once again has done a very good critique of the galley. Other readers I wish to thank are William Rusche, Vern Schanilec and Faye Schanilec.

The cost of my son Clay's creative writing education at the University of Iowa has once again paid off as he has done the copy-edit of *Ice Lord*. Likewise my daughter Kris's education. She did the final proof along with Hap McCleery, the publisher.

Thank you BJ for the use of your business name, *Lakes Brewed Awakening*. The same thanks goes to Laura for *Bookin' It* book store in Little Falls. Thank you Josh Hanson for *Spanky's*.

Scripture references have been taken from the Bible *New Living Translation* second edition. This novel in no way whatsoever intends to discredit the Bible and its supporters.

ICE LORD

For Judy
05-09-2015
Have a great summer

By: Ernest Francis Schanilec

Also by Ernest Francis Schanilec

Blue Darkness

The Towers

Danger in the Keys

Purgatory Curve

Gray Riders

Sleep Six

Night Out in Fargo

Gray Riders II

ICE LORD

Author - Ernest Francis Schanilec
Publisher - J&M Printing, Inc. - PO Box 248 - Gwinner, ND 58040 - 1-800-437-1033

International Standard Book Number: 978-1-931916-56-1

Printed in the United States of America

DEDICATIONS

THIS NOVEL IS DEDICATED TO ALL THE READERS of my books, especially if they had a good experience.

1

THE FISHERMAN LUNGED AT THE DOOR. He slipped and dropped to all fours. Bob Keller had been in his fishing house since dusk on the first Sunday in January of 2008. He pushed the palm of one of his hands against his forehead to support a hammering headache. Bob gasped for air, the inner lining of his nostrils burning fiercely.

He got to his knees and grasped the door handle with both hands. It turned. Then he thrust his left shoulder against the door. It opened only slightly, letting in a whiff of cold air. Bob inhaled deeply. "Damn! That door should open," he muttered, sounding like a whining calf.

My lungs! My lungs! he exclaimed to himself. What's wrong? I can't breathe! He lowered his body to the floor and rolled over on his side, gasping for air.

Terrifying thoughts raced through his mind. Someone has plugged the vent outside. I've got to smash through that door. Dizzily, he got up on his feet. In spite of his wobbly legs, he made it to the door a second time. Then he gave it a push with his shoulder. Nothing happened. It didn't even open a crack as it had minutes ago.

The fishing hole—oxygen! He dropped to his knees and crawled toward the hole that he had cut into the ice earlier. Bob extended his neck as far as he could and rested his chin on the rugged edge of ice. He inhaled over and over again, attempting to satisfy his need for oxygen. In seconds, he recovered. I've got to get out of here, he said to himself.

His thoughts flashed back to a few minutes earlier when he had heard a snowmobile approach and stop nearby. Bob remembered hearing the crunch of footsteps in the snow.

Panicking, Bob crawled back toward the door. If it's partially open—even a small crack—it will save me, he thought. He got to the door and pushed on it with the top of his head. Again, it didn't budge. He slowly raised his right arm, his forefinger feeling the handle. Bob tried to stretch his arm farther. Then it dropped. His mind drifted.

Momentarily, his brain awoke from a burst of air. He heard the latch click and the door open. His lungs hurt and he heard gurgling noises coming from his own throat. Then he was being dragged along the floor. The smell—someone is in here. He felt his rear end being plunked down on the chair. The helpless fingers of his right hand got jerked forward. His left arm got moved onto his lap.

He heard footsteps on the floor, then the slam of a door—then a click. His head moved slightly when he heard a snowmobile engine. It got louder for a moment, and then slowly the sound dissipated. Except for wind slapping against the small structure, it became deadly quiet. Deep sleep followed.

JOHN OLSON FLIPPED CHANNELS with his remote looking for a television program that fit his fancy. He and his bride had just finished watching a movie on one of the premium channels. John looked forward to Sunday evenings—spending them with his wife. John purchased the house the previous fall. He fell in love with the sunsets on Lake Sallie, a few miles from the city of Big Lakes.

The sound of a snowmobile caught his attention. He saw the lights fanning out across the snow on the lake. It stopped next to a cluster of fishing houses. Sort of late to be going out fishing, he thought and clicked the remote again.

"Do you want some popcorn?" Sharon asked, her voice muffled by the wall between the kitchen and where he sat.

"Yes, honey, lots of it," he answered and glanced out the window.

The roaring sound of the snowmobile dissipated in the distance, as did the headlights. John's face broke into a smile, energized by the smell of popcorn.

"What's on? Anything interesting?" Sharon asked as she set the popcorn bowl down on the end table.

"Naw, just a bunch of rot. We have close to fifty channels and most of 'em are junk. That was a darn good movie, though."

"You should start reading, John."

"Yeah...yeah...someday."

He brought up a fistful of corn to his mouth. "It sure didn't stay long," he said with a mouth partially full.

"What didn't stay long?" Sharon asked.

"The snowmobile...out there."

"What about it?"

"Usually the fishermen—" John continued to chew and swallowed. "—are gone by now. The last one just left."

"Bone chilling...who'd want to be out there on a cold night like this anyway? Some of your friends are nuts."

John laughed and looked back to the television. "Ah, there's the news. Time for bed right after that."

Sharon returned into the kitchen.

A FRESH LAYER OF SNOW CARPETED THE GROUND in the Lake Sallie area on Monday, the next morning. John sipped his coffee. He backed his chair away from the table and walked to the window. "Hey, Sharon, a snowmobile is still out there—next to Bob Keller's house."

Sharon walked into the room, all dressed for work in a neat pair of black slacks and a red sweater. Her black onyx necklace bounced slightly as she walked to the window. "Hmmm, maybe he couldn't get the darn thing started."

John shook his head. "No one knows snowmobile engines better than Bob."

"Well, it happens to you a lot, doesn't it? Why couldn't it happen to him?"

John shrugged his shoulders and left the room. He returned with his coat on. "Time for me to go to work." He walked over to the window. "Maybe I should call Vern at DNR—check out Bob's fishing house."

2

THE SUN EMERGED ABOVE THE RIM OF TREES to the southeast for the first time since before Christmas, spreading shadowy spikes over the snow-covered bay. Tom Hastings, cup of coffee in hand, looked out his window that same early January Monday morning.

The upper branches of the tall oaks and ash trees swayed with the breeze that delivered cold air from Canada. He watched a gray squirrel claw at the organic remains that had dropped from a tall Black Hills spruce. The rodent successfully loaded his mouth with supplies and scurried up the trunk.

He thought about the C-SPAN television program he had watched the previous evening. His friend Julie testified for the better part of a day before a senate committee investigating the McDougal-Togolese financial relationship.

Tom thought the senator was in big trouble. He also thought Julie would never return to Border's Lake. His spirits momentarily lifted thinking about the good times that the two of them had had over the years. It's all done...I'm totally alone again.

Well, not exactly alone, he said to himself, watching a gray squirrel attack his bird feeder. He couldn't believe that the aggressive rodent would take the risk of plunging into the tube, clawing at the thistle feed. Tom was angry because the feeder was the fourth one that he had purchased within the last month.

Tom eyed his pellet gun, loaded and leaning against the wall near the door. I hate killing animals, he thought, but....

Returning to the kitchen to refill his coffee cup, Tom hoped the squirrel would vacate the feeder before he returned to his dining-room table. I wonder what the upcoming year has in store for me this time around. Tom chuckled, thinking about the barn and cornfield he got caught in during the recent senator's residency last summer.

The phony Department of Agriculture project is gone, he said to himself. The corn has been harvested and the field is covered with snow. The plastic bubble is gone. Hans is gone. The military guys are gone. I can now safely go for a ski run or walk.

Tom Hastings's home was on the shoreline of a bay extension of Border's Lake, four miles from the town of New Dresden. It was one of the lakes that surrounded the town of approximately 400 residents. During the past three years, he had gotten caught up in serious conflicts and his life and well-being had been threatened.

He clicked his teeth together thinking about the monster machine that almost ran over him in his neighbor's cornfield. The ambitious senator from North Dakota had engaged a German scientist to condense the oxygen from the top of a corn stalk and pass it over a new element discovered deep in the ground in Togo, Africa. The generated heat was transferred to the drive train of a Ford mustang, powering the car. Tom's curiosity had gotten him into trouble with the militant guards that protected the senator's secret.

It's time to go into New Dresden for the mail, Tom thought. He put on his jacket and stood by the door, staring at the artistic glitter in the icicles, hanging from the roof before the bright sun. Life goes on, he thought, smiling, as he backed his vehicle out of the garage.

He passed by a dairy farm and caught up with four snowmobiles zigzagging across the bottoms of the ditches, narrowly missing the power-line pole support cables. Geez that looks dangerous, Tom thought. But then, I used to do the same thing.

Tom pulled his gray SUV up at the curb next to the post office after doing a perfect U-turn. He watched a man walk up the handicap ramp and hurry into the building. Tom left his vehicle, entered the mail-box room and saw the same man standing next to the counter. The man glanced at Tom and quickly looked away. Geez, that's a strange-looking face, Tom thought. A weird white—sort of like the surface of the dumplings my mother used to make.

The man soon left without saying a word. Tom walked out onto Main Street and followed him toward the grocery store. The man sped up, crossed the street at an angle and kept going in spite of a semi-truck approaching the intersection. Its hissing brakes slowed it in time to prevent an accident. Tom held his breath watching the truck make a wide turn and head toward Nabor's Service Station. Dirty fragments of icy snow fell from its wheels and lay in the street. Tom expected to see the man after the truck had passed, but he had disappeared.

TERRY PENDLETON GLANCED BACK TOWARD MAIN STREET. He entered his house and tossed the mail on the kitchen table. Why did that man look at me so suspiciously at the post office? he said to himself. I was just minding my own business...that man and others in this town need to do that also.

He had bought his house within the past year, moving from Big Lakes where he owned and operated a shoe repair shop. Terry had sold his home in Big Lakes because his neighbors spied on him. Every time I drove up into my driveway, they all stared at me, he thought. They must've thought I'm awful stupid, not noticing the movement in the curtains.

Terry took off his shoes and entered his private room—his sanctuary, he called it. Inside the room, two fish tanks, each set on four legs, took up one wall. A single tank occupied the side opposite. Across from the door, a bench hosted two multiple candle holders. He pulled out a drawer and picked out a match to light the candles. *It's ready....*

His short stocky legs supported a paunchy frame, a large chest and wide shoulders with long dangling arms. He knelt down and clasped his hands together. Murmuring, he said, "I have obeyed you,

Lord. Those that disobey you must be penalized. Thor at your service…."

Thor moved his lips in silent prayer. Minutes later, he stood, feeling theocratic—anointed by God. He creased his narrow lips and blew the candles out. Thor gently closed the door and walked to his closet. He put on his coat and cap. *Alright, Terry, let's go to work.* He backed his car out of the garage and headed for his place of business in Big Lakes.

3

BIG LAKES COUNTY DEPUTY IZZY FELTON sat in a chair in her office. She glanced at the clock on the wall. This day is really dragging by, she said to herself. Minnesota has slowed to a crawl.

Her dark brown ponytail bounced on a stiff collar that tightened firmly around her narrow neck as she moved her head. She wore large plastic-framed glasses, the thick lenses slightly distorting her sky-blue eyes. Her phone rang. "Felton."

"Hi, Izz, this is Vern."

"Oh, yeah, DNR, right?"

"You got it."

"What can I do for you today?"

"I'm calling from Lake Sallie. We gotta dead guy in a fishing house over here—one of those small boxes on a lake. Sort of looks like his gas heater outlet plugged and he died of carbon monoxide. The fella is frozen solid."

"Huh, that sounds God awful," Izzy said.

"There's something weird here, though."

"What's that?"

"The man was cradling a Bible in his left arm."

Silence.

"Izzy, are you there?"

"A Bible? Now that's a new one. Better leave everything alone. I'll get the ball rolling and we'll be out there shortly."

"Okay, but bring snowmobiles—ice should be okay for cats, but don't trust it for a vehicle."

"See you in about an hour."

IZZY FELTON HAD JOINED THE BIG LAKES SHERIFF'S STAFF the previous year. Her first investigative case came when a U.S. senator's secretary was murdered on Border's Lake. That crime and other lawless activities baffled Izzy and her partner. Because of the complexity of the case, they became deputized by the police in Fargo. She and her partner participated in the solution to the crimes at a country club in Fargo.

She shook her head thinking about Tom Hastings, the man who risked his life attacking the murderer. His evening date, Julie Huffman, was grabbed and held as a hostage by the perpetrator against a wall. I couldn't believe what Hastings did, she thought. He put his shoulder into the two of them and successfully forced the gun out of the murderer's fist.

Izzy rode in the first of two SUV vehicles. Each pulled a trailer with two snowmobiles. Her driver turned off Highway 59 onto Shoreham Lane. She saw the sign *Shoreview,* a local bar and grill.

Finally they turned onto the public access road. Both vehicles stopped, and they unloaded the snowmobiles. "Hey, Izzy, you take the red one. Ya know how to run it?"

"Is the pope Catholic?" Izzy said, smiling.

Two men stood next to the door of one of the small houses when they arrived. Izzy dismounted and stood. She slipped and almost fell making her first step.

"Hi, Vern, good to see you again," she said.

"This is one of my associates, Brent."

Vern's associate had the looks of an average man in the 40's. His dark brown hair clung to his head, every hair appearing to be in perfect position.

"Hi, Brent, I'm Deputy Felton. Nice to meet you."

Agent Vern opened the door to the fishing house.

Izzy peaked in. "Holy smokes—just like you described it, Vern."

She took a step inside and turned her head. "Val, get me a bag big enough for this book, will ya?'

Izzy put on plastic gloves and gently raised the Bible. She grasped a corner of the open page and bent it inward. Then, she closed it and handed it to another deputy next to the door. "Hand me a flashlight, would ya, Val?"

She slowly scanned the insides of the fishing house and used her flashlight to light up all the dark corners. After examining the victim, she stepped outside. "All right, Val. Lets get 'em on one of the machines. The ambulance should be over at the access by now."

Izzy cringed as the men carried the body outside and loaded it onto the rear part of a snowmobile seat. She had seen her share of victims during her career, but still felt the reality of someone losing their life. She walked over to one of the snowmobile drivers. "Would you spin this machine around and stop it right under the exhaust pipe on the other side of the building?" One of the other deputies had already photographed the tracks near the building.

Izzy stepped up onto the snowmobile and reached a hand to the top of the pipe. "There's something in it, guys. Have you got a blade or something, Val?"

"I feel stupid that I didn't check that before," Val said. He opened up a switch blade and pried out part of an object. "Huh...an apple, Izz."

SHERIFF DAVE JOHNSON STUDIED THE TWO SHEETS OF PAPER lying on his desk. "What do ya make of it, Izz? I don't know much about this Bible stuff."

He ran a hand up his forehead and through his thinning, blond hair. His blue eyes and neatly manicured fingernails suggested he may have been a college professor.

Izzy cleared her throat. She grimaced. "Could be suicide. That would explain the Bible: The guy plugged up the vent intentionally. He then prayed 'till he lost consciousness…then died."

The sheriff nodded.

Izzy held up her hand. "There are a couple of things that bother me, though."

Dave's eyes widened. "And?"

She smacked her lips together. "Why would the guy still be fishing? The Bible should have been held in both hands if he was waiting to die."

"And what else?"

"We have a couple of witnesses." She opened a page in her notebook. "A John and Sharon Olson. They're the ones who called Vern first thing this morning. They saw the lights of a snowmobile coming—and then leaving."

"And what time was that?"

"News time—just before they went to bed."

The sheriff sighed. "Not unusual though for snowmobiles to drive around at night."

"Yes, but, this one went to the fishing houses and then shut down. The Olsons estimate about ten minutes of time elapsed between coming and going."

"What was used to clog the exhaust pipe?" the sheriff asked.

"An apple."

"An apple! What the heck? Did you find a lunch kit or bag in the shack?"

Izzy shook her head.

"So the guy brings an apple and a Bible and a fishing rod. He fishes for a while—then goes out and clogs the pipe."

"Yeah, but why wouldn't he reel the line in?"

The sheriff shrugged his shoulders.

"Something else, too," Izzy said. She waited for the sheriff to respond.

Dave smiled. "Okay, what else? Let's have it."

"We couldn't find the padlock."

"What padlock?"

"Most all fishing houses are locked with a padlock when the owner isn't there. That house had a hasp...but we couldn't find the lock. It should've been hanging there."

"Maybe this guy didn't use one?"

"Maybe not...but...but from what I've heard, most everyone does."

"Do you know of anyone that would know?" the sheriff asked.

"No, Dave, but we're working on it."

He shrugged his shoulders again.

4

TOM HASTINGS MADE THE TURN onto the county highway and headed for New Dresden on Tuesday. Most of the fresh snow had been blown off the surface of the road by a piercing western breeze. The snow glistened from rays of the sun in the cemetery where his wife rested eternally.

After getting his mail and buying a *Fargo Forum* at Stillman's Super Market, he entered Border's Café. Henry, his friend of many years, sat at his usual table under the menu board. Tom took off his coat and sat down across from him.

"When are you headin' south?" Tom asked.

"Couple of weeks."

"Goin' to the same place?"

"Yup."

"Would you like to order, sir?" a waitress asked.

"The special and coffee."

The waitress nodded and hastened away.

"What's new, Henry?"

"If you open that paper to the fourth page, you'll notice that an ice fisherman died on Sallie a couple of days ago."

Tom brought the page up closer to his eyes. "Hmmm, a Bob Keller found dead in a fishing house. Did you know him…or of him?"

"Yes, very much so. He used to work for us."

"Says here that he was asphyxiated," Tom said, grasping his coffee cup.

Henry nodded. "It doesn't say it in the paper but he was holding a Bible when he died."

Tom's eyes widened. "I suppose that could happen, especially if it was a suicide."

"No way," Henry said.

"Why not?"

"Bob was an atheist. He didn't know a Bible from a fence post."

Tom raised his eyebrows. "Maybe at the very end…."

Henry's eyes narrowed, smiling. "I think there's more to Bob's death then the cops have told us."

Henry stood, dropped a bill on the table and headed for check-out.

THE MICROWAVE CLOCK READ 4:30. Tom walked over to his wood stove and dropped in another log. Time for my walk, he thought.

The crunching sound from his boots in the snow disturbed a downy woodpecker as Tom walked his trail toward the tennis court. The colorful bird skipped out of sight to the back side of an oak tree—one that had an exaggerated base. Tom stopped to listen to the rat-a-tat of the beak digging into the bark.

He continued past the court and reached the edge of the woods next to an apple orchard. Years back there were twenty apple trees. An extra-cold winter killed most of them. Only two trees remained. They provided food for the deer. Tom stopped. A short distance away, two deer stood in the grassy snow. He felt amazed. The buck's rack is the biggest one that I've ever seen, he said to himself, not moving a muscle.

The doe lay down in the grass as the buck continued to watch him. That has to be Prancer's son, Tom thought, thinking about his experiences involving a special deer about three years ago. The big deer lowered its head and munched on the grass. Then, the animal lifted his head high, revealing a spectacular rack. Tom continued to stare in amazement.

Tom took one step and the two deer bounded off. He watched their white tails disappear into the woods, still feeling awed by the size of the antlers.

He felt an eastern breeze, carrying with it a chill after passing over the ice of the lake. Tom entered his house, took off his outer clothes and headed for the kitchen. He saw a snowmobile heading toward a cluster of fishing houses. Geez, there're seven of the little boxes out there today, he said to himself. A new one added lately.

TOM SPENT HIS EVENING WATCHING A MINNESOTA GOPHERS BASKETBALL GAME. Aren't they ever going to win a Big Ten game? he asked himself. He dozed off during the second half, awakening after the game had ended. He pressed the off button and walked into the kitchen. A narrow pair of headlights streaked toward the cluster of fishing houses. Someone's gonna be fishing late, he thought.

Before going to sleep, he thought about the phone call that he had gotten earlier in the day. One of his former friends had called from Kansas City. Jolene Hunt had accepted a position with a realty company in Big Lakes. Geez, she's comin' back, he said to himself. What's that going to mean for me? Only the spirits know. We got pretty close to each other back then. Heck, we could've even gotten married.

The image of a railroad locomotive crashing into a pickup on Main Street in New Dresden wandered into his mind. It was her dad that got killed...a victim of a money-hungry nephew. The people of the town of New Dresden lived in fear for several months until the perpetrators were brought to justice.

I wonder, he mused, why Jolene is coming back.

5

TERRY PENDLETON LOOKED OVER THE FRAME of his glasses and examined a shoe that needed new heels and soles. “I can have those ready for you next Tuesday.”

The senior gentleman accepted the slip. “Thank you very much. See you then.” He supported his frame with a cane and made his way to the door. Terry watched as he left and limped his way to his car parked on Washington Avenue.

Terry read *5:30* on the clock in his shop. He sat down on his stool next to his bench and continued where he had left off, repairing a pair of Red Wing boots.

He had felt greatly troubled the past two months since the fishing houses first appeared on local lakes. *Sundays are reserved for the Lord, he said to himself. Those that pursue the innocent on Sundays will die a fiery death and spend eternity in Hell.*

Year after year he felt depressed driving around the lakes and seeing vehicles parked on lakes on Sundays. He threaded the last stitch into the heel area. Terry brought the boots up close to his eyes and examined them carefully. They’re ready, he said to himself, and placed them in a plastic bag on the shelf above his bench. He opened a drawer and brought out his invoice pad. Terry wrote down the price and stapled the slip to the plastic. Then he wrote up the shoe tag and stapled that, too.

Terry shut the drawer and opened up the one directly below. He gingerly removed a Bible. He set it down on the bench and left his stool to lock the front door. He flipped the cardboard sign to show the public that he was closed.

He returned to the bench, picked up the Bible and sat down in a heavily worn easy chair. Terry flipped open the book, using his marker as a guide. He read slowly and silently: *But those who have become defiled and do not purify themselves will be cut off from the community for they have defied the sanctuary of the Lord.*

Terry closed the book, returning it to the drawer. He put on his black coat and black cap. "Thor is here now, Lord," he muttered and exited the back door. He got into his black SUV, started the engine and put his head down to pray. *Lord, give me the strength to carry out your will.*

THOR STARED AT HIS SNOWMOBILE perched on a trailer in his roomy garage. He pressed a button and watched the overhead door close. Thor walked slowly toward the back door of his house. He felt peace of mind as he entered his kitchen.

He had bought the small house last year. I got it for half price, he said to himself, smiling. My house in Big Lakes sold for twice the money. His new house and lot were located in the southwest section of New Dresden. Thor checked the thermostat and rotated the control. Bitter cold outside.

Thor opened the refrigerator door and fingered through his choices for dinner. He brought out a package of frozen fish and set it down on the counter. *Today I obey the Lord and eat his deliverance.* Pausing by a door, he slowly pushed it open.

He studied the fish and lit the candles.

GARTH SABOLIK EASED HIS ARTIC CAT ATV down the trailer ramp. He pressed the starter and grinned when the engine roared. He backed the machine to the hitch of his fishing house he had brought over earlier in the day. After securing them together, he slowly drove the ATV down onto the ice-covered bay on Border's Lake.

He pulled the square-looking structure westward toward a cluster of other fishing houses. Garth disconnected the trailer hitch and used his blocky frame to tilt the fishing house upright. Garth opened the door and released the catch on a bracket that had been used to attach his ice auger to the wall.

The auger started on the third pull and he drilled a hole in the ice. Judging the hole satisfactory, he walked outside and hauled in his 20-pound tank of LP gas. After connecting it to a metallic heater, he opened the valve and struck a match to light the gas burner. Garth walked back outside and checked the exhaust pipe of the house. Nodding, he carried in a chair, a cooler and fishing gear from a box suspended on the rear frame of his ATV.

Garth opened his tackle box and baited a hook. Dropping the line into the water, he reached into the cooler and brought out a can of beer. Raising the can, he took a sip and smiled. This is as close to heaven as you can get, he said to himself, thinking about his wife Nettie's displeasure that he would miss church again on Sunday morning.

He fished for two hours, catching a crappie and two bluegills. Garth looked at his watch. The football playoffs were scheduled to start in an hour. He closed the valve on the gas tank and organized his gear. Minutes later, his ATV roared back up the snowy roadway toward his pickup and trailer.

6

TOM HASTINGS STOPPED AT STILLMAN'S SUPER MARKET to pick up the Sunday newspaper. The clerk informed him that the thief, who had broken into Quality Supply twice, had been caught. According to her, the robber had stolen a car in Pine Lakes, then driven it to New Dresden to rob the store. He escaped in the vehicle and returned it to his home in Chilton Mills. It had just snowed and the officers followed the tracks and found the stolen vehicle parked in front of a house. An immediate arrest was made.

Tom chuckled, adding to the noisy chatter of patrons hanging around the checkout counter.

He headed north in his vehicle, passing the ball diamond. Geez, they never did get those bases picked up last fall, he said to himself. Oh well, they'll be ready to go in the spring after the snow melts.

Tom walked into his kitchen and saw an ATV leave the fishing house area down below on the snow-covered bay. He grabbed a bottle of beer from his refrigerator and headed back into his den. The New York Giants were playing the Dallas Cowboys in the National League final for the right to go to the Super Bowl.

He read the story about the fisherman found dead in his fishing house on Lake Sallie. The police had concluded that it was a suicide. Tom looked up at the ceiling, remembering what Henry had said about the victim...an atheist. Why the Bible? Tom asked himself.

JOLENE HUNT LOOKED IN THE MIRROR in her new bedroom. Not bad for a senior citizen, she said to herself. Tom is going to like me being slim. She had permanently moved from Kansas City to be near her half-brother Steve Steiger. They had discovered each other a couple of years ago after their paternal father was criminally killed in a train crash. The victim owned and operated a hog farm with his brother, who was murdered later, but in a different manner. Steve currently operated the hog farm.

She walked into the living room and sat on the couch, patiently waiting for her buzzer to announce the arrival of her date. She felt anxious to see him after leaving the area to move back to Kansas City. She had accomplished her objective to override the jurisdiction of the local sheriff and investigate her father's death on her own.

Jolene smiled thinking about how she coaxed her new friend into a sneaky visit to the Talbot farm. We actually got away with it...well not quite. I got arrested by the sheriff. Tom had to shoot our way past the punk of a nephew out in that field. Then, we all got caught, Tom, me and my brother Steve. She laughed. The corrupt sheriff was going to blow us up in that machine shop. Thank God that Deputy Johnson and the other officers showed up when they did.

The buzzer went off. "Hello, Tom. Come on up."

Her heart fluttered as she walked toward the door. She heard the knock and nervously turned the knob. Tom's big smile erased her anxiety. She accepted his massive hug. Jolene gasped and coughed lightly as he finally released her.

"You look great, Jolene."

"So do you."

"Come on in and lets have a glass of wine. Still drink some, do ya?" she added.

"Yup, sure do."

TOM AND JOLENE CHATTED as he drove his vehicle to Bayside Restaurant. The classic bar and grill was one of the few in the area that remained open in January. Jolene got another hug after they entered. This one came from her former classmate Brenda, who managed the restaurant.

"This place looks as inviting as ever," Jolene said after she sat down on the chair that Tom had pulled back for her.

Tom nodded and opened a menu. "How about a bottle of Chardonnay? Got a good one here from Australia."

Jolene laughed. "Remember when we used to go out to Mary Ann's?"

"Yeah, I sure do—how could I forget?"

Jolene continued to laugh. "That young punk sure whacked you one."

"It didn't feel very funny to me," Tom said, taking another sip of wine. He set the glass down.

"Well, they're all either in jail or dead—and here you are safe and sound."

Tom raised his eyebrows. "You're gonna have a hard time talkin' me into trouble again."

"Oh shucks. You remember Steve, don't you?"

Tom nodded.

"Well, he has a deluxe fishing house on your lake. I thought we could make dinner out there some evening."

"So that's who owns the big one. There must be a dozen out there—one of them looks like a house."

Jolene laughed. "It's even got a bathroom."

"Would you like another glass of wine?" the waitress asked.

"Yup, sure would," Tom said.

Jolene's face tensed. "Better be careful there, young man. I may have to drive you home."

"That's my last one. No more."

TOM AND JOLENE GOT UP FROM THE TABLE. He carried the slip and his check over to pay. "Are you okay to drive, Tom?"

"Yup, that cup of coffee did the trick," he said.

Tom pushed on the outside door.

"Cripes, it's cold out here," Jolene said.

He dashed ahead and pressed the switch on his key fob. Then he opened the door.

The drive to Jolene's apartment took only a few minutes. "Come on in for a bit if you wish," she said.

Tom sat down on the couch and flicked on the TV. Fifteen minutes later he fell sound asleep.

"Tom, wake up, it's two o'clock."

He jerked upright. "Did I fall asleep?"

"Fall asleep! You've been out for over three hours."

"Impossible." Tom stood.

"Not impossible. I went to bed—didn't want to disturb you. Do you think you feel well enough to drive home?"

"Drive home? Ah—yeah—drive home. I'll be fine."

Tom left Jolene's apartment shortly after 2:00 a.m. He left town on Highway 59, heading south. He turned onto a county road a few miles later that took him into New Dresden. He felt good when the lights of New Dresden appeared after passing over a hill. Tom slowed his vehicle to 30.

Suddenly two persons ran across the street directly ahead of him. Tom hit the brakes. What the heck are they carrying? Looks like a bag of grain, he said to himself. They had come from the direction of the gas station. The man on the street side opened the back door of a car parked at the curb, next to the bank. He tossed inside whatever he was carrying. Something had fallen to the pavement. He stooped to pick it up and held it for a moment. Geez, that's a crowbar, Tom said to himself. The man tossed it into the back seat, too.

Tom stopped at the stop sign and pressed the knob to open his window. The man opened the driver's side door and turned his head. Tom stared into a pair of dark, beady eyes. The person wore a tight black stocking cap. He had a narrow face partially covered with dark whiskers.

The man quickly got in and closed the door. The rusty white car's front wheels spun and screeched as the vehicle jerked onto the street and headed up the county highway in the direction of Highway 59.

TOM WOKE UP THE NEXT DAY WITH A HEADACHE. Way too much wine, he thought. He strode down the steps and fired up the woodstove. Then he started the coffee pot. "Dinner in a fishing house!" he muttered. What will she think of next? he asked himself.

It's the third Sunday in January, he thought. No game today... shucks...a whole week to wait for the Super Bowl. He looked out over the lake. He saw one ATV and a snowmobile. The reddish machine was parked next to the large house. That must be Steve's.

He filled his travel mug with coffee, draining the last of the dark liquid from the pot. Tom headed out to the garage. He drove into town. The bases on the ball diamond were more visible than the day before with the temperature hovering at 20 degrees above normal.

He stopped at the Main Street stop sign and thought about the two men he had seen the previous night. Tom recollected Ellie at Stillman's Super Market telling him about a previous robbery at the same station. Geez, I suppose I better report what I saw to the cops.

7

THOR PARKED HIS BLACK SUV AND TRAILER in the public access lot on the northern shore of Big Lake. He unfastened his Polaris snowmobile, grunting as he tugged. It slowly slipped off. Using his gloves, he wiped off the snow particles from one side of the cowl, exposing the white markings. His watch read 10:15 p.m.

A few minutes earlier, he had witnessed two snowmobile loadings. There should be only one left, he said to himself. He turned the key and the engine roared. Thor knelt on the seat as he pulled on his helmet and snapped the strap shut.

A regular superhighway, he thought, as he continued riding toward a cluster of over thirty fishing houses. Thor rotated the throttle and slowed as he approached the first house. His headlights flashed across the back end of a vehicle. He stopped his snowmobile a short distance away and turned the switch.

Thor inhaled. He smelled the exhaust coming from the pipe above the only occupied fishing house. He reached into a bag attached to the rear of his seat. His bare hand brought out an apple. He slowly walked toward the house, stepping as quietly as possible. Thor looked up at the sky. "Thou shall receive your punishment, soon," he whispered. *This is the fruit which God forbade you to eat. Now it will kill you.*

Two more steps and he stood quietly next to the small structure. Reaching up, he used his palm to push downward on the apple, closing the orifice of the pipe. Then he stepped around the fishing house and gently grasped the padlock, snapping it shut.

Thor held his breath for a few moments, slowly making his way back to his snowmobile. He anxiously waited. Suddenly, he heard a pounding sound. Thor waited in silence, wringing his hands together. He held his breath as the pounding sound lessened. He heard a shuffle. Soon all was quiet. Thor continued to wait, checking his wristwatch often. After ten minutes had passed, he reached into his case in the back and pulled out a bolt cutter, pausing to look toward the road to see the headlights of a noisy truck in the distance.

Snap! The padlock flew off and fell into the snow stacked against the base of the fishing house. He reached down with his bare hand, attempting to recover the lock. "Cold!" he exclaimed, sticking his hand into his pocket. Thor ignored the lock and opened the door. As he had expected and hoped, the fisherman lay in a heap on the floor. Thor grunted as he raised the limp body onto the seat. He pushed the torso against the wall, balancing it so it couldn't fall backwards. Thor rushed back outside and returned with a Bible.

DEPUTY IZZY FELTON CLENCHED HER TEETH and sucked in a lungful of air as she listened to the phone. She shook her head. Hanging up, she got up from her desk and walked down the hall. "Are ya busy, Dave?"

"Yes, I am, but—" She remained in the doorway and Dave frowned. "Somethin' big—ah can feel it."

Izzy nodded. "Another one, Dave."

"Another what?"

"Fisherman dead—dead with a Bible."

Dave whistled. "Uh-oh. Where did it happen? Same lake?"

"No. Big Lake this time."

Dave stood and walked to his coat rack. He put on his coat and hat. "We better get out there. Have you told Kelly yet?"

"Not yet, he was on the phone."

"Best he comes along."

"Okay."

THE DRIVE TO THE PUBLIC BOAT ACCESS on Big Lake took only five minutes after leaving the sheriff's office. DNR snowmobiles had been removed from their trailers and sat on the snow-laden slope, each with a male driver. Izzy got on a snowmobile and stretched her arms around the driver's waist. He turned the key and the engine started. The machine roared onto the lake. She put her nose against the back of his coat to escape the bitter wind.

She turned her head and saw Sheriff Johnson and Deputy Martin snuggled up to drivers as she was. The fourth machine carried a large bag of equipment behind that driver.

Izzy thought about the victim they investigated on Lake Sallie. He, too, had a Bible cradled in his lap. Goodbye to the suicide theory, she said to herself. The snowmobile stopped.

Sheriff Johnson and Deputy Martin stood by the door of the fishing house. They had their flashlights on. Izzy peaked through the door. "My God, it looks a ditto."

"It's a ditto alright," the sheriff said. "A suicide is not in play any longer," he added.

"Yeah, I thought the same thing on the way out here," Izzy said.

Deputy Martin dragged his boot in the loose snow alongside the base of the small wooden structure. He stooped down. "Hey, look at this. A padlock."

Martin shone his light directly on the object. "It's been cut, Kelly," Izzy said. "See that?" She pointed.

"Well for cripes sakes. Izzy, do you remember if we saw a padlock at Lake Sallie—the other one?"

She shook her head. "No, we didn't find any. According to people that we had interviewed, there should have been one. The guys use it to lock their fishing houses when they're gone."

Dave cleared his throat. "We must have missed it—probably still in the snow."

Izzy shone her flashlight all along the wooden floor of the victim's fishing house. "What the heck are those?" she said.

Martin stuck his head in. "What are you talking about?"

"Those funny looking things on the floor. They look like what's left when a cat gets done with a fish."

Izzy slipped on a pair of plastic gloves. She reached in her jacket and brought out a plastic bag. Izzy knelt down and picked up several small items and dropped them in.

"Those are fish tails," Martin said.

"Yeah, I think so...actually minnow tails."

"Well, you have secured 'em. You're doin' your job. They may or may not have anything to do with this crime."

Izzy stepped outside and heard two other snowmobiles drive up. "The ambulance is here."

Kelly and one of the DNR men helped place the body in a bag and load it onto a sled attached to the rear of one of the snowmobiles.

Izzy stepped inside the fishing house for one last look around. She came out. "I'm anxious to see if this Bible is opened to the same page as the other."

"Did you mark it before?" the sheriff asked.

"I turned in the corner of the page."

Dave nodded. "Right on the ball...good work."

Izzy looked out across the frozen lake. "All the photography is done. So far the evidence points in the same direction as the other case—the one on Sallie. Except for...."

"Except what?'

"The minnow tails."

"Ha," the sheriff grunted.

8

TOM PARKED HIS VEHICLE IN STILLMAN'S parking lot. Inside, he grabbed a *Forum* and placed three quarters down on the counter, immediately scanning the front page.

"Have you heard the latest?" Ellie asked.

"No, what's up?"

"Another fisherman dead."

Tom looked away from the paper. He narrowed his eyes and raised his chin. "Hmmm."

"You won't find it in there. It only happened late last night."

"Same lake?"

"Nope. Big Lake this time."

"Another suicide?"

"Nope. Likely murder!"

His mouth partially opened. "Murder? Both then, huh?"

Ellie nodded. "You better get over to the café. Henry should be there. He'll know more than I do. Also...."

"Also what?"

"The station across the street was robbed again."

Tom's froze in his tracks. "When?"

"Sunday night, someone said."

Tom narrowed his eyes, thinking about *glaring, dark eyes...a tight black stocking cap...a partially shaven face.*

"You look like you've seen a ghost, Tom," she said, frowning.

He blinked. Should I spit it out, he wondered? The police need to be told first, he thought. Would they believe me? Deputy Izzy would.

"Tom, are you okay?" Ellie asked.

"Oh yeah. Gotta go. See ya tomorrow."

He felt a pair of eyes staring at his back as he left the grocery store.

Tom hurriedly crossed the street and opened the door of the restaurant. He felt disappointed not seeing Henry at his usual table. The chatter didn't stop as he looked around, noticing several sets of eyes staring at him. Geez, they're all talking at once, he said to himself. He closed the door and headed for his vehicle.

DEPUTIES FELTON AND MARTIN WALKED INTO Lakes Brewed Awakening, a new eating establishment. Izzy insisted on having lunch there as she had heard so many good reports about it. They walked to the counter where customers placed their orders.

"What can I get for you?" a young woman asked. Her tan name tag read *Katie*. The two officers studied the menu.

Izzy said, "I'll have the veggie-wrap…and coffee."

Kelly nodded his head. "Same for me."

Izzy carried her coffee and a number tag to an open table. She sat down, placed the bag that she carried on the table, and took a sip of coffee. "Yum good, Kell."

"Nice place," Kelly said.

"Have you heard about the two food shop robberies in New Dresden?" Izzy said.

"No, I haven't. What's the deal?"

"Apparently it was mostly cigarettes taken. They were both pretty well cleaned out."

A second young woman arrived with two plates. "Hi, I'm BJ. Thanks for coming over. I hope you enjoy your lunch."

Izzy smiled. "Your restaurant is new, isn't it?"

"Yes, it is…I opened it last fall."

"Best of luck to you with your new business," Izzy said.

Kelly smiled and lifted his cup.

"Come see us again."

"We will," Izzy said and took a big sip of coffee.

The officers ate in silence. Minutes later, Izzy wiped her lips with a napkin. "Time to go, Kell."

The two officers left the eating establishment and headed up the sidewalk. "I'd like to check something out at Crafter's Charm in the mall. We can check Bible sales at Inspirations at the same time," Izzy said.

They crossed the street and entered Big Lakes Mall. "This is it," Izzy said and led Kelly into the store that had different categories of gifts organized into cubicles.

"Hi, I'm Pat. Can I help you?" the tall, attractive woman behind the counter said.

Izzy smiled. "Just lookin' around." Minutes later she brought over a book with a white police car on the cover. "This looks interesting."

"It certainly is. So are all the other books in that display," Pat said.

"I'll give this a try. If I like it, I'll come back for more."

Kelly picked up the book off the counter. He read the back cover synopsis. "Hmmm, *Purgatory Curve*…fascinating, especially with a police car on the cover."

They continued moving up the mall concourse, stopping at Inspirations, a Christian gift shop. "I'm Deputy Felton and this is Deputy Martin," Izzy told the dark-haired girl behind the counter. "And you are…?"

"Denise."

"Denise, you carry Bibles right?"

"Sure do."

Izzy reached into the plastic bag and showed the clerk the Bible. "Do you carry this kind?"

Denise squinted. "Don't think so…but let me check."

The deputies followed her to the far wall. "Doesn't look like we do."

Izzy smiled. "We appreciate your help, Denise."

"Yeah, thanks," Kelly said.

"Just a second, Kell, I need a card for my niece's birthday." Izzy said and walked over to a rotating floor-mounted display populated with greeting cards. She fingered some of them and made a selection. "How much for this one?"

Denise walked back behind the counter. She smiled at a young man who had just entered. "Two-fifty."

Izzy lay a five-dollar bill on the counter. "I'll take this one."

"Oh, that's so cute," Denise said.

Izzy dropped the change into her coat pocket. She smiled at the young lady and led Kelly out of the store. "My...an attractive girl," Izzy said.

Kelly rubbed his palms together. "You sure got that right."

They walked back outside and crossed the street at the crosswalk. "Hey, slow down!" Kelly yelled at a car.

"Those hot tomatoes! Don't they realize that their whole lives will be ruined if they hit someone—especially if they kill 'em?"

"Some people never learn," Kelly said and opened the door to the Book World bookstore. They entered.

"Hello. Could you direct us to the Bible section?" Izzy asked. She read the name *Angella* neatly embossed on the ID tag pinned to the woman's sweater.

The young woman pointed. "It's over there, at the very end of that aisle."

The two officers walked to the far end. They stopped. Izzy pointed. "That's the one—right there."

"Aha, we found it. I wonder why they didn't have one of these at the Inspirations store? They had a lot of other versions, though."

Izzy grabbed the book and they headed back to the counter. "Miss, could you tell me if anyone has bought a Bible just like this one in the past thirty days?"

Angela said, "Yes, there was a gentleman who bought two of 'em recently."

Izzy's eyes widened. "Is there some way we could get a name?"

"If they paid with a credit card, you can. Let me check."

The deputies waited by the door.

"I've got it!" Angella exclaimed.

"Yes?"

"The name who I have listed here is Tom Hastings."

"Well, blow me over! You gotta be kidding!" Deputy Martin exclaimed.

"How long ago did he buy the two?" Izzy asked.

"Well he got the first one on December 20. Then the second one on January 3."

"Are you sure they were exactly the same as this one?" Izzy asked.

Angella nodded.

"Are you the manager?" Izzy asked.

"Yes, I am."

"Deputy Martin and I are investigating a crime. We need a copy of the two sales. You have the right to refuse us, but we can get a court order if needed."

Angella scratched her left ear. "I suppose it would be okay. You're from the sheriff's office, right?"

Izzy nodded.

Angella placed the two slips in the copying machine. "I can give you copies—not the originals."

"Do you have an envelope we can steal?" Kelly asked.

"Sure." Angella handed the evidence to the deputy.

9

THOR KNELT DOWN IN FRONT OF HIS ALTAR. "You had to pay the price—the Lord commanded me," he whispered. His lips moved as he read a passage from the open Bible on the bench. The shadows on the far wall fluttered in the candlelight. Thor prayed.

He kept his hands clasped together and lowered his face to the floor, almost touching the carpet with his nose. *You must not make for yourself an idol of any kind, or an image of anything in the heavens, or on the earth, or on the sea.* "The taking of fish from under the protection of the winter ice is sinful," he whispered.

Thor stood. Perspiration beads slid down his forehead, forcing him to close his eyes. "They will sin no more, Lord. They are cleansed."

He blew out the candles and softly closed the door.

Thor's nightlight next to his bed lit up the page of the Bible. He read, *Observe the Sabbath day by keeping it holy, as the Lord your God has commanded you.*

He set down the book and flicked off the light. Thor closed his eyes and thought about the past.

Terrance sat at his desk in the assembly at the high school. He felt great. His freshman year had been successful and there were still close to five months left.

His thoughts drifted to a terrifying period of time in his life at age six. He couldn't bear to watch his father push his mother around the room. He heard a loud slap and a scream. Terrance heard a thud. Terrance peeked through the fingers of his hand as his father stomped out of the room. His eyes opened wide—his mother lay on the floor, blood dripping from the corner of her mouth.

The sound of the front door slamming sent shivers up his spine. He turned his head, relieved that his father had not returned. The brute has left the house, he said to himself. His mother continued to sob, her head buried between her arms. Terrance stood and rushed to his mother.

"You okay?" he said anxiously, getting down on his knees and gently holding her with his arms.

She tried to clear her throat and whimpered, "We have to leave."

She staggered, trying to rise. Terrance did all he could to help her. "Where can we go?" he whispered.

Years later, he still woke up sweating from the nightmares. Terrance had adjusted to living in a small apartment with his mother in Big Lakes, Minnesota. She worked long hours at a series of restau-

rants to put clothes on their backs and food in the refrigerator.

Then one day, Terrance couldn't wait to get home after school. He had made the football team as a freshman, and he stomped up the stairs, anxious to tell his mother. Then he stopped. He heard noises. He knew. The shouts sounded familiar...from many years previous.

Terrance crept up the two remaining steps and quietly pulled on the door. It wasn't locked. He entered. The voices came from the television room. Terrance hastened into the kitchen and grabbed a large knife from the wooden block.

He peeked around the door frame and saw his father's hands grasping his mother's throat. Terrance grabbed the handle with both hands and advanced, raising his arms. His father turned his head. Terrance drove the blade into his father's heart.

THE COLD JANUARY MORNING FOUND deputies Izzy and Kelly in Pine Lakes. Kelly had heard through the grapevine there was a pastor in that town who was considered a Bible expert. Martin turned the sheriff's car off Main Street at Sixth Avenue SW, right next to the police station. "I wish we had more time. We could stop and visit with Chief Brian," Izzy said.

"So far, he hasn't had to deal with any fishing house murders," Kelly said.

"Not yet, but don't count your winnings yet," Kelly said.

Kelly slowed the car. "There it is, Izz. Just the way the guy described it."

He did a U-turn at the intersection and parked the car next to a curb across from a quaint, brick-faced structure. The blunt steeple was part of an entry extension of the building. It had a white double door entrance, above it a large decorative window, pointed at the top. It matched two other windows next to the entryway, and five other windows on each side of the building. Matched pairs of evergreen bushes partially covered the bottoms of the two front windows.

Izzy got out on the passenger side. "Hey, look at that brick...and the house next door…and look, the building across the street next to our car. Chicago, I think."

"Chicago? What's that mean?"

"The big fire…when a cow kicked over a lantern and almost the entire city burnt to the ground…lots of brick left. It got sold all over the country. I think we're looking at some right now."

Kelly cleared his throat. He shrugged his shoulders and led Izzy across the street. They walked up four concrete steps. "Pastor Tereka said he would meet us inside."

Izzy turned to face Martin. "This should be interesting."

She grabbed the door handle, squeezed the catch and pulled. It creaked open. "The pastor should be here."

A dim light shone down on them from the ceiling of the entryway. The vestibule wallpaper reminded Izzy of a place that her parents took her when she was a little girl. She remembered looking up at strange, white-looking angels on a dark maroon wall. The extra-wide wooden trim suggested a very old building.

Izzy walked forward and opened a large inner double door. She stepped onto a dark red carpet in the center aisle. Izzy whispered, "He's probably in the back area somewhere."

She heard the sound of soft footsteps to her left. A figure approached slowly.

"Sir, I'm Deputy Felton and this is Deputy Martin. You must be Pastor Tereka."

A hoarse voice said, "Yes, I have been expecting you two."

They shook hands. The pastor led them up the aisle and turned just before the altar. He opened a door. "Let's go into my study."

The police officers followed the man into a room much brighter in color than the vestibule and the large area with pews. Izzy and Kelly sat down next to each other on an overstuffed divan.

The pastor sat on a wood-framed rocking chair. "Now, what can I do for you?"

Izzy explained some of the details regarding the crimes that they were investigating. She opened the Bible that she carried to the page the murderer had selected and handed it to the pastor.

"Since this is a police matter, I assume it is urgent and will make this a priority. You will have a written report by the end of the week."

"We really appreciate that. You are helping us serve justice." She handed the pastor her card. "Please call me when it's ready. We'll come by and pick it up."

The pastor nodded and stood.

"Thanks, Pastor Tereka. We'll let ourselves out," Kelly said.

The sounds of their footsteps echoed off the walls as they walked toward the front vestibule.

They returned to their vehicle. Kelly said, "It's a long shot but we have nothing to lose."

"Sure an interesting church," Izzy said. "Did you notice the pointed arches? If my school days served me correctly, they were initiated during the Gothic…Medieval times."

"Anything you say, Deputy," Kelly said, chuckling.

10

TOM TIGHTENED THE STRAP OF A SNOWSHOE across his boot. He stood to push the toe of his other boot into the harness. A white car pulled up in his driveway. "Sheriff's car," he muttered. "What the heck now? Surely they wouldn't know about what I saw the other night."

Geez, I remember those guys, he said to himself. It's Izzy and the Martin guy.

Tom removed the shoe and waited for the doorbell to ring. He took a deep breath and opened it.

"Mr. Hastings, do you remember us? I'm Deputy Felton and this is Deputy Martin."

"Yup, I remember. How could I forget?" Tom thought about his close encounter with Birdie Hec. She mistakenly thought that I was her sixth target. She had the blade of a knife right next to my throat in a store in Chilton Mills. If the cops hadn't showed up when they did, I might have been a dead man.

"Can we come in? We need to ask you a few questions." Deputy Felton said.

"Oh sure." Tom retreated into the room and pointed at a couple of chairs parked at his dining-room table.

Tom sat down. "Go ahead."

Izzy's lips tightened. "Mr. Hastings, you may have already heard of the two fishing house deaths in this area."

Tom nodded.

Izzy continued. "Both of the dead men had a Bible cradled in their left arm—both, just like this one." Izzy laid a Bible on the table.

Tom nodded. "I bought one like that for my brother for Christmas."

"Tom....can I call you Tom?" Izzy asked.

"Sure. You've done so in the past."

The deputy smiled. "Tom, all we need from you is evidence that your brother received the Bible. Where does he live?"

"Washington...the state that is."

"Maybe if you give me his number, I can call him and clear this up," Deputy Martin said.

Tom took a deep breath. "The first one never got there."

"Never got there! And why not?" Martin exclaimed.

"The box that I sent it in must have broken open and the postal department lost it."

Izzy lay the palm of her hand on the table surface. "How about the second one?"

"I just mailed it the other day and since it went *media* rate, he likely doesn't have that one yet, either."

Deputy Martin stood. He took two steps, then he suddenly turned and pointed his finger. "Hastings, we need to know—and soon."

Tom's face reddened. He rubbed his right thumb across the mustache above his upper lip. "I'll call him today."

Izzy stood, too. "All right then—you let us know right away

when your brother gets that Bible." She gave Deputy Martin a chiding look.

"I will." Tom felt his heart racing. He should have reported what he saw at that gas station that night. Could he tell them now? No, he decided, too many days have passed.

The deputies walked through the door and moved onto the sidewalk.

"Just a second!" Tom exclaimed.

They stopped and turned.

"This has nothing to do with the fishing house murders, but—"

"But what?" Deputy Martin took a step forward.

"I saw two guys run across the street from Quality Supply late Sunday night—about two in the morning."

Both deputies stepped toward him. "Mr. Hastings, we're not part of that investigation, but I'll pass the word on to those who are," Izzy said.

She made a notation in her notebook. "Thank you, Mr. Hastings, we appreciate you coming forward with that information."

Tom watched the two deputies get in their vehicle and drive off, thinking—no, this can't be happening again.

DEPUTY IZZY SLAMMED THE CAR DOOR SHUT. "Kelly, I don't think you had to pour it on like that."

He turned the key and the engine started. "Don't you think the coincidence is just a little too much? Gads, two dead guys, each with a Bible. Our suspect bought two Bibles—the same kind."

Izzy frowned. She took a deep breath. "You were wrong about him once before or don't you remember?"

Martin scowled. "Well, why didn't he call the police sooner about what he saw at the gas station?"

Martin hit the accelerator and the car sped up the Hastings's roadway. "I'll bet you five bucks the second Bible he claims to have sent to his brother—that's gonna get lost, too."

"You're on, buddy," Izzy said, staring straight ahead.

JOLENE HUNT and a co-worker walked from their offices to Lakes Brewed Awakening. They took a seat next to a window. Jolene wore a long skirt and a tan, leather jacket. She felt exhilarated. Her first property sale had closed the previous day. "This is going to be fun, Jan."

"You're going to enjoy working for Big Lakes Realty. They're a nice bunch of people. No one is going to stab you in the back."

Jolene nodded and smiled.

"Say, have you read about the fishing house murders?"

"Not really," Jolene said, curious.

"Two guys dead. Each with a Bible."

"A Bible?"

"Yes, a Bible. Oh by the way, do you know a guy with the name of Hastings?"

"I do, but what's that got to do with the murders?"

"He bought two identical Bibles recently…and…."

"And what?"

"According to what I heard, the police investigated and the books have disappeared."

"The police have disappeared—or the Bibles?"

Jan laughed. "The Bibles, you nut."

Jolene looked up at the ceiling. "So let me get this straight. Hastings buys two Bibles. Each one of the victims is found dead holding an identical Bible—two victims—two Bibles."

Jan leaned forward. "You've got it."

Jolene's face turned rigid. "Oh my gosh!" She thought about the past and her relationship with Hastings. Has he gone off the deep edge this time? Do I really know that man?

"Hey—wake up," Jan said.

"Oh! Sorry, I drifted into the past—lost it for a moment."

"Ah, don't worry about it—everyone knows that you had something going with Hastings a couple of years ago. Nothing wrong with that."

Jolene flushed. "I may as well tell you. You'll find out anyhow.

Our offices are a regular newsroom."

Jan smiled.

"I've already had a date with the gentleman. He took me out to Bayside last weekend."

"You don't think he's the fishing house killer, do ya?"

Jolene shook her head slowly. "No, I don't—"

"You look as if you have some doubt," Jan said.

"I don't know what to think. Say, by the way, is there a shoe store in Big Lakes? I broke a heel yesterday."

"Sure. Terry's Shoe Shop on Washington. About a block from here, toward the lake."

"Thanks."

11

JOLENE PARKED HER VEHICLE NEXT TO THE CURB on Washington Avenue across the street from *Lakes Brewed Awakening*. She grabbed her broken shoe from the passenger seat and partially opened the door. Jolene waited for a truck to pass and quickly stepped out. She hurried to get off the street as a pickup gathered speed after going through the intersection.

"I hope you get to where you're going on time, ya nut," she murmured, grimacing as she brushed slush off her coat. Jolene looked up at the store signs, walking along slowly. She saw *Terry's Shoe Shop* and headed for the door.

Jolene entered. A series of bells hanging on the door announced her arrival. She approached the counter but didn't see anyone at or behind it. Jolene stopped and looked toward the rear of the space behind the counter. Shoe repair tools surrounded the small vacant space on the workbench stationed next to the wall. Gads, it's quiet in here, she said to herself.

"Can I help you?"

Startled, she turned, covering her mouth with the palm of her hand. Jolene looked into the small, dark, beady eyes of a pale-skinned face. The odd-shaped man, with short stubby legs, wore a plastic visor that filtered out the overhead light, spreading a bluish sheen over his face. The surface reminded Jolene of dumplings her mother used to serve for dinner.

"Oh, I've brought in a shoe." She held it up. "Look, a broken heel…needs fixing."

The man grabbed it and held it up to the light. "Yeah, I can fix that." He flipped up a section of the counter and walked behind it. He got a receipt book out and set it on the counter. "Name?"

"Jolene Hunt."

"Phone number?"

"847-3421."

"Be ready next Wednesday."

Jolene nodded, barely able to contain her fear. "I'll be back."

She walked back quickly to her vehicle and got in. What a weird character, she thought. He gives me the chills.

JOLENE DROVE TO HER APARTMENT after leaving the shoe repair shop. It was quite the day, she thought. First, my friend Jan as much as accuses my friend Tom of being the fishing house killer; then I meet the strangest man at the shoe shop. Whew!

She parked her vehicle in the lower level lot and walked to the elevator. Jolene pushed the button and the door opened. She heard footsteps behind her. "Hold it, please!"

Jolene turned. A man approached. "Thanks," he said and they both entered. "I'm Paul Minton. You must be one of my neighbors."

"I'm Jolene Hunt."

"I get off here," he said. He stepped out and held the door open. "I see you work for Big Lakes Realty."

Jolene smiled and looked down at her badge. "Yes, I do."

"Are you a broker?"

"Yes, I am."

"Hey, tell you what, I'm looking for a place to buy. There's this place for sale in New Dresden. How about you and I getting together?"

"Why, yes, of course. Give me a call," Jolene said and handed him her card.

"Where's your office?" Paul asked, widening his perpetual smile.

"On Washington Avenue, next to Lakes Brewed Awakening."

"Hey, that's your *For Sale* sign out there, right?"

Jolene nodded.

He blew her a kiss and released the door.

She rode up to her floor. Wow, that guy is a looker, she said to herself. He's got the hair of an angel, wavy—so cool.

Jolene unlocked the door to her room and took off her coat. She picked up the phone. "Tom, we've got to talk."

She held the phone close to her ear and told Tom about her Bible conversation with her co-worker. "Let's go out for dinner and we can talk about it then."

She listened to his suggestion.

"Where's Spanky's?" she said. Jolene nodded. "Oh, the old Mary Ann's—yes, I sure do remember."

She placed a hand over her mouth and promptly withdrew it. "Hey, why should you drive over here first? I'll pick you up at your place," Jolene said. She listened for a few moments. "See you at 6:30 then." She hung up.

TERRANCE TURNED THE DOOR KNOB. He walked through the rear door of his business establishment, immediately changing to a different person, like a snake shedding its skin. "I'm Thor, an agent of God," he whispered, his eyes opened wide. Thor jiggled the outside handle, making sure the back door was locked. He looked up at the sky. "Thor at your service, Lord," he whispered again.

Thor slid into the front seat of his black SUV. Taking a right on

Willow Street, he headed for Highway 59 and New Dresden. On Lake Sauer, he noticed that the fishing houses had been positioned mainly in the middle. Two pickups and an ATV were parked in the fishing area.

Thor thought about the good-looking blonde that brought over a broken heel just before closing up. *I hope she doesn't fish on the Sabbath,* he said to himself. *She's too beautiful to hurt, swallowing the thought. The Lord does not allow exceptions!*

"Lord, help me!" he exclaimed when his vehicle veered over the white line on a curve. "Thank you," he whispered after his vehicle returned to the right side of the road.

A couple of miles down, he felt the vehicle vibrate as it came abreast of a freight train. The last boxcar had passed as he drove up and over the final hill before the outskirts of New Dresden.

The blonde woman remained on his mind as he pressed the garage door button attached to his visor. Thor entered his house and opened the refrigerator door. Nothing for dinner there, he thought. I'll have to have my dinner at Spanky's.

12

THE HEADLIGHTS FROM JOLENE'S TOYOTA lit up the wall of trees east of Tom's driveway. He had been sitting at his computers awaiting his date's arrival. He quickly stood and put on his hat and coat. Locking the door behind him, he headed for Jolene's vehicle, a light-gray Toyota 4Runner.

"Feels great—nice and warm," Tom said as he closed the passenger door behind him.

"So when did Mary Ann's become Spanky's?" she asked.

"Last fall."

Jolene glanced at Tom. "Has it changed much?"

"Yeah, it has—all kinds of fishing stuff on the walls."

"Speaking of fishing—remember, I talked about doing a dinner in Steve's fishing house. We need to set a date."

Tom shook his head. "Dinner in a fishing house. Somehow it sounds fishy." Tom looked at her. "No pun intended." He laughed.

Jolene snickered. "You're the one who's fishy."

She waited for a vehicle to pass and turned the Toyota onto the county highway. Minutes later, she drove into Spanky's parking lot.

"I'm anxious to hear what you've heard about the Bibles."

"Let's wait until we get seated, okay?" Jolene said.

They settled down at a booth close to the wood burning fireplace. Tom looked up. "Hi, Amanda, this is my friend Jolene. Do you remember her?"

Amanda stood with pencil ready. "I sure do."

Tom laughed. "No trouble this trip."

Tom ordered a wine and Jolene settled for a glass of water.

The wine arrived and they ordered. Tom took a deep breath. "Okay, now what's the news?"

"I was having lunch with one of my co-workers at Lakes Brewed Awakening the other day. She asked me if I knew you. Reluctantly, I had to admit it."

"Thanks."

"Well anyhow, she said that you were a suspect in the fishing house murders because—"

Tom grimaced. "Because I bought two Bibles."

"Jan has a friend who works in the sheriff's department. The man said that you couldn't account for the two Bibles that you purchased recently."

"Hi, Jolene," someone nearby said.

Tom looked up. He saw a tall, good-looking guy grinning from ear to ear. The man sat down next to Jolene.

"Tom, I want you to meet Paul. He's interested in some property on Loon Lake. Not far from the highway. You can see it from the road."

Tom reached over to shake his hand. He didn't appreciate the intrusion. I don't trust that smile, Tom said to himself, watching the man talking a mile a minute to Jolene. It looks perpetual—usually phony. The man wore blue jeans with a wide black belt, and a denim blue long-sleeved shirt. Minton was slim and tall. He had thin lips that exposed large front teeth. Tom noticed that the man had a unique habit of turning his head and looking at a person out of the corner of his eye.

Five minutes later the man was still there and Tom began to fidget on the seat and scratch the back of his head. "Excuse me, I'm heading for the washroom," Tom said.

Tom returned and felt relieved that the man had left. "That man is the mother of all table-hoppers," Tom quickly said after sitting down.

Jolene shook her head. "He could be my first sale and I need to be friendly to my customers."

Tom gulped down the rest of the wine in his glass. "I'll have another one," he said to Amanda as she set their entrées onto a portable stand next to the table.

"He may be a customer, but he sure looks like a pest to me."

"Come on, Tom. Relax—you can't control everything—for cripes sakes."

They ate in silence.

"So, Tom, what happened to the second Bible?"

Tom scoffed. "As I said, the first one got lost in the mail—the other is en route."

"Route to where?"

"My brother. I'm not a Bible guy but he is. So I sent him one for Christmas. Well it never got there. So I sent him another one. I called his house earlier today."

"Has he gotten it yet?"

"No—"

"Okay, tell me what happened."

"My brother didn't answer the phone. He and his wife left for the Caribbean yesterday."

"Blazes! Will they be gone long?"

Tom ground his teeth together at the thought. "Three weeks."

Jolene shook her head slowly. "Uh-oh."

"There's more to the story."

"More! Now what?"

"This is a separate issue, but since I've told the cops, I'll tell you."

Jolene leaned forward.

"I think that I witnessed the gas station robbery in New Dresden on Sunday night."

"Oh my."

He told Jolene what he had seen.

"What did the cops say?"

"They're going to pass the information on to whoever is investigating the robbery."

"So you'll have more visitors."

"Likely."

Jolene took a sip and set her glass down. "Have you ever had a shoe repaired in Big Lakes?"

"No, is there such a place?"

"Yes, on the main street...Washington. Close to that new restaurant...oh, what is its name?"

"You mean that place that specialized in veggie wraps. Heck, I can't think of the name either. Anyhow, what about it?"

"Nothing, I just took one of my high-heeled shoes there—well, maybe more than nothing. The guy scared the daylights out of me."

"What did he do?"

"I walked in—nobody around—quiet as could be. Suddenly this man crept up behind me—"

"Did he touch you in any way?"

"No, he didn't—and he's got such a snake-like voice. Oh, now I remember. The veggie wrap place is Lakes Brewed Awakening."

PAUL MINTON SAT DOWN ON A STOOL at the bar and ordered a Calvert's on the rocks. Randy, the bartender, set the icy drink down. Paul pointed. "Do you know that couple over there?"

"Sure do. The guy is Tom Hastings. He lives not far from here. The lady—"

"I know the lady," Paul said and took a sip from the glass.

Randy smiled.

"Ah, are they a—a couple?"

The smile widened. "Can't answer that, but I do know they met right here—'bout five years ago."

Randy side-stepped to take another order. Paul glanced at Jolene and Tom again. He lit a cigarette. Taking a deep drag, he exhaled three perfect smoke rings. Paul felt a brush against his left shoulder.

He looked into a pair of dark, beady eyes. Whiskers covered most of the smiling face of a stocky man who slid his rear end onto the stool next to Paul. "A Bud," the man said to Randy.

"Ya new around here?" the man asked Paul.

"Yes, as a matter of fact I am. I'm in the process of buying some property on Loon Lake—and you?"

The man lifted the bottle to his face. He plunked it down and wiped his lips with his sleeve. "Lived here all my life. Hey barkeep, I'll have another."

Garth Sabolik pulled out a pack of cigarettes. He lit one and blew the smoke ahead of him. "Do any fishin'?"

Paul rubbed his chin with his fingers. "Not yet. I'm hopin' to buy a new place soon—a deluxe fishing house comes with it."

Garth took a deep drag from his cigarette. "I got mine down today—the long narrow bay on Border's Lake—fishin' good there most of the time."

Paul looked the other way. He didn't appreciate the man's odor. The guy smells like a dead fish, he said to himself. I don't need that right now. Paul lit another cigarette and blew the smoke in the shaggy man's direction. The guy coughed. Paul looked the other way. He saw Jolene and her date leave their booth. His eyes followed them as they headed toward the checkout counter.

THOR SAT ALONE IN A BOOTH AT SPANKY'S where he could watch most of the tables and the bar. He wore black pants and a shirt, his black beanie cap pulled down low over his forehead. Thor took a sip of red wine from a tall glass. Without moving his head, his eyes followed the tall, slim wavy-haired man who walked across the room and sat down next to a woman. Lord heavens, that's the same blonde who brought in that broken heel yesterday, he said to himself.

The guy sitting across from the woman appears to be irritated with the intruder, Thor thought. He looks angry. A passage from the Old Testament came to his mind: *There is violence everywhere—even the wild animals, the birds of the sky, and the fish of the sea are disappearing.* He watched with amusement as the man's irritation intensified. The tall blond man got up from the booth and stomped off toward the bar. Thor turned slowly and watched the man sit down on a stool next to a stocky guy.

I know that bearded person, Thor said to himself, smiling. *That sinner goes out fishing almost every day...the past two Sundays for certain.* Thor smiled. The tall man shifted his butt on his stool to move away from the stocky one.

Baggy jeans...that's what most everyone wears here. Cheap tennis shoes, too. Thor counted 26 people that he could see. All of them wore blue jeans. Doesn't anyone dress dignified anymore? he asked himself. *This is the dining room of the Lord. They're all like a herd of sheep waiting for the Master to cull one out for the sacrifice.*

TOM OPENED THE BLACK VINYL FOLDER. He glanced at the numbers and reached into his coat pocket for his wallet.

"Let's share that," Jolene said.

"It's not—no big deal. Don't worry about it." Tom assisted Jolene with her coat.

"Thank you," she said.

He glanced toward the bar area. Tom saw the man who had annoyed him earlier waving his arms. Loud laughter followed. The jerk appears to be entertaining the people around him, Tom said to himself. He's probably stuffed with dirty jokes. Tom's eyes locked on those of another man sitting in a booth. "Looks like Johnny Cash," Tom murmured.

"Who looks like Johnny Cash?"

Tom narrowed his eyes and signaled by moving his chin.

Jolene frowned and narrowed her eyes. "Weird, but I think that's the shoe repair store guy."

Tom laid the folder and his check on the counter.

"Have a good night," the hostess said.

"Can't miss," Tom returned.

Jolene cleared her throat. "We shall see."

Tom opened the outside door. "I suppose you saw that other guy in Big Lakes, too—the table-hopper."

"As a matter of fact, I did."

Tom shook his head and guided Jolene toward her vehicle.

13

THE BRIGHT BLUE SKY AND CLEAR WHITE SNOW on the lake sandwiched the long slab of drab, brown trees on the far side of the shoreline. Tom sipped his coffee and glanced at the temperature gauge: *two below zero*. The weather is just teasing us right now… preparing us for spring, he said to himself. All weather is good really. When living in Minnesota, you've got to expect this. After all, it's a Sunday in January.

A pileated woodpecker swooped once, swooped twice and settled on a red oak tree a short distance from Tom's house. It hurriedly moved up and down the trunk, pausing occasionally to peck at the bark. I wonder how many bugs they find in there this time of the year, Tom asked himself, watching with interest.

Tom's mind focused on his date with Jolene the previous evening. Damn that intruder, he said to himself. The table-hopper spoiled our evening. Jolene's eyes flashed with excitement after the dog-head sat down. The big woodpecker swooped over to another tree. Hmmm, a tree-hopper—just like last night. A hopper is a hopper...they're looking for something. I need to learn more about this Paul guy. He could be a problem for me.

Tom spent most of the daylight hours working on his income taxes. At 4:00 p.m., he took a break and dressed up for a ski run. Tom got his skis from the garage and snapped them onto his boots.

The snow depth felt perfect as he moved up one of his many trails. The gray body of a deer flashed past the edge of a small clearing. He counted seven more as they followed the same path as their leader.

He paused by the break in the trees where he had walked into a cornfield last summer. Tom grimaced, thinking about the monster machine that had run over him—an Oxybeast they called it. Fortunately, the wheels missed my body. He shuddered. Good god, that thing was about two stories high. He remembered it passing up and down the field, sucking up oxygen. Then the machine passed the oxygen over an element dug out of deep mines in Togo, Africa. The energy it produced successfully propelled a Ford Mustang. Tom thought about Senator McDougal and how political quagmire prevented further development.

Tom continued to stare at the tops of the harvested corn stalks that dotted the snow-covered field. The barn beyond the field adds character to the scene, he thought. That picture would make a good jigsaw puzzle.

He followed the trail until it turned and looped back toward his home. He chugged up a hill and stopped. Tom chuckled remembering his friend Julie who used to come out for weekends. They went skiing frequently and always paused here. I named the spot after her—*Julie Hill.*

Tom felt invigorated after returning back to his house. He put his skis away in the garage. He walked across the driveway area and spotted a bald eagle perched on a tree branch. The beautiful predator didn't appear to pay any attention to him as he entered the house. Tom got out his camera and took a series of photographs of the huge bird.

He studied the photograph of the eagle on his computer screen and printed a copy. Tom thought about Jolene's suggestion that they have a dinner at her brother's fishing house. The idea sounds a little crazy, but I'm probably stupid enough to go for it. On the other hand, it could be great. He picked up his binoculars and scanned all the fishing houses—nobody around right now.

Tom put his boots and coat back on and headed down the front slope of his home toward the lake. The snow and ice partially covered the pontoon boat and dock. He walked onto the lake and stopped to listen, expecting to hear a snowmobile engine. The world was deadly quiet.

Tom struck out toward Steve's fishing house. Geez, this is the first time I've set a foot down on the lake for a long time, he said to himself. What is that woman doing to me? Heck, I'm perfectly satisfied to watch the lake from above and watch the vehicles driving to and from their destinations.

He marveled at the size of Steve's fishing house, comparing it to all the other ones. Tom stood next to it and gazed at the surroundings—winter-brown trees on the slopes of the shorelines probing at the white puffs of clouds that moved gently across a bright blue sky.

Tom slowly began the trek back toward his house, listening to the crunching sounds of his boots. The distant sound of a snowmobile engine caught his attention. He stopped and turned his head. A set of bobbing headlights came around a bend and headed for the fishing houses. I wonder if the local fishermen think about the two men who were murdered—in their houses, he thought.

GARCIA STOOD JUST INSIDE THE DOOR OF THE GARAGE. He watched four Mexicans load the final bag into the box of a used truck that he had bought from the local furniture dealer in Chilton

Mills. Garcia exchanged conversation with the leader of the four. In Spanish, he told them they and their families could live in the house for the time being, but they would have to help with packaging in the near future.

Garcia had talked with his upper-level contact from Big Lakes earlier in the day. He had learned a large storage building would soon be available where they could safely package the cartons of cigarettes and ship them.

Ernesto Manual Garcia had entered the United States illegally in 2005. The families living in the big house were also illegal immigrants but they were not his relatives. The women had all found jobs doing housekeeping in motels in Big Lakes and Pine Lakes. The men were without work during the winter months. They will soon have work, he said to himself.

Garcia stood at slightly over six feet, much taller than his counterparts living in the big house. From his recent conversations with the tall American, he expected that pesos would flow his way and toward his unemployed Mexican male friends.

Thus far, Garcia had moderated the delivery of six loads of cigarette bags, delivered by two crude-looking Americans. He didn't know their names but knew they drove a rusty, white car. According to his contact, another delivery was expected soon.

GARTH SABOLIK FLIPPED THROUGH THE CHANNELS. He settled on a hunting scene. Three guys dressed in camouflage gear walked in a field of tall grass. There go three greenhorn city slickers, Garth said to himself. Two of the men carried rifles, the other an apparatus that looked like a pack of metal rods…uh-huh, a tripod… funny.

The next scene showed one of them opening up the apparatus and setting up the tripod. They fastened one of the rifles to the top. Garth chuckled. Real city slickers for sure. Shooting from a tripod of all things, he said to himself. "What next, a rocket launcher?" he murmured. Garth laughed louder.

Nettie walked into the room. "How's the quilt comin'?" Garth asked.

"Good. Should finish it tomorrow. I'm tired and goin' to bed."

"Good night," Garth said.

A strange bear-like animal loped through the tall grass. It stopped. The camera showed the hunter lining up the rifle that perched on top of the tripod. Garth saw a puff of smoke. The animal lurched sideways and dropped to the ground, disappearing into the tall grass.

"Bet it will cost 'em a ton to mount that one," Garth murmured.

He looked forward to the next day. Garth planned on fishing after getting his job done finishing the painting of the walls in the kids' two bedrooms. The brats won't be back until Sunday night, he said to himself. Garth didn't care for Nettie's offspring, the result of a previous marriage. Two teenyboppers—a boy-brat and a girl-brat.

Garth fell asleep on the couch. He woke up. The wall clock read 2:13 a.m. He staggered to the bedroom, undressed and slipped under the covers.

14

GARTH GLARED THROUGH THE WINDOW. His heart sank watching his two step-kids get out of a car. He sneered as the driver's side door opened. His wife's ex-husband walked onto the sidewalk and the three arrivals gathered for a family hug. Garth gritted his teeth as the two teenagers were handed their bags. They hugged one more time. The man raised one hand, smiled widely, and got into the car and sped away.

"Good riddance for that, but here come the brats," Garth stammered. Time to go fishin', he said to himself.

Garth quickly walked over to the closet and put on his coat. "You leaving already?" Nettie asked. "Why don't you stay a bit and visit with Katie and Tommie?" she asked, frowning.

"I'll talk to them later. See ya."

Garth walked out the side door into the garage. He brushed off the look of disappointment on his wife's face. Garth had gotten fishing bait earlier when he had gone into town for the newspaper. All the equipment he needed lay in the back of his Nissan SUV. He congratulated himself for previously hooking up his snowmobile trailer.

The drive to the boat launch took only five minutes. Garth bounced out of his vehicle and released the catch on the trailer. He slid the snowmobile onto the snow-packed ground. Garth fetched a plastic bag of goodies and a container of minnows from his vehicle and locked the doors. He felt a heavy snowflake that landed on the tip of his nose.

The Artic Cat started on the second turn of the key. The falling snowflakes got larger and denser as he drove the machine onto the ice. Taking a left turn, he rotated the handle throttle and sped toward his fishing house.

A column of the falling snowflakes glistened from the bright pole light high above the garage of the nearby home on the north shore. The boxy outlines of fishing houses appeared as he approached his. Two ATVs marked two of them that were in use. Garth pulled up next to his fishing house. He turned the engine off and briefly listened to the muffled sound of falling snowflakes. He walked to his door and placed a key in the padlock, then walked to the backside of the house and opened the gas tank valve.

Garth returned to his snowmobile and grabbed his supplies. At the door, he stomped his boots, shook off most of the snow on his cap and coat, entered and turned on the heat.

He used a small ax to smash through a layer of ice that had closed his fishing hole. Garth grabbed the end of his line from the rattle wheel and grabbed a minnow from his bucket. He dropped the minnow that he attempted to attach to the hook. "Come 'ere ya little weasel," he muttered. After three tries, he successfully attached the minnow and dropped the line into the water.

Moments later, bells jingled and he jerked forward from his sitting position. Garth worked the rattle wheel and retrieved a mid-sized bluegill. The fish jiggled as he released it from the hook and dropped it into a pail.

That's thirteen, almost enough for a meal, he said to himself. The slivers of light showing through the cracks around the small window had faded, showing Garth that daylight had ended. He yawned and looked at his watch. Too damn early to go home, he thought. The brats are likely still at the house…probably cleaning out the refrigerator. Surely, they'll both go out for the evening…soon as their bellies are full.

Some time later, the sound of a snowmobile jolted his sleepy mind. Garth awoke fully and looked at this watch: 8:45. Suppose I best get home, he thought. The brats will be gone and Nettie will be working on her quilt. Huh, he scoffed. She's doin' two of 'em. One for each.

The snowmobile motor sputtered and stopped. Garth yawned again. He heard the sound of footsteps crunching in the snow. Someone had come out to fish late…probably Erick, he said to himself. Another yawn. Garth patted his mouth with the palm of his hand. I'm really getting sleepy.

Suddenly his head began to ache. He placed a palm against his forehead, then lowered it to his throat where his breath became short and raspy. God awful stuffy in here, he thought. I better open the door. Garth attempted to step forward. He fell to the carpeted floor. Something is wrong…the air….

He got up on his knees and grabbed the door latch, giving it a twist. He pushed on the door. It opened slightly but he met resistance as he continued to push. Garth felt total panic. He used all the strength that he could muster and stood up. Leading with his shoulder, he lunged at the door. The entire wall broke away. His body fell again. Garth gasped for air as he lay with his head tucked between his arms.

THOR STOOD ON THE SNOW COVERED ICE, a bolt cutter grasped in both hands, patiently waiting for the noise in the fishing house to cease. The wall suddenly smashed to the ice. Thor jumped back. His body went rigid, Thor's eyes wide in disbelief. Thor gasped as he watched his adversary lying on the fallen wall. His victim's face lay buried in both arms. The torso heaved violently. *What do I do now, Lord?* he thought. *What do I do?*

Thor stepped forward. He raised the bolt cutter slightly, but resisted the temptation to strike his victim on the head. Quickly, he backed away and trotted toward his snowmobile. He turned the key and spun the machine around, roaring toward his pickup and trailer.

Thor drove the machine onto the trailer. He stopped the engine and listened...no sound except for vehicles on the highway. The lights in the windows of the house on the north shore of the bay didn't appear to change. He tilted the trailer bed, locking it automatically. Thor searched the compartment on his snowmobile for the bolt cutter. Where was it? He panicked and yanked off his gloves, desperately searching along the floor of the snowmobile with his naked fingers. Nothing. Oh no, it's still out there. I can't go back there...too risky. The guy has likely recovered by now.

He secured the snowmobile and got into his SUV. "My Lord has forsaken me," he murmured. *Then perhaps there is a reason*, he said to himself and waited for a vehicle to pass before turning his pickup onto the state highway. Thor arrived at his home minutes later. Backing the trailer into the garage, he unhitched it. He turned his vehicle around and parked it, too. He pressed the button and the door closed.

Thor carried a book in his left hand as he unlocked the door with the other. He set the Bible down on the small table and hung up his coat. Grabbing the book, he entered his holy room. Thor patted the cover gently and set the book down on top of four others. He knelt in front of the altar after lighting all the candles. *Come, let us return to the Lord. He has torn us to pieces; now he will heal us. He has injured us; now he will bandage our wounds.*

TED STEVENS AT THE SHERIFF'S DEPARTMENT took the call. "Some b… tried to kill me!" a man's ranting voice exclaimed.

The dispatcher straightened and set his feet down on the floor. "Hold it a minute—slow down a bit."

The dispatcher exhaled, cradling the phone between his cheek and shoulder. He grabbed a pencil and wrote down *Sabolik*. "You said what?" He wrote down *Border's Lake*. His eyes narrowed. "We'll be out soon as we can. Please repeat the address." The dispatcher hung up.

15

"HOW DO YOU LIKE BEING AN INVESTIGATOR NOW… huh, Felton?"

Izzy yawned. "I could think of worse things."

"Yeah, like what?" Deputy Kelly Martin asked.

"Well, I could've been turned down for this job."

Kelly laughed. "You're a trooper…no doubt about that."

The two officers hustled down the stairway and walked toward one of the parked sheriff's vehicles. Kelly got behind the steering wheel. He flicked on the siren and flashing light switches and drove onto the street. Minutes later, they reached the city limits and Kelly increased their speed heading southeast on Highway 10. The deputy sped close to 80 miles per hour in the left lane.

They drove in silence until Kelly steered the police car onto the approach that led to New Dresden. "We'll be there soon. Would ya read me what you got so far?"

"Some guy name of Sabolik called. Said someone locked him in—in his fishing house."

"Cripes sakes. Sounds like the same MO," Kelly said.

Izzy turned the page. "Sure a different result, though."

"Yes, a living victim witness. I wondered about the other two cases...why they didn't break out the wall," Kelly said.

"The way the doctor put it is, 'different people react differently to carbon monoxide. Some are gone almost right away—some not'."

Izzy responded to a buzz on the police radio. "Okay, we'll meet you at the landing. First we have to talk to the victim."

Kelly held onto the steering wheel with both hands, anxiously watching for other vehicles.

"Uh-huh—uh-huh." She returned the mouthpiece.

"We'll have snowmobiles on the site when we get there. That's good news. I'd sure hate to walk at this temperature—below zero."

The deputy turned off the siren and flashing lights after they exited the federal highway and turned onto a county road. They passed by Spanky's restaurant. "Hey, different name," Martin said.

The sheriff's car rounded Purgatory Curve and approached the railroad tracks. It slowed before crossing. "When you come to the stop sign, take a left. The Sabolik house is about three blocks beyond the intersection, on S Unit Avenue," Izzy said, studying the map.

"There it is—the one with a shovel by the door."

Kelly turned the wheel and stopped the car in the driveway. Izzy led the way to the door. "Are you Sabolik?" she asked.

"Yup. I'm your guy."

"Okay then. I'm Deputy Felton." She pointed. "This is Deputy Martin."

Garth opened the door wide and waved an arm. "Come on in. Have a seat."

The deputies sat down and took out notebooks and pens. "Tell us in your own words what happened first. Then we'll drive out to the site," Deputy Martin said.

Garth stumbled with his words. The deputies listened, taking notes.

"After crawling back into the remains of my fishing house, I wanted to warm up by the heater. Smoke was coming out of my heater. I finally got up on my feet and walked around to the back. There was something stuck in the pipe."

"What was it?" Izzy asked.

"Not sure. I grabbed it and it was sort of slimy."

"Did you hold onto it?"

"No, I threw it into the snow."

"Was it an apple?"

"Huh?" Garth shrugged his shoulders.

Martin stood. "Okay, let's get out there. We want you to come along, Mr. Sabolik."

IZZY STARTED UP HER SNOWMOBILE. "Get onto that one, right behind Kelly," she said to Garth.

Sabolik nodded. Izzy smiled. He looks disappointed, she thought. She allowed Martin to lead, knowing that Garth would direct him. "Thanks, guys," Izzy said to two officers standing nearby. "Shouldn't take too long."

The fishing house has really had it, Izzy thought after stopping her machine a few yards away. One wall lay on the ice, the roof partially collapsed. She got off and walked around the defunct house. "Sabolik, which direction did you throw the app—ah, the plug?"

The man took a few steps and stopped. "Right about over there."

Izzy walked cautiously. "You stay where you are. I'll find it." She got down on one knee and with her gloved hand picked up a dark-brown, small object. She brought it up to her nose for a moment and placed it into a plastic bag.

She walked back to the fishing house. "Kelly, we're gonna need to take that door off."

"Let's have Bill and Terry do it after we get back to our car."

"That'll work," Izzy said.

Kelly looked toward the north. He saw a house and other buildings on the shoreline. "Who lives there?"

"You've met the guy, Kelly. That's where Tom Hastings lives."

Kelly nodded. His cheek muscles firmed. "Hot tomatoes! I wonder where Mr. Hastings was last night?"

He looked at Garth. "You said about 8:00 or so, huh?"

"At least 8:45. That's what it was when I looked at my watch—last time I did that."

Kelly took a few steps toward Hastings's house. He turned. "Izzy, come on over here." He pointed at an object partially covered with snow.

Stooping over, he picked it up by the ends of the handles. "A bolt cutter!"

Martin took a walk around the periphery of damaged fishing house. He returned and said, "There's a set of footprints that look a little suspect."

Izzy tilted her chin.

"One set of tracks—coming from the Hastings's house—and going back."

JOLENE GOT THE CALL SHORTLY AFTER 9:00 A.M. "Okay, why don't you stop by and we'll drive out and have a look?"

She hung up the phone. Wow, this is great, but I better not tell Tom. He'll be ticked, she thought. She hesitated for a few moments and looked up at the ceiling, then she opened the file cabinet. I've got to make this sale—my second one. "Yippee!" she expressed gleefully.

She took a sip of tea and Paul Minton walked into her office. Wow, he must have been directly outside when he called, she thought. He walked straight toward her and held out a hand. "I'm Paul Minton. We've met before. The other day, remember?"

"Oh yes, I do remember."

"I hear you have a choice property for sale."

Jolene released his hand and sat back down. "Just got this listing a week ago. The owners had to leave the area hurriedly."

"Is it that one in New Dresden, on Loon Lake, close to the highway?"

"Why yes, it is."

"Good, when can I see it?"

"How about right now? It'll take me a couple of minutes to get the paperwork together. Please have a seat."

Jolene left the room and returned moments later. "I have what we need. How about if I meet you out there?—say in fifteen minutes."

He stood. "Why don't you ride out with me? I can drive you back."

"Ah—I'd rather drive out by myself—got a couple of stops to make," she said.

"Suit yourself." He stood by the door waiting for Jolene.

He touched her shoulder with his hand as she walked by. She walked quickly to the outside door. Paul opened it, allowing her to pass under his outstretched arm.

"All right, Mr. Minton, I'll see you at the site in a few minutes."

"Paul—please call me Paul."

"Paul it is."

JOLENE TURNED OFF OF THE COUNTY HIGHWAY onto Park View Road. She drove all the away around a loop surrounded by new homes. She pulled into the driveway of a two-stall garage. The large storage building to her right, about twenty feet from the house, blocked her view of the neighboring home next door. She got out and heard a vehicle pull up right next to her. Jolene reached into her carrying bag and brought out a ring of keys.

"This is a nice place, Paul. I can see why you are interested in buying it."

"One of the things that turned me on was the garage space and the extra storage building." He pointed.

She felt his hand on her shoulder as she opened the front door and entered. Quickly stepping forward, she set her zippered black case on a small table and brought out a folder. "2,120 square feet." Jolene stepped away and added, "Let's start with the kitchen." She gently rubbed her fingers on an oak cabinet door. "Nice wood."

"Yeah, it's a good-looking place…blisters!"

"What."

Minton laughed. "Just an expression of mine...blisters."

Jolene walked into the living room. "How about that rock fireplace?"

"Awesome...great guns."

She stepped toward the windows that overlooked the lake. Jolene pointed. "Fantastic view."

Minton continued to smile. He walked up next to her and put a hand on her shoulder. She quickly pushed it away, showing anger.

"Sorry," he said.

Jolene led him toward the bedrooms and bathrooms, spending very little time at each stop. She felt tension and wanted to get the showing over as quickly as possible. He makes me extremely uncomfortable, she said to herself.

They returned to the kitchen. Jolene's forehead furrowed slightly. "Four and a quarter. What do you think?"

For the first time since they met in the driveway, Minton didn't smile. "Three fifty," he said.

16

TOM SLOWED HIS VEHICLE APPROACHING THE CITY of Big Lakes from the east. As he had expected earlier, the sheriff's department had phoned him. A deputy Jackson requested an interview regarding the gas station robbery. Since Tom had other business in town, he agreed to meet the deputy in the county facility rather than in his own home.

He arrived in Big Lakes early so he decided to have lunch at Lakes Brewed Awakening. Tom parked in the shopping mall parking lot and stopped to browse at a craft shop inside. He walked down the entire concourse and exited onto Washington Avenue. Tom was waiting for the light to change at the intersection. A car turned the corner almost on two wheels. He quickly stepped back onto the sidewalk. That's it...the car used to rob the food shop in New Dresden... it's white and has a lot of rust. His eyes followed the vehicle as it sped to the next intersection, drawing a horn at a four-way stop. Tension built in his body as he crossed the street and headed for the restaurant. Tom ordered and ate his usual sandwich, the veggie wrap, still thinking about the robbers. He looked at his watch. It's time to go see the sheriff, he said to himself.

Tom headed back to the mall and walked through it to access the western exit that accessed the parking lot. He heard footsteps behind him...he turned. The footsteps stopped. Two men stood a few feet away. They both stared at the far wall. One of them had long, narrow sideburns and black, kinky hair. The other one looked like a ball. He had a round head, arms, legs and hands. Suddenly he knew. *They were the two guys who robbed the gas station in New Dresden.*

Tom rushed through the door and hurried to his vehicle. He pressed the unlock icon on his fob and grabbed the handle. He felt a hand on his shoulder. Turning his head, he looked into a pair of beady eyes set deep into a narrow face. "What!" he exclaimed.

The man grabbed Tom's shirt at the neck and pulled it forward. "If you want your life to remain peaceful, you shut your mouth. Do you understand?"

"What the heck are you talking about? Get your hand off of me!"

Tom felt the push. His torso slammed against the car door.

"You know damn well what I'm talkin' about." The man placed a fist against Tom's chin—pushing it upward, stretching his neck until it hurt. Then the assailant pulled it back, turned and rapidly walked away.

Tom opened the door and sat down. The deep, sinking feeling in the pit of his stomach didn't go away. He started his vehicle and drove to the County Offices building, almost hitting a pickup truck at the second intersection. The blaring sound of a horn jolted his brain back into reality.

TOM WALKED UP A CORRIDOR IN THE COUNTY BUILDING, following a set of wall signs that led him to a frosted glass door emblazoned with *Big Lake's County Sheriff.* He entered and approached one of the two peep windows.

"Can I help you?" the woman sitting behind the counter asked.

"I'm here to see Deputy Jackson. I have an appointment."

"Name, please."

"Tom Hastings."

"Just a moment." She left her station.

Tom felt tension building in his chest. A minute later, a side door opened. A tall, lean, smiling deputy stood in the doorway. "Hello, Hastings, I'm Deputy Todd Jackson."

Tom shook his hand.

"Come on in. I appreciate you doing this."

Tom nodded and followed the deputy into a large room. Four people sat in a semi-circle in front of computer screens.

"Right this way, sir," the deputy said, his left eye squinting.

Tom followed the deputy into a small office. The deputy pointed at a chair in front of the desk. Tom sat down and looked around the room. The door opened and a second deputy entered.

"Hastings, this is Deputy Evers. He's my investigative partner in this case."

Tom and the new deputy shook hands.

"So what's this about you seeing two men in New Dresden late Sunday night?" Deputy Jackson asked.

Tom explained what he had seen. The deputy penciled in a notebook. Then he looked up. "Would you recognize either of the two if you saw them again?"

Tom looked up at the ceiling.

"Mr. Hastings, are you okay?"

The deputy stood. "You've been threatened! Haven't you?"

Tom gritted his teeth and nodded. The tension in his chest eased considerably.

"Mr. Hastings, we need to know the whole story. Best for you—best for everyone concerned," Deputy Jackson said.

Tom told the deputy everything that had happened at the meeting with the two men.

The deputy got up from behind the desk. "Mr. Hastings, we appreciate all that you've told us. I'm not exactly certain what sort of threat those two men are to you. However, I'm gonna give you a special cell phone." The deputy opened a drawer. "This one—you carry it with you at all times."

Tom thought about the $20,000 incident he experienced the previous year. He had been blackmailed. The sheriff set up a scene where he would hand over the money...and they were supposed to catch the perpetrator on the site. It failed. Tom eventually got his money back but it took almost a year.

Tom stood. The deputy walked over to him and showed him the button he needed to press if a problem arose. Tom reached out with his hand and dropped it into his jacket pocket, watching the deputy's left eye squint.

"The department appreciates you coming in, Mr. Hastings. We hope to have the bandits in custody soon."

Tom nodded. "The sooner the better."

He walked out into the receiving area and out through another door. Tom walked quickly up the corridor that led to the exit. He bounced down the marble steps and waited for two cars to pass before crossing the street to his vehicle.

Tom felt more secure with the special communication device in his coat pocket. He thought about his automatic sitting on a shelf in a closet in his bedroom. As he took a right on the avenue that led him to U.S. Highway 59, he noticed that a rusty white sedan took the same turn and followed behind. The vehicle glinted in his rear view mirror.

Tom waited for a line of four vehicles to pass before turning left onto the federal highway. He set his cruise to 60 and glanced at the temperature gauge. It read eight degrees. The sedan remained about three car lengths behind. Tom pushed his foot on the accelerator, speeding up to 65. The car behind him sped up also.

He took a left onto a county highway towards New Dresden. The white car also made the turn and remained close behind. Tom gripped the steering wheel tighter. He slowed for a sharp curve two miles later. Tom increased his speed to 50. The car behind him did the same. Okay, wise guys, he said to himself. He reached in his pocket and pulled out the phone. He pressed the red button.

"Sheriff's dispatch. Pullman here. How can I help you?"

"This is Tom Hastings. Please notify Deputy Jackson immediately! I'm being followed!"

"Okay. You must be on County 17, right?"

"Yes—about four miles from New Dresden."

Tom heard noises in the background during the pause. "Hastings, this is Jackson. What type of vehicle is it?"

"It's a rusted white sedan."

"Okay. Stay at slightly slower than normal speed—about 50—and then take a left at the stop sign in New Dresden. Pull over to the curb and park. Make sure your doors are locked. If your pursuers get out of the car, drive your vehicle a few feet ahead—not much, just a little."

"Okay."

17

HUB SCHMITZ'S TONGUE DARTED OUT to moisten his cracked lips. His eyes focused on the rear bumper of the gray SUV directly ahead of him. His almost chinless, slim face had barely enough space for a narrow set of lips and a black, thin mustache. Hub's kinky, black hair looked like a rug, except for a pair of long, narrow sideburns.

His leering expression magnified each time he slowed or sped up to stay close to his target. Hub turned his head toward his partner, Tyke Carlson. His laugh ended and his voice spiked up an octave. "Look at the scared son of a bitch. He knows who we are."

Tyke Carlson needed money badly. He had been fired from a job in Pine Lakes, working for a locksmith. His car and snowmobile had been repossessed.

Tyke had the opposite build of his partner—everything looked round: his face, eyes, hands, arms, shoulders, chest and stomach, except the shadowy dimple in his chin, marking the beginning of a brown goatee. His thinning hair was combed straight back. Tyke wore baggy blue jeans held up with suspenders.

Tyke had been evicted from his apartment. Thank god Hub took me in, he thought. My ex-wife continually harasses me for child-support payments. No way am I going to support her high and mighty lifestyle.

'Twas my lucky day running into Hub at the bar in Pine Lakes, he said to himself. Not only do I have a place to live but a new source of income. Even though my cut is only 5 per cent for each pack or carton of cigarettes we deliver, it amounts to a lot more than I made working with that tightwad Irvin.

At least a dozen times, he had helped Hub rob a convenience store, resulting in an astonishing inventory of cigarettes. Tyke's computer expertise led to the use of Internet eBay to open up a huge market. They sold the cartons at a sizable discount. No taxes—sales or income.

Then everything changed. Hub met this man Garcia at a bar in Alexandria. Tyke smiled. No longer do I have to spend my days on the computer and shipping the bloody things, he thought. Instead we haul the loot to an old house on the outskirts of Chilton Mills. Everybody there is a Garcia. We count the packs and cartons and get paid with an envelope loaded with cash. I don't know who the Mexicans sell them to and I don't care. It's what's in here that counts, he said to himself, patting his jacket pocket.

Tyke looked at Hub with his large, round steel-gray eyes. "Why are we messing with that stupid guy, Hub? He can't hurt us—the cops have nothing."

"I can't call you a dumb butt, Tyke, 'cuz you've got a lot more moxy than I do in certain situations...such as the computer. But, we need to stay on top. The dink head ahead of us got a look at our faces last Sunday night. He needs a strong message…something for him to remember."

TOM SLOWED HIS VEHICLE just before he passed the 30 miles per hour sign in New Dresden. Okay, ya two bullies, you're gonna get yours and real soon. He stopped at the stop sign. The white car must be only inches away from my bumper, Tom thought. He pressed the door-lock button and heard the multiple clicks.

Slowly, Tom made the left turn, looking for a place to park. He flicked on his right turn signal and touched the brakes. The car behind him held back for a moment. Tom pulled up next to the curb in front of Ace Hardware. He anxiously watched as the white car came to a stop directly behind.

Where the heck are the cops? he asked himself, straining his neck to see the intersection behind him. Two men got out of the car, one of them short and skinny, the other built like a Santa Claus. Come on, cops. I need you now. Where are you? His lungs felt like they were going to burst. His pursuers closed their doors. Tom held his breath as he jerked his SUV ahead a few feet. The two men behind him darted back toward their vehicle.

Suddenly, sirens and flashing lights exploded onto Main Street. Thank God, Tom said to himself. Whew, that was close. Sheriff's vehicles appeared from all directions. One of them parked right behind the white car. Officers jumped out, yelling and pointing their weapons toward Tom's pursuers. Another sheriff's car pulled up against the traffic, next to Tom's vehicle. More deputies jumped out.

Within minutes, the pursuers had their hands handcuffed behind their backs. Tom slowly opened his door and got out. For just a moment his gaze met one of the robbers'. He saw hate in the man's eyes just before a deputy placed a hand on the man's head and pushed him into the back of the police car.

Minutes later, Deputy Jackson arrived. He hurried over to Tom. "Good job, Hastings. You don't have to worry about those two thugs any more."

Tom nervously smiled. “Your men came through.”

“You go on home now, Hastings. Sooner or later, you’ll get a call from the prosecutor. They’ll need your testimony.”

Tom got back in his vehicle and drove across the railroad tracks. I hope the deputy is right, he said to himself.

THOR BLEW OUT THE CANDLES. His thoughts ran deep. *I have failed you, Lord. I must have revenge…make up for my failure.* He sat down on his couch and read again the line he’d memorized from the Bible. *Therefore, I will send down fire on their cities and burn up their fortresses.*

Thor opened his garage door and backed his vehicle out onto the street. He turned left and drove down to the stop sign. He continued on through Main Street and took a right at the hardware store corner. Thor parked and entered the store, walking into the aisle of tools. “Can I help you?”

He turned. The woman looking up at him wore a red vest. The badge pinned to it read *Tammy*. Not a proper biblical name, he said to himself. “No, thanks, I’m just looking,” he said.

The woman clerk walked away.

Thor stared at the bolt cutter. It’s just what I need, but do I dare buy it here. He looked up at the ceiling thinking of a specific verse in the Old Testament. *No one has caught me cheating! My record is spotless!* Thor removed the bolt cutter from its two supports. He carried it to the counter and laid it down. Then he quickly walked into the other section of the store and brought back a red, one-gallon gas can.

He paid with cash and quickly walked toward the door. Thor collided with a big man who had just entered from the Main Street side of the store. The bolt cutter fell to the floor.

“Sorry about that,” the man said. He picked up the bolt cutter with his huge hand and handed it to Thor. The diamond in the ring on his forefinger glistened. Thor grabbed the bolt cutter and didn’t say a word. The man shrugged his shoulders and walked up the aisle.

Suddenly, sirens seemed to come from all directions. Thor didn't dare move. He felt nauseated. *Why are you treating me, your servant, so harshly? Have mercy on me.* The wails tailed off, but had sounded very close to the building. He feared that officers would burst through the door at any moment and arrest him. Thor nervously set his purchases down on a box next to the aisle, as if to disassociate himself from them.

Thor thought about making a run for the back door. My legs… they're glued to the floor. He heard footsteps approaching. A man whom Thor recognized as the owner walked briskly toward the front of the store. He paid no attention to Thor and opened the door.

"Whoa, what have we got here?" the red-shirted man exclaimed.

Three other people joined the owner at the door. "Look at that, they're slapping cuffs on those two guys," one of them said.

The tallest of the employees, a woman also wearing a red shirt, said, "Wonder if it's the gas station robbers…or just maybe…the fishing house murderers."

Thor shuddered under the employee's glance before he followed the others outside. He took a deep breath, exhaled and experienced the icy feeling leave his body. Thor quickly picked up the can and bolt cutter, and snaked through the door. He dangled the bolt cutter so it paralleled and nestled against his left leg. Thor walked as fast as he dared, bumping into people along the way. He found an open space next to the building and hastily walked toward his vehicle in the grocery store parking lot. Thor opened the rear door and set the bolt cutter and the gas can on the floor, then he hurried around and got into his car.

More police cars had arrived and the bystanders increased as Thor backed his car up and drove it toward the back alley. He felt liberated after leaving the noisy scene. Thor parked next to a pair of gas pumps at Nabor's service station. He filled his vehicle with gas and opened the rear door. He set the new tank on the ground and poured fuel into it until the liquid rose to within a few inches of the top.

18

HUB SCHMITZ SNEERED at the jailer after walking down the steps to the county jail area. He rubbed his wrists after an officer removed the handcuffs. "I want to call my lawyer!"

"In due time, sir," the jailer said, and directed Hub to a chair next to a counter.

"What do ya mean 'in due time'? I need 'em now."

The jailer ignored the request. He placed a sheet of paper down on the counter. "You fill this out." He glared at Hub.

Hub glanced behind him. His partner, Tyke, sat on a bench awaiting his turn. Grabbing the pen handed to him, he read the heading: *Employment*. Hub laughed and looked up at the jailer. Should I write down *thief*? he asked himself. He laughed deeper.

"What's so funny? Come on, let's get it done. I have further plans for you," the jailer said.

I wonder who I hate worse…the guy in front of me or that Hastings, he asked himself, thinking bitterly about getting set up and nabbed in New Dresden.

He signed the document and shoved it forward. The jailer picked it up and said, "You need to date it," and set it back on the counter.

Hub sneered at him. He roughly picked up the document, scribbled in the date and flipped it forward.

The jailer picked it up. "You know, your attitude isn't going to make your stay here any more pleasant."

"I don't plan on staying long," Hub shot back.

Minutes later, the jailer escorted Hub and Tyke down a narrow, dingy corridor. He swung a creaking cell door open. "Right in there, gentlemen. Enjoy your stay."

THE SHERIFF TURNED TOWARD THE DOOR. Someone had knocked. "Come on in, Todd."

The tall, light-brown haired deputy entered the room.

"Have a seat."

Sheriff Dave Johnson leaned back in his chair and placed both hands behind his head. "Okay, guys, let's have your reports. You first, Todd."

The tall deputy licked his upper lip. "I've got some good news and I've got some bad."

Sheriff Dave Johnson nodded slightly. "The good first, please."

"We've got the two gas station robbers in jail. They threatened the witness Hastings, who...who cooperated wonderfully, leading the two bandits into a trap on Main Street in New Dresden."

"The bad news?"

"We have not been able to locate the stolen property...mainly hundreds of cartons of cigarettes. The two crooks live in a trailer house, just outside of Chilton Mills."

"What about neighbors? Any luck?"

"None," the deputy replied. "But, we're still working on it."

"Good. It might be a little tough to convince the prosecutor to formally charge them without the real evidence."

The sheriff leaned forward, flipping a page of his notebook. "Izzy, Kelly, what's the latest on the fishing house murders?"

Kelly Martin looked at Izzy. She nodded. "Kelly, go first."

"Dave, we have two dead victims, and one not-dead victim. A man by the name of Garth Sabolik successfully knocked out the wall of his fishing house and avoided carbon monoxide asphyxiation. All three crimes were committed on a Sunday evening.

"In all three cases, an apple was used to close the outside heater vent. All three involved a padlock and a bolt cutter.

"The two cases where the victims died—cradling a Bible in their left arm—opened to the same page, 110."

The sheriff ran one of his hands over his forehead. "Have you had any luck with a Bible interpreter?"

Izzy interrupted. "Yes, we visited the pastor of a church in Pine Lakes. He's well known as a Bible expert. He's also a psychologist. I have in my possession his interpretation of what he saw in the Bible and what type of person the killer is."

"Good. We'll go over that soon as we're done in here. Go on, Kelly."

"Lots of tracks at all three sites—both snowmobile and ATV. Nothing big to go on yet." The deputy paused and glanced at Izzy. "I did find a set of footprints in the Border's Lake case—different from the others."

The sheriff leaned forward.

"The tracks came directly from Tom Hastings's house. The return tracks did the same."

The sheriff smiled. "Not him again. Have you talked to him about the tracks?"

Izzy interrupted again. "Not yet, but we will soon. We're still waiting for his verification that the two Bibles he bought were in fact shipped to his brother in Washington."

"Oh yeah, I remember hearing about that. That Hastings guy seems to be everywhere." The sheriff ran a hand against the front of his shoulder, remembering the gunshot wound he had gotten at the hog farm a couple of years ago. Hastings was one of three victims tied up against the wall. Then, last year, he got involved in the North Dakota senator's escapades.

"Anything else? Izzy?"

"Locks and a bolt cutter and minnow tails."

Deputy Martin smirked. "Oh yeah, I forgot. You're gonna love this one."

Izzy continued. "The lock we found in the second case on Big Lakes was a standard padlock—pretty much for sale at any hardware store—pretty much the same for the bolt cutter that showed up in the snow on Border's Lake. The killer obviously snapped the locks shut to trap his victims. Then he used a bolt cutter to gain access."

"What about the fish tails?" the sheriff asked.

Izzy took a deep breath. "The strange-looking remains that we found on the floor are fish tails…minnow tails. Now get this! They matched the victim's DNA."

"What the heck does that mean?"

Izzy swept the back of her hand across her mouth. "It means that the victim bites the tails off his bait before he puts it on his hook."

"Ugh!" Martin exclaimed.

The sheriff laughed. "Well, Kelly, what do you think now?"

"I think we should pay Hastings another visit and see if he has any new explanation for the two recent Bible purchases…and explain the tracks coming from his house."

Silence.

The sheriff's eyes focused on Izzy. "All right, why don't you and Kelly go visit that guy again…Hastings. We need to get that cleared up, and the sooner the better."

The sheriff looked at his watch. "Thanks, everyone. I've got an important phone call coming in about a minute. Kelly and Izz, please remain in the building. I want to go over the pastor's report right after the call."

The deputies left the room.

"OKAY, WOULD YOU READ THE REPORT, IZZ?"

Izzy held a single paper in her hand and lifted it closer. She read:

The person (likely a male) who you are seeking for the two fishing house murders has some major mental problems:

1. He has been abused as a child.

2. The abuse likely came from a parent or someone close to him, such as clergy or a teacher.

3. He lives alone and hides from the public as much as he can.

4. He has made a covenant with his God to reward those who follow his law and punish those who don't.

5. His choice to kill fishermen who fish on the Sabbath could be based on the Bible proverb that forbids man to idolize anything, including fish in the sea (this is stated on page 110).

The Ice Lord will strike again.

"I would like a copy left on my desk," the sheriff said. "Make about three so we can each have one. This will take some independent thinking."

TOM FELT DISTRAUGHT AFTER HANGING UP THE PHONE. He walked into his den and sat down on the couch. Returning to the kitchen, he poured himself a glass of wine. Tom set the glass down on a table. He lowered his forehead into the outspread fingers of his right hand. "Butch is gone," he whispered.

A very close friend and former baseball teammate had died. In his remorse, he picked up the glass and said, "Here's to you, Butch."

Tom sat quietly, listening to music, his thoughts bringing to mind many years ago when he played American Legion baseball. Butch was one heck of a player. He often led off by getting on base. The second batter bunted. Before the opposition knew what happened, Butch was sliding into third. The only two-base sacrifice I've ever seen, he said to himself. And he did it so many times.

The doorbell rang.

Tom cleared his head and hastened to the door. He looked out the window and saw a sheriff's car. Uh-oh, here we go again, he said to himself. He opened the door.

"Hello. Remember us?" Deputy Martin asked.

"Yup. What can I do for you?"

"Only one question. Where were you Sunday night between 8:00 and 10:00?"

"Ah geez. I went out with my friend. We had dinner in Big Lakes. I got home a little late. Hey, that's the night I saw the two gas station robbers!"

"Your friend's name?"

"Jolene Hunt."

Deputy Martin stared at Tom. "Do you have an address and phone number?"

Izzy put up her hand. “Look, Tom, there was an apparent, attempted murder Sunday night. Right on your bay.” She pointed.

Tom frowned. “Murder. Another one?”

“Hastings. Because of not being able to account for two Bibles that you purchased…and because you live right here…it’s very important that you have an alibi for that night. Now that you’ve given us a name, we’ll check it out.”

“Look, guys, I’ve been telling you the truth about the Bibles. When my brother gets back from the Carribean, he will verify that.”

Izzy said, “Why don’t you call him on his cell phone?”

Tom gasped. “Not everyone has cell phones. I’m conservative just like my brother. Neither one of us has one.”

Deputy Martin glared at Tom. “There’s one more thing.”

“What’s that?”

“We found a set of foot tracks that connect your house to the fishing houses over there.” The deputy pointed.

“Oh, I went for a walk late Sunday afternoon.”

“By yourself?”

“Yeah, exactly that…by myself. My friend has been talking about having dinner in her brother’s fishing house one of these days. So I simply took a walk out there…to check it out…the distance.”

“Did you see anything unusual?” Izzy asked.

“No, there wasn’t anyone around. Only when….”

“When what?” Deputy Martin asked.

“When I got back, a snowmobile was on the way out there. It came from the public launch.”

“Did you see where it parked?”

“Naw, didn’t pay any attention. I went back up the hill and into my house.”

Deputy Martin said, “Come on, Izzy, let’s get back to the office.”

Tom watched the deputy’s car disappear around a bend of naked trees. His thoughts about his old friend Butch had gone up in smoke. That deputy…Martin…he always seems to give me a bad time, Tom said to himself, sitting back down on the couch.

19

AN ENVELOPE WITH A RETURN ADDRESS OF Big Lakes County Court showed up in Tom's mail. The prosecutor requested Tom's presence at the preliminary hearing for the two gas station robbers. I sure as hell don't cherish looking at their faces again, but I've gotta do it, he thought. The main thing is that the charges stick and they both go to jail.

Tom had tense feelings on his way to Big Lakes. He looked at his watch and realized that in half an hour, he needed to be at the courthouse. Stopping for groceries at this time was out of the question, he said to himself, pushing his foot down on the accelerator.

Tom softly stepped on the marble steps and heard the clatter of footsteps coming down. He entered a large entry room and stopped to read the marquee. Tom opened the door of the hearing room, drawing the gazes of several of the occupants. He recognized the clean cut, young man sitting on a high back chair. Jack McCarthy, the county prosecutor, had a set of light blue eyes, light brown hair and a trim physique.

Tom cautiously stepped into the room. His eye caught that of Hub Schmitz, one of the gas station robbers. Tom quickly looked away and welcomed the smile of the prosecutor who walked forward and reached out his hand.

McCarthy pointed. "The hearing will start in a few minutes. Would you take a seat over there?"

Tom sat down and felt as if most people in the room stared at him. He glanced at the witness chair, knowing that soon he would be sitting in it. I've got nothing to lose, he thought. Those two goons are guilty and the law is going to put 'em away. Tom grasped the frame of his glasses and pushed them tight against his face.

A robed judge strode into the room. A clear voice broke the silence. "The honorable Judge Bernanke presiding—everyone rise."

Tom watched the judge struggle getting up the two steps to his chair behind the desk. The humpbacked man raised both hands and everyone sat down. I don't like the looks of this, it looks so formal, Tom thought. I imagined a simple *say what you have to say and go home*.

The next few minutes filled with splashes of words amongst the judge, the defense and the prosecution. Finally the judge whacked his gavel on the desk and said, "Let's begin."

The two sides presented their opening statements. Tom focused on his ski trails. His mind drifted to where he wanted to be. Then he heard, "Mr. Hastings!" He straightened in his chair. "Would you take the witness stand, please?"

Tom felt every bone in his body creak as he stood and walked toward the witness chair parked on a platform next to the judge's bench. He sat down and took a deep breath.

McCarthy stood and approached him. He seemed to be stretched to one side fighting off an attempt to smile. "Would you give the court your name, please?'

Tom stated his name and address, watching the attorney's face turn into an expressionless mask. Mr. McCarthy approached. He smiled. "Mr. Hastings, please tell the court what you saw on the night of January 14, a Sunday—well, actually during the wee hours of Monday the 15th."

"It was about two o'clock. I was coming into town on County 17."

"What town?"

"Ah...New Dresden."

"Go on."

"About a block from the main intersection, I saw two guys carrying some bags across the street. They came from the direction of Quality Supply. As I slowed for the stop sign, one of them opened the door of a vehicle and threw the bags in. The other guy opened the trunk and did the same."

"What kind of vehicle?"

"A white sedan with a lot of rust."

"Did you see the faces of either one of the guys?"

"Yes. The one who dumped his load in the trunk came around and opened the driver's side door. When the light came on, he turned toward me. I had a good look at his face."

"Mr. Hastings, do you see anyone resembling that face in this courtroom?"

Tom's face turned slightly. "It was that man sitting over there."

The attorney quickly walked over to the defense table. "Was this the man?"

Tom nodded. "Yes, it was."

The prosecutor had Tom tell the judge the details of being accosted in the parking lot and followed all the way to New Dresden. Tom pointed at the two men whom he had led into the trap. He felt the glare of the narrow-faced one.

Mr. McCarthy finished his questioning and sat down. The judge peered over the top of his glasses. "Combs, your turn."

The balding attorney sitting next to the defendants pushed his chair back. He walked slowly towards Tom. His sport coat opened, exposing a generous midriff. He hitched up his pants with one of his hands and tucked in the front of his white shirt. "Mr. Hastings, what brought you to New Dresden at two in the morning?"

"I was visiting a friend."

"A friend. Man friend or woman friend?"

Tom gritted his teeth. "Woman friend!"

"Did you have any alcohol to drink that evening?"

"Yes, I did."

"Please tell the court how much."

"I had three glasses of wine at Bayside. Then I had two more at Jolene's apartment."

"Five glasses of wine, huh?"

"Yeah, but none since about nine o'clock."

"So after nine, you didn't drink anything?"

"Only coffee."

"When you pulled into New Dresden, what did you see?"

"Two men carrying bags, crossing the street."

"Did you see where they came from?"

"No, but they were coming from the direction of the convenience store."

"Did you actually see them come from the building?"

Tom shook his head.

"That means no?"

"Yes, it means no."

"When the two men were crossing the street, did you see their faces?"

"No."

"Then how could you conclude that one of them was my client?"

Tom gritted his teeth. "When the driver opened the car door, he turned toward me and I could see his face."

"How long did that take?"

"Ah, a second or two."

"For a flash."

"Yeah, for a second or two."

"What were you doing just before you got into your vehicle and drove toward New Dresden?"

"I fell asleep on the couch watching a movie. Must have been close to ten o'clock. Then my friend awakened me about one-thirty. I left for home shortly after…well, after two cups of coffee."

"So when you arrived in New Dresden, were you alert—or were you fighting off sleep…getting sleepy?"

"I was alert."

"What kind of a night was it…outdoors that is?"

Tom straightened his back and shrugged his shoulders. "Just another night. It wasn't snowing or drifting."

"Were there any vehicles parked on Main Street?"

Tom hesitated. "I don't think so…don't remember seeing any."

"According to my client, you said something nasty to him in the Big Lakes mall. What did you say?"

"He's wrong. I didn't say anything. I just walked out to my vehicle and he attacked me."

"My client disagrees and soon he will tell us his version." Combs pointed toward his client. He walked back to his chair and sat down. "That's all, Your Honor."

20

THOR CLASPED HIS HANDS TOGETHER IN PRAYER. He stared, mesmerized by the flames of his candles. *Yes! A fire! The house must burn! I shall turn it to fire on the Sabbath, he said to himself.* Then his hands began to tremble. He felt guilty. Thor asked the Lord to help him make a decision, shifting from a kneeling position to sitting on the floor with his head buried between his hands.

I must close the leak in the impenetrable wall of my brain, he thought. Sometimes a leak occurs. *My conscience is clear. I am doing the Lord's work.* Thor breathed a sigh of relief. A huge burden had disappeared.

"Yes," he whispered.

The mournful whistle of a freight train rumbling through town roused him from his deep thoughts. He rose, blew out the candles and walked to his bedroom. Four separate blasts from the locomotive warned the local citizens that it was about to cross Main Street. Moments later, the rumbling lessened and the town became silent again.

Thor slipped under the covers. He visualized leaping flames. *The house of the devil will be destroyed.*

TOM CHECKED HIS COMPUTER CALENDAR to verify the time for his medical appointment in Big Lakes. He knew that by leaving early, he would have time to stop for the mail and a newspaper. Tom turned onto the county highway and set his cruise at 58. He approached a farm and touched the brakes when a red pickup truck rolled onto the highway just in front of him, ignoring his right-of-way.

The vehicle drove slowly at first, but sped up as Tom signaled for a pass. It hardly slowed down at the state highway stop sign and failed to signal. Tom laughed. Most of the local drivers make up their own driving rules, he thought.

There was only one vehicle parked at Stillman's Super Market, not uncommon for a January day. Tom pulled in and parked a safe distance away. He turned the key and dumped it into his coat pocket. Main Street was mostly vacant.

Tom entered the grocery and picked up two newspapers. He got in line behind a woman whose cart almost overflowed. After she finished writing out a check, she asked to buy a lottery ticket. Geez man, pity us who don't gamble, Tom thought. We have to wait in line anyway.

The woman picked up her two bags and left. "Have you heard?" Ellie asked.

"Heard what?"

"The gas station robbers were both let out of jail."

"What!"

"According to what I heard this morning, the judge upheld the charges, but they are out on bail."

"Out on bail."

"Yup, some rich guy from the Cities put up the $100,000. The trial is supposedly scheduled for mid-March."

TOM TURNED RIGHT AT THE MAIN STREET INTERSECTION and headed toward Big Lakes. I can't believe what happened, he said to himself. Those two thugs are back out on the street. At least my evidence led to an official charge. That crumb-of-a-lawyer's tactics he used against me didn't work. It didn't sway the judge. Geez, trial not until March. I wonder if the sheriff's office is going to warn me. I better keep an eye out for trouble. Tom thought about his pistol again. Surely if they try something stupid, their bail money will be revoked. Yet, I'll be testifying at the trial, he said to himself. And... it's my testimony that convinced the judge. Naw...they wouldn't try anything. They wouldn't dare.

Tom turned off Highway 59 and headed toward the medical clinic. He crossed a single set of railroad tracks and slowed for a school crossing. The signal light a few blocks ahead turned red. He stopped and turned right, then signaled a left for the clinic parking lot.

The fish tank in the waiting room appeared to be getting most of the attention of the people waiting. A young mother picked up each of her small children in turn and allowed them to see through the open top.

"Mr. Hastings."

Tom jumped off the seat. He followed the nurse up a corridor and stepped onto a scale.

"Follow me, please."

The nurse motioned toward an open door. Tom sat down on one of two chairs next to a small desk.

"Uncross your legs," she said, and strapped the blood pressure apparatus around his right arm. She squeezed the black pump until Tom's arm felt as if it were going to explode. She released the pressure and sat down at the desk.

"How much?" Tom asked.

"One hundred-thirty over eighty-four."

"Hey, that's great. The doc's gonna like that."

The nurse smiled and said, "The doctor has ordered an electrocardiogram. You know why, don't you?"

"Because of the irregular heart beat, huh?'

"Yup, that's it."

"Where do I go for that?" Tom asked.

"You don't. The nurse will be here...oh, here she is now."

Tom took off his shirt and watched as the nurse glued a series of wires to his body. "Please don't move until I'm finished."

Tom nodded.

The test ended and the nurse pulled the stickers from his chest and packed up her equipment. Without saying a word, she rolled the apparatus out of the room and closed the door. Tom put his shirt back on.

Ten minutes later the door swung open and Dr. Rickter entered. "Good morning, Mr. Hastings. How are you today?"

"Fine so far."

"Ah, your EKG was basically okay, but it showed some signs of weakness."

"Weakness? What kind of weakness?"

The doctor explained that Tom had some valve leakage and atrial fibrillation: an irregular heart beat. He wrote out a prescription for two different medications. "I want to see you back in three months."

Tom placed the papers in his pocket. "Thanks, Doc."

He had the prescriptions filled in the clinic, drove uptown and parked in the mall lot. I'm starved, he said to himself, and turned right in the mall, heading for Lakes Brewed Awakening. He walked in and stopped. Jolene Hunt sat at a table next to the window...and a man sat across from her. It was the *table-hopper*.

JOLENE WALKED DOWN THE MAIN STREET SIDEWALK. She felt badly that Tom Hastings had seen her visiting with Paul Minton. She fully understood that he, Tom, detested the man. Jolene paused next to the large window in front of Terry's Shoe Shop. She peeked in hoping to see the proprietor and not get surprised like she had the last time.

Mr. Pendleton sat on a high stool behind the counter. The overhead light, penetrating his visor, created a green sheen that covered part of his pale face. He looked up. "Hello there. Got your shoe fixed." He reached down under the counter and held it up for her to see.

"Looks good. How much do I owe you?"

"Eight-fifty."

Jolene handed him a 10-dollar bill. He rang it up and gave her the change, also handing her a plastic bag with the shoe in it.

She left the store and tightened her shoulders. That man gives me the creeps, she said to herself. Not sure of the Minton guy. He doesn't exactly do the same, but I have the feeling that he's a front for something sinister within. I'll have to be up front with Tom when I see him again.

21

HUB SCHMITZ STOMPED THE SNOW OFF HIS BOOTS. He nudged his partner, Tyke Carlson. "This is the place."

Tyke tapped Hub on the shoulder. "Hey, going in there could send us back to the jug—parole I mean."

"Ah stuff the parole. There's no one watching us. The cops' law can go to hell as far as I'm concerned," Hub said, swiping at Tyke's arm.

They walked down three steps and entered a bar on Washington Avenue in Big Lakes. He stopped and looked around. "Follow me, Tyke," he said and worked his way around several tables, heading for the far corner where two men sat. One of them had dark skin and a black mustache. The other wore sunglasses that covered about half his face.

The dark-skinned man with a bushy black mustache stood. "*Sī, señors,* have a chair." He sat back down.

Hub and Tyke both lit cigarettes, exhaling streams of smoke that gathered into a cloud over the table. They stared at the man wearing the sunglasses. Hub felt the tension. Garcia had told him in Alexandria that they could become part of a syndicate and make much more money.

The man with Garcia spoke softly in a husky voice, "You are

both here because Garcia tells me you're trustworthy."

Hub nodded. He poked Tyke with his elbow.

Tyke jerked his shoulders and smiled. "You can trust me."

"Good. I need to trust you both. I need your skills."

Tyke listened with a frown on his face and narrowed eyes as he heard the man tell him that his experience as a locksmith would be needed. He will need to lift a set of master keys from his former employer. No more use of crowbars…only in an emergency.

"And you, sir."

Hub flinched under the man's stare, inhaled and embarrassingly gave off a croaking sound.

"You are the delivery man. You drive to and from jobs. You deliver the merchandise to Garcia's place. Understand?"

Hub nodded, feeling the blood rush to his face. "Look, angel man, I'm not interested in someone telling me how to run my business. I only want someone to sell my product to. I've got the product…remember?"

The man's face showed no expression as he talked, moving only his lips and lower jaw. "Exactly. You and I will get along perfectly. You go now. You will hear from Garcia when I need you. Understand?"

Tyke nodded. He stood, catching himself from falling after tripping on one of the chair legs.

Hub crunched his cigarette in the ashtray. He pushed back his chair. "It will be a pleasure to do business with you."

Garcia smiled, his large dark brown eyes reflecting light. "Gentlemen, I will be calling you soon."

Hub and Tyke walked away.

Garcia leaned over and whispered in the man's ear.

The man shook his head slowly. "No worry. They won't get caught this time. But if they do, we don't know them."

Garcia nodded.

Hub pulled the outside door open and turned his head. Both the man and Garcia were gone. "Hell, let's have a beer."

They reversed their direction and took a table in the opposite corner. They both lit cigarettes and ordered a beer.

"Can you get 'em?" Hub asked.

"Get what?" Tyke said.

"The keys, you dummy. Remember what the man said. No more crowbars. A key opens the door quietly. "

Tyke's round face glowed. "Yeah...yeah, I'll fetch the extra ring with a full set of masters. No one will miss it...at least not right away."

"We don't want a trail. You have copies made of each one and then return the originals, understand?" Hub said.

"Hey, that should work. Yeah—"

Smoke rose in columns from the two as they sipped beers. Hub glared at his partner. "Tyke, we'll need the keys for our next job."

"When's that supposed to be?"

"Not sure, but it'll be soon. You can count on that."

Tyke set his beer down. "I'll get 'em tomorrow."

"Good."

They smoked and drank, not saying anything for a few minutes.

Tyke said roughly, "Don't wanna go to jail, Hub. What if something goes wrong?"

"Now that we're in with the big boys from Minneapolis, we don't have to worry. They'll take care of it. That's what Garcia told me."

"Yeah, but what about this Hastings guy? He saw us!" Tyke exclaimed.

"Don't worry about him. Garcia told me they have a lawyer that's never lost a case."

"What if we got rid of Hastings before the trial? We wouldn't have anything to worry about," Tyke said.

Hub set his beer down with a bang. "Tyke, you idiot! If something happened to him, they'd come looking for us. We'd lose our bail...and our freedom."

Tyke lowered his head.

Hub placed a hand on Tyke's shoulder. "Sorry, I didn't mean that. You're not an idiot. You're one of the smartest guys I know."

Tyke sneered.

"But on the other hand, if we could make it look like an accident...alibis included...yup, it's a possibility. I'm gonna bring it up with Garcia."

TOM PULLED UP IN FRONT OF JOLENE'S APARTMENT BUILDING. The tension he felt preparing for the evening grew dramatically. He didn't know what to say to her after seeing her with that other man...that table-hopper. Maybe it was just a business deal, he said to himself. Tom entered the vestibule and pressed the button next to her number.

"Hi," Jolene said.

"I'm here."

"Okay, come on up."

Tom heard the buzzer and he opened the door. He walked to the elevator, entered and pushed the number three button. The hallway on floor three smelled of fried fish as he walked toward Jolene's door. He knocked.

The door opened. "Hi, Tom. Come on in."

Tom grabbed her around the waist, holding her close. "I missed you. It's lonely out there."

She pecked him on the lips. "Good. Would you like some wine?"

"Sure would." Tom followed her into the kitchen. She reached into the refrigerator, removed a bottle and filled the two glasses on the counter.

They clinked glasses and Tom followed her into her sitting room. They sat down on the couch. "What's the latest on the gas station robbers, Tom?"

"They're out."

"Out? I thought they were in jail!"

"Someone paid their bail. They're loose until the trial in March."

Jolene slammed a palm down on the table. "What?" She shook her head. "The law sure has its loopholes."

Tom nodded, frowning.

They finished their wines and Jolene led them back into the kitchen.

"Ready to go?" Tom asked.

"Ready as I'll ever be," Jolene said, smiling.

Tom helped Jolene with her coat and they headed for the elevators. "I haven't been to Bayside in quite awhile," Tom said.

After arriving at the restaurant, they were greeted by Jolene's cousin, Brenda. Tom lightly grasped Jolene's elbow with his hand as they followed the hostess to a table. He politely pulled out a chair and she sat down. Tom parked on the chair across from her. He faced the windows that exposed the expanse of a beautiful lake with a background of land and sky in the distance.

Tom ordered a bottle of wine and they studied the menus. "What looks good, Tom?"

"The third rack of ribs," he said and set the menu down.

The waitress arrived and they ordered. Tom held up his glass and they clinked. "Here's to our health."

Then it happened. Tom looked up and saw the slim, smiling Paul Minton approaching. Surely, he's not going to bug us, Tom thought.

Paul walked right up to the table. He grabbed a chair and sat down. "Greetings, Miss Jolene. How are you?" He turned his head. "Hastings."

Tom feared the worst. His blood began to boil. If this guy hangs around very long, I'm not going to be able to survive, he said to himself.

Jolene and Paul chatted for what seemed to Tom like hours. He squirmed on his chair, nervously sipping from his glass. Tom kept telling himself to have patience. Then he saw Paul place his hand over Jolene's.

Tom said firmly, "Paul, would you mind? We're having dinner."

Paul's smile disappeared. His eyes locked on Tom. "Blisters, you're not very friendly, are you?"

Tom stood. "Paul, I don't give a damn what you think. I want you to leave this table right now. You're not welcome at my table."

Paul stood. His cheeks reddened. "Great guns!" he exclaimed, turned and briskly walked away.

Jolene's mouth opened. She said softly, "Tom, what were you thinking? Paul's one of my customers."

"I don't give a damn what he is. He should mind his own business. We're out for dinner, remember? You're my date! Besides, I haven't much use for table-hoppers."

"Oh, Tom, you're overreacting. He stops by because of our business deal."

"Was it all business at Lakes Brewed Awakening the other day, too?"

"Huh?"

"Oh, never mind. It isn't any of my business."

Jolene reached over and touched his arm. "You're jealous." She laughed.

"I have no right to be jealous—" Tom gritted his teeth. "But I am."

Jolene laughed. She leaned over and pressed her head against his shoulder. "I like it when you're jealous."

Tom smiled and kissed her on the forehead.

THOR WATCHED THE COUPLE LEAVE. He thought about his abusive father. That man who disrupted the couple reminds me of him, he thought, anger building in his heart. *The sinner appears to get joy from irritating someone…the mind of a sadist destined for hell. The Lord gives both death and life; he brings some down to the grave but raises others up.*

A waitress brought his bill and set it down on the table. Thor raised his hand. "Who is that man over there, the one with the smile and wavy hair?"

"Paul Minton. He lives on Loon Lake. You can see his house from the road. It's new." She left.

22

TOM GLANCED AT THE CLOCK IN HIS VEHICLE. He left Jolene's apartment at 12:30 with mixed feelings. They had had a productive talk and reached an understanding. That Paul creep is all business with her, he thought. He's not the problem. There's something else. Something missing in our relationship. We seem to advance and then run into a brick wall. Time will tell.

He approached the crest of the last hill before he could see the town of New Dresden. Tom felt relieved that he didn't see anyone in the vicinity of Quality Supply as he slowed for the stop sign. Main Street appeared vacated except for a cluster of vehicles parked near William's Pub. Tom drove across the railroad tracks and looked forward to a good night's sleep.

Tom switched his headlights from dim to bright after turning off the county highway. His tires gnawed at the gravel as he made his way up and down a series of small rises before reaching his roadway. Tom held his breath. He saw a car parked on the shoulder of the road just short of his roadway. Tom slowed his vehicle to a crawl and almost stopped as he passed by, straining to see inside. It's empty, he thought. The color…it's dirty but…is it white like the sedan?

Tom didn't know what to expect. Is there somebody lurking about? he asked himself, watching the roadsides like a hawk. He flicked the headlights to bright and approached his driveway cautiously. He parked in front of the garage door, quickly withdrew the keys and got out. He locked the vehicle and headed for the house. Nothing appeared to be damaged or out of place.

He got inside and bolted the door without switching the light on. Damn, should have gotten the license number, he said to himself. Tom shut off the rest of the lights and dashed around his entire house, checking his security and looking out the windows.

Tom racked the slide of both his shotgun and pistol, making certain they were loaded. He set them down on the floor next to his bed. The special sheriff's phone lay on his night table. It's gonna be tough to fall asleep, he thought.

PAUL MINTON HELD THE CELL PHONE tightly to his ear. "What do ya mean, ya need the money now? I thought we made a deal."

He struck his fist against the back of the chair. His smile vanished, replaced by a deep frown. "What? Hey, I can't! Huh?"

Paul threw the phone down on the couch. "Why those dirty sons of …."

He walked into the kitchen and kicked the door of the refrigerator. Jerking it open, he grabbed a beer. He returned to the couch and recovered his cell phone. Forcefully, he punched in a series of numbers. "Hello. Oh damn, wrong number. Sorry." Paul repeated the process…slower.

"Garcia?"

Pause.

"It's me."

Paul listened for a moment and nodded. "Look, Garcia, I gotta have at least two heists by this coming weekend. Hub could do Dunvilla. What about your Alexandria team?"

He listened, shifting his lower jaw back and forth. "You better!" Paul hung up.

23

HUB DRESSED IN HIS BLACK WARM-UP PANTS and black turtleneck shirt, glanced at the clock on the table next to his bed and walked through the bedroom door. "Come on, let's go," he said to his partner Tyke. "It's close to one o'clock. Are you awake?"

Tyke, wearing a dark green plaid shirt and baggy blue jeans, sat on the couch, his legs stretched out to full length. "I hate this job," he growled.

Hub kicked Tyke on the side of his shoe. The heavyset man groaned as he pushed his right hand down on the armrest and stood. He opened the closet door and put on his jacket. Tyke stepped down the trailer step and walked around to the other side of the white sedan. He lit a cigarette, opened the door, and sat down.

"Ya got the key ring?" Hub asked after starting the engine.

Tyke reached into his jacket pocket and held up the ring, heavy with keys.

"This Garcia is a smart man—key instead of a crowbar," Hub said.

A freight train rumbling through the town of Chilton Mills held up their vehicle at the tracks. Smoke drifted out of both partially-open rear windows as Hub and Tyke watched the boxcars roll by. "How long is this crate anyhow?" Hub muttered.

The last boxcar rolled by and the flashing gates rose. "Come on you, dirt bag," Hub yelled at the car in front of him. He slammed a hand down on the horn.

They crossed Highway 10 and turned onto County 29. "How far is this Dunvilla place?" Tyke asked.

"Ten to fifteen miles," Hub said. "Garcia said 20 minutes," he added.

Hub slowed the vehicle to 50 approaching Spanky's restaurant, in spite of a speed limit of 30. "I bet that Hastings guy isn't getting any sleep," he said and laughed. Garcia's got good ideas. "Scare the pants off 'em, he said."

He slipped the vehicle through New Dresden, not stopping at the first stop sign, taking a sharp left. He didn't stop at the second sign either and sped up as he approached the outskirts of town headed southwest.

"Huh," Tyke groaned. "Ya got through that little jerk town in record time."

Heavy snow fell from the sky, forcing Hub to slow and grab the wheel tighter passing through Crystal-Lida. Outside of town, he sped up and hit the brakes going around a curve. Hub lost control. The car slid at an angle until coming to a stop just short of the ditch.

"Hub! For Christ sakes take it easy. What's the hurry anyhow? The cigs aren't goin' anywhere."

"THERE'S NO ONE AROUND," Hub said, chuckling as he turned off Highway 59. The snow had already blanketed the parking lot. It continued to fall heavily. He drove toward a small building that looked like a gift shop, and took a left to drive behind the main structure, disappearing from view of the highway. He stopped the car. "Get yar damn keys out and see if they work."

Hub remained in the vehicle with it running as Tyke hurried over to a back door. He fidgeted nervously glancing into the rearview mirror occasionally. Suddenly, Tyke turned the handle and the door opened. Hub turned off the engine and put the keys in his pocket. "Hey, you look like frosty the snowman," he chided, laughing as he opened the back door and grabbed a bunch of canvas bags. Hub hurried toward the door.

Tyke snapped on his flashlight and they followed a corridor that led to the main part of the building. He came to a door and turned the handle. "Damn, it's locked, too." Tyke tried the same key that worked on the outside door. It turned. In moments they stood in front of the huge cabinet that contained stacks of cartons of cigarettes.

Hub removed the small crow bar that hung from his belt and pried on the edge of the glass door. Something snapped. Tyke pushed aside the glass and began to toss the cartons on the floor. Hub got down on his knees and used his arms to slide them into a bag. "Takes care of those." Hub pointed. "Give those sliding doors underneath the counter a tug." He cleared his throat.

Hub laughed each time he heard the snap of glass breaking as Tyke pried open each door. "Look at that! A bunch more!"

"Let's get the hell out of 'ere," Hub said, and began dragging four of the bulky bags toward the door. "This is too much. Let's get half of them to the car and come back for the rest."

"Look at that, our tracks are already covered," Tyke said after opening the outside door to a whirl of snowflakes. They finished loading the bags into the back seat.

Hub entered and started the vehicle. "We're outta here."

TYKE WATCHED THE ROAD LIKE A HAWK. His driver had successfully gotten them past Crystal-Lida. He worried about the curves ahead, especially in places where the road's edge had no definite outline. He started feeling better after they passed the County Highway 41 sign. It's not very far to New Dresden.

"Wonder when that place is going to be on our list?" Hub asked, pointing toward the lights of a service station just southwest of the town.

"Hundart's?"

"Yeah, Hundart's."

Tyke felt more secure when the lights of New Dresden came into view. So he doesn't stop at any of the stop signs, he thought. No cops around here this time of the night anyhow. They crossed the tracks and he felt better as Hub slowed going around Purgatory Curve...long way to the bottom if he misses that curve.

Tyke's back straightened and tightened. Hub hit the brakes and the car skidded. He released his breath when it came to a stop and they were still on the road, but barely. The front wheels spun as Hub backed the car up and successfully left the state highway, continuing on the county road. He sped up as they climbed the hill before passing by a dairy farm. Tyke leaned forward. Hub hadn't slowed for the red markings ahead that signaled a sharp curve.

"Slow down!" Tyke exclaimed.

Hub lost control as the car slid sideways and snow exploded as the rear end buried itself in the ditch.

Tyke shook his head. "You son of a—"

"Stop the engine! The exhaust pipe is buried," Tyke said, disgusted with his partner. What a loser, he thought.

Hub paid no attention.

Tyke reached over and turned the ignition key. "What are we gonna do—stay here and freeze?"

"Look," Hub said.

A pair of headlights rounded the curve, coming from the direction of New Dresden.

Hub saw a small man get out of a Ford pickup. Striped bib overalls peeked out through an open coat. The man's jerky movements quickly brought him to the driver's open window. "Hey, you're in the ditch!"

"No kiddin'. Hey, ya gotta chain?" Hub asked.

"Nope. No chain."

"Maybe you can call a wrecker for us."

"Gotta rope, though."

Hub turned and struck Tyke in the shoulder. "Get out there and help this guy." Hub shivered, watching the desperate look on Tyke's face. "Come on! We've got to get out of 'ere."

Tyke opened the door and let in a blast of cold air. He watched through the windshield as a hooded man carried over a rope and dropped it to the shoulder of the road. Tyke pulled the door partially open.

The man wearing the striped overalls yelled in his high-pitched voice, "Start the engine and set the drive to low-D. Then, when you feel a tug, give 'er hell."

Tyke clapped his gloves together over his head as the white sedan stubbornly backed up onto the road. He reached in his billfold and brought out a bill.

The man saluted. "Forget it. Glad to help you out. Nasty night." The man threw the rope into the pickup box.

"Turn this thing around—and for cripes sakes, watch it!" Tyke exclaimed.

24

PAUL HELD THE PHONE TO HIS EAR. "What! The idiot drove into the ditch?"

He listened.

"Any idea who pulled 'em out?"

Paul scratched his chin and listened. "Edgar who?"

He smiled. "Well, at least they got out. Imagine what would have happened if they didn't and someone found the stash."

He walked around the room holding the phone to his ear. "Your guys need a new rule…no heists unless the roads are okay. Just a second," Paul said, getting another cup of coffee. He returned to the couch. "You still there?"

Pause.

"You need to have the Alex team make their heist right away—soon as the roads are safe."

He shook his head after listening further. "Look, the snowplows will have the roads cleared by tomorrow."

He listened some more. "How about this Hastings guy?" Paul asked.

Paul laughed at the response. "Your goin' to give 'em a call? That should slow him down a little."

"Okay." Paul hung up.

Jesus, I feel tired, Paul said to himself after the phone call. No way could any of my contacts identify me if they got caught. This includes Garcia.

PAUL SLIPPED UNDER THE COVERS. He thought about his wife, Susan, and Dilup Industries. We had the world by the tail back in Indiana. I was the CEO. She ran the front office. If her father hadn't got so picky, I'd have still been there. The surprise audit! I never had a chance. Then the old fogy called the cops.

Hell, I'd have paid it back, he said to himself. My luck was bound to change. That damn dealer at the casino. He screwed me good. I had the winning hand. So there were a couple of cards on the floor. The big lug that dragged me off. I'd like to get another shot at 'em.

So I broke bail. Paul snickered. I wish I could've seen the look on the jerk attorney's face when I didn't show up for the trial, he said to himself. I didn't want to leave Susan but didn't have any choice. Imagine spending three to four years in the slammer. No way!

Jolene! She reminded me of Susan just as soon as I laid eyes on her, he thought. What's she doin' with that old man anyhow? I should be able to take her away from him in a....

His forehead furrowed and he felt depressed. I bet that my old buddy Don has got somethin' goin' with my Susan by now. Nuthin' that I can do about that now. After I take care of Hastings, and my job here is done, I'm goin' back and take care of him, too.

THE NIGHT SEEMED TO LAST FOREVER as Tom tossed and turned, occasionally getting up to gaze out the windows. I've been here before, he thought, remembering being stalked after the murder of his neighbor and friend, Maynard Cushing.

He walked down to the kitchen shortly after 7:00 a.m. and started the coffee. The sky in the east began to lighten. Tom started a fire in his wood burner and headed back up into bed, taking one last look out the window overlooking his driveway.

Sleep didn't come. He got out of bed and dressed with two layers of clothing. His lower level in the house had warmed up some, and he sat at his dining-room table eating a banana and sipping coffee. His vehicle in the driveway appeared undisturbed.

Despite his uneasiness, Tom felt great because of the talk he had with Jolene the previous evening. They agreed to have dinner at Spanky's Saturday evening. He fixed himself an oatmeal breakfast and caught up with the news on the Internet. Then he put on his coat and headed outside. He started his vehicle and returned inside to have more coffee while the SUV warmed up.

The phone rang. "Hello."

"Hello."

Tom heard a crackling sound. A hoarse voice spoke slowly. "If you testify, you will die."

"Hello. Who is this?"

The line went dead.

"HELLO, THE SHERIFF'S OFFICE."

"This is Tom Hastings. I need to speak with Deputy Todd Jackson. It's urgent!"

"Please hold, I'll check to see if he's in."

Tom waited.

"Sir, Deputy Jackson isn't here right now. Can I refer you to another deputy?"

"Yes, Deputy Izzy."

"Izzy Felton?"

"Yes."

"Just a moment."

Pause.

"Hello, this is Deputy Felton."

Tom told her about the threatening phone call. She sounded concerned. "I'll talk to Sheriff Johnson and we'll get back to you."

"I'm going in for the mail. How about if I stop at your office…

say in an hour?"

"Okay. I'll be here."

Tom carried his automatic pistol to his vehicle. He laid it down on the passenger seat. Then he remembered the communication device. It was still in the glove compartment.

He wondered if the white car would be parked at the head of his roadway. Moments later he had the answer—the car had left. Tom stopped his vehicle and carefully stepped around the ground where the white vehicle had parked. He found seven cigarette butts and two crushed empty beer cans. He heard a vehicle approaching and looked up the road. A pickup headed toward him. Tom jumped in his vehicle and eased it to the right side of the road. The pickup passed and took a left toward Rocky Point.

Tom turned his SUV around and drove back to his house. He entered his kitchen and removed a box of plastic bags from a drawer. Tom grabbed his camera bag and drove back up his roadway. He photographed the butts and cans before carefully placing them into plastic bags.

He drove into New Dresden and made a quick mail stop. Then he headed for Big Lakes and the sheriff's office.

"HASTINGS, I'M IMPRESSED," Deputy Izzy Felton said. "What do you think, Todd? He's doing our work."

"I picked them all up using plastic examination gloves, so none of them would have my fingerprints," Tom said.

Jackson's left eye squinted. He whistled. "You're a wonder."

The deputies took notes while Tom told them about the parked car and the threatening phone call.

Deputy Jackson said, "I guess that I forgot to get back the communication tool from you, Hastings. Why don't you just keep it for now, considering the circumstances?"

"Thank you, I will. It's in my glove compartment."

"I wish we could help you more right now. If you get one more threatening call, let us know, and we'll put a tap on your phone."

Tom nodded. "Meanwhile, what do I do, shoot the bastards if they show up at my home?"

"The best thing to do is to call us. If they threaten you physically, then—"

"Then what?"

The deputy smiled. "Other than calling us, use your best judgment."

Tom nodded and left the sheriff's office. He glanced around the street before crossing and getting into his vehicle. He didn't see a rusty, white car.

25

GARTH SABOLIK HAD THE USUAL EXCUSES TALKING TO HIS WIFE. "I gotta get out and get some air." He left the house shortly after her two children arrived on Sunday evening. Garth pulled into the public access, glad there were no other vehicles. Typical, he thought. I like fishing by myself…gives me time to think.

He walked around his fishing house and turned on the gas valve. Garth smiled. No way is the crucifier going to get me this time, he said to himself. The special type of vent and door lock is my security. He patted the left pocket of his jacket. Just let the Bible guy try something. He'll get his due.

The evening wore on. Garth napped for about half an hour and awakened to the sound of bells jingling. He grabbed the line and pulled up his sixth fish, a two-pound northern. He released the hook and dumped his catch into a pail along with two other northerns and three pan fish. Garth stood and stretched, then opened the door and gazed in all directions. Nobody around, he said to himself. The crucifier is out of business. Garth returned to his chair.

THOR LIFTED THE DECK LID AND PLACED THE GAS CAN INSIDE. I won't be using the bolt cutter tonight, he said to himself, setting it down on his shop bench. He pulled on the chain fastened to the skis of his snowmobile. It's tight enough. Thor started his SUV and drove slowly onto the street. He slowed for the bumpy railroad tracks and took the state highway out of town.

As he had hoped and expected, there was only one vehicle and trailer at the public launch. Thor released the chain and pulled the snowmobile off his trailer. He looked into the container fastened to the rear of his seat. He could tell from its weight that the small gas can was full.

Astride the snowmobile, he turned the switch and the engine roared. The run toward the cluster of fishing houses took only a minute. He didn't stop but drove past about the length of a football field. Thor released the throttle but allowed his engine to keep running. He grabbed the gas can and walked toward his target. Then he changed his mind by retracing his steps and turning off the machine.

In this way, I will demonstrate my glory to the nations. Everyone will see the punishment I have inflicted on them and the power of my fist when I strike.

He slowed his pace and walked gingerly as he approached the fishing house. Thor stopped a few feet away and marveled at the changes. The vent had been moved to an external position to prevent a backup of smoke inside. Also, the door had a conventional lock eliminating the hasp and padlock. No longer could he plug the vent, or lock the door from the outside. My victim plans well, he thought.

Thor listened and didn't hear a sound from within. He screwed the cap off the can and placed it in his pocket, at the same time grabbing the lighter. Softly he walked around the fishing house and splashed gasoline against the outside walls of the structure. He set the can down onto the snow and replaced the cover. Again walking slowly with light-footed steps, he returned to the small structure.

He leaned over and flicked on the lighter. In moments, flames engulfed the entire exterior. "Curses." The right sleeve of his coat caught fire. Panicking, Thor dropped the can and slapped at the flames with his other hand. He thought about a specific Bible passage. *When he prayed to the Lord the fire stopped.*

He almost passed out from the immediate pain even though he had successfully snuffed out the fire from his sleeve. Thor held his burned hand away from his body as he hastened back toward his snowmobile. The engine started. He raced away from the burning house toward the public access, his wound tucked between his elbow and ribs.

GARTH HEARD THE SOUND OF A SNOWMOBILE ENGINE. He stood and peeked out his new window. He nervously watched the headlights approaching and sighed with relief when they turned slightly away from his fishing house and passed by. He returned to his seat. The noise gradually faded and totally vanished in moments.

This is the life, he thought as he lifted a can of beer to his mouth. He licked his lips and anxiously watched his line as it twitched. Garth thought he heard footsteps. He tilted his chin upward. Then he heard nothing. "Hey, I got another one," he muttered, his line bending sharply.

Suddenly—intense heat! Flames broke out inside the lower part of all four walls—the insulation melted and flowed like water. He dropped his beer and smashed through a wall. Flames engulfed most of Garth's entire frame. "Holy God!" he exclaimed. "I'm on fire!" He screamed and rolled in the snow...back and forth...over and over again. The pain felt unbearable. Scattered fragments of his clothing dotted the path that he had created. Intense heat turned into bitter cold.

TOM WATCHED A MINNESOTA WILD HOCKEY GAME on Sunday evening. The second period ended and he got up off the couch and entered his kitchen. As he filled a glass with water, he saw flames. Geez, there's a fishing house on fire. He quickly returned to the den and punched in 911 on his phone.

"Hi, this is Tom Hastings from Border's Lake. There's a fire in the bay in front of my place. Looks like a fishing house burning!"

"35204 Rocky Point Road…between me and Highway 228," Tom added.

He anxiously listened. Tom nodded and hung up. I should run right out to the fire, he thought. But then, what can I do? He delayed a decision for a few moments. I've got to go down there and help if I can. Tom hurried to his front door and put on his boots, then his coat and gloves. He used the door accessing the deck to leave his house. Tom trod down the steps and onto the front slope. He heard an explosion. Tom froze in his tracks. Flaming particles flew in all directions…much like fireworks on the fourth of July, he thought.

Tom reached his dock area in moments, the burning fishing house about two football fields distance. Suddenly, a new source of flames appeared, sending a blazing stream about 30 feet into the air. He stopped again, thinking he was too close. When the fire appeared to be subsiding, he continued.

Tom broke into a trot but slowed, feeling his heart rate increase. Then he heard someone yell, "Help! Help!"

He ran, ignoring his rapid heartbeat. Tom was close enough now to see that the fishing house had been reduced to a framework of glowing cinders. Nearby he saw a glowing bulk. "Oh my God, that was a snowmobile," Tom muttered. Then he saw a dark, beefy form lying on the snow. He heard groans. Tom knelt down by the person. He covered his mouth with a glove, nauseated by the odor of burning flesh.

The person faintly moaned, "Help me. Help me."

"Help is on the way!" Tom exclaimed.

Tom took off his coat and draped it over the man's legs. Then he heard the siren. "They're coming. Hang in there, man."

"Help me."

He saw the flashing lights on the state highway. Geez, I hope they pull off at the public access where I told them to, he said to himself. I hate to feel so helpless. Tom patiently waited and watched. At last he saw a pair of headlights.

The emergency rescue vehicle, a pickup truck from New Dresden, pulled up. Two men with flashlights jumped out. "What's happened here?"

"This man is badly burned!" Tom yelled.

They knelt down by the victim. "Let's get the gurney. He needs a hospital right now."

Tom watched them carefully load the man onto the stretcher. He helped them place it into the rear compartment of the pickup. "How do you think he is?"

One of the two gurney men turned. "No way to know at this point. Thanks for your help."

Moments later, they drove away. Tom watched the taillights and then walked over to the fishing house remains—mostly a pile of ashes except for the metal remains of the gas tank. Geez, I've lived here so many years and nothing like this has ever happened before, he said to himself, shaking his head. Tom slowly walked back toward his house, turning occasionally to watch the flashing lights on the state highway.

26

"I'M GETTING A TON OF PRESSURE FROM THE COMMISSIONERS," Sheriff Dave Johnson announced to his investigators.

"Whoever this eccentric is—the *Ice Lord*? He's a slippery one. Not even one witness. We've interviewed all the people within visual site of the crimes," Deputy Izzy Felton said. "We haven't got any fingerprints—only a padlock and bolt cutter," she added. "And three spoiled apples."

Kelly Martin scowled. "I know that you all don't think that Hastings is the so-called *Ice Lord*, but darn it...there he was again... at the crime scene...first one, too. I don't get it." Izzy opened her mouth as if to speak. Kelly interrupted. "I think we should bring him in for questioning. I don't think he's telling us the whole truth."

Izzy shook her head. "But Kelly, why would he have placed his coat over the victim? Then waited for fire and rescue...and on such a cold night? Why wouldn't he be the first one there? He lives the closest."

The sheriff forced a smile. "*Ice Lord*. It fits."

Deputy Todd Jackson said, "What's the latest on the victim?"

Dave shook his head slowly back and forth. "He's hanging on for his life at MeritCare Hospital in Fargo. The latest I heard was that he had less than fifty percent chance to make it." The sheriff ran his fingers through his thin blond hair. "Yeah, sixty percent of his body has third-degree burns."

Izzy gritted her teeth and shook her head. "What's our next move, Dave?"

"I want you guys to split up. Divide the stores I have on this list. I want every single one checked out for the sale of bolt cutters within the past two weeks."

The sheriff ran fingers over his forehead. "By the way, I've had Stamms contact all the medical clinics in the area. The *Ice Lord* could have burned himself lighting the fire, especially if he used gasoline to start the fire...and it looks that way."

A knock on the door drew everyone's eyes. A woman peeked in. "Dave, the press conference is set for this afternoon at 1:00 p.m. at the community building on Willow Street."

DAVE JOHNSON, BIG LAKES COUNTY SHERIFF, stopped at the front door to shake hands with a man and woman who represented the *Big Lakes Tribune*. He glanced back at the street. "Looks crowded...every television station from Fargo...and most of the newspapers."

The woman led the sheriff into the large meeting room. They stepped into the dazzling lights blanketing the podium. The whirr and click of cameras drowned out the murmur of voices. The woman knocked on the podium stand. The room quieted. "Thanks for coming," she said. After introducing the sheriff, she took a seat in the front row.

"Ah...." He took a deep breath and gently rubbed the top of his forehead. "Two people have died in their fishing houses. A third almost did." The sheriff went on to explain the asphyxiations, how the victims' vents had been plugged, how each one held a Bible in his arms, how the third victim escaped but was attacked a second time—with a fire. He completed his statement and looked around the room. "Any questions?"

"Were the Bibles opened to the same page?" a reporter asked.

The sheriff cleared his throat. "Yes, the same page...110 or something like that. What does it mean? Not sure. We have an expert studying the pages to help us answer your question."

The editor of the *Pine Lakes Enterprise* stood. "Sheriff, has your staff given the...the perpetrator a name yet?"

"Yes, Lou. My deputies call him—or her—the *Ice Lord*."

Clicking of laptop keyboards increased to a higher level.

"Do you have any suspects?" a female reporter asked.

"Nothing definite."

Half an hour had passed and the sheriff looked at his watch. "I thank you all for coming, but I have to go. You should all understand why."

The sheriff followed a deputy toward the door.

"Oh, Sheriff!" a young male reporter standing by the door exclaimed loudly.

"Yes, what?"

"Are the cigarette robberies related to the *Ice Lord* killings?"

"Don't know, but we're certainly considering the possibility."

PAUL MINTON MADE HIS FINAL PHONE CALL ON WEDNESDAY. Then he dumped the list in a wastebasket. There's hope, he said to himself. My income has tripled since last Friday. Paul clenched his fists and raised both arms high. The heists at Dunvilla and Carlos should put me over the top. If I have another good day tomorrow, I can meet the payment on time next Thursday...get those turkeys off my back....Blisters!

He glanced at the newspaper and saw the photograph of the burned fishing house. Paul picked it up and began to read. Well, I'll be damned. A fishing house fire...potential arson at that. How could you make any money burning down a fishing house? He shook his head.

He looked up at the ceiling. "Damn, I forgot." He punched in another number on his phone. "Garcia! It's me."

Minton listened.

"Alexandria tomorrow, huh? Tell you what, tell your local boys that we have some more jobs for them...and there'll be enough in it for 'em to hire a better lawyer. They'll be needin' one in March."

Paul listened for a few moments and smiled. "I got four more sitting ducks for ya to consider. Forget about another hit at Quality. They likely installed security. I want you to look into Nabor's and Buzz's here in New Dresden, then the station in Dent—and the one in Deer Creek."

Paul scratched the top of his forehead and swiveled his lower jaw back and forth for a few moments. "Okay! I'm countin' on ya."

Paul hung up. I'm one giant step closer to the goal...riches and a woman.

IZZY PARKED THE DEPUTY SHERIFF'S VEHICLE at the curb next to Ace Hardware in New Dresden. She looked at her list. Finally, my last call for the day. She walked onto the sidewalk and looked around. Izzy smiled watching all the vehicles slow down coming from the northeast. They've seen my car, she said to herself.

She walked into the store, stopping to look at a display of unique, lighted, decorative miniature buildings. Then she proceeded to the checkout counter. "Could I have a moment with the manager?" Izzy was ushered to a short stairway leading up to a cubicle. "Oh, hello up there. You're the owner?"

"Yup, what can I do for you?"

"I'm part of a criminal investigation. We're looking for sales records of bolt cutters—mainly within the past six months."

A man in a red shirt sitting in a chair nodded. "Step up here and we'll check it out on the computer."

Izzy stood behind the man and peered at the screen. She saw samples of red-handled bolt cutters. There appeared to be three different lengths. I bet that short one would take out a padlock, she thought.

"This is the one we carry," he said. "We should have two on hand, after selling one a week ago."

"A week ago!" she exclaimed.

He nodded and worked the keyboard. Then he turned his head. "The customer paid cash."

"Do you think any of your employees would remember the person?"

"It's possible...wait a minute...the day those two robbers got caught out front. A man in the aisle had a bolt cutter in his hand. I talked to him."

Izzy's eyes widened.

"Yeah, I headed to the front door after hearing the sirens. This man stood in the last aisle next to the ladders. He carried something else, too." He paused. Then he raised a finger. "A gas can. One of those one gallon jobs."

"This is very important, Mister...."

"Nelson, Matt Nelson."

"It's essential that we identify the person who you were just talking about. Can you give me a description?"

"Ah, I really didn't pay much attention to him...but wait. I do remember seeing a white face in a black background."

"How about your staff? Could you ask them...every one of them if they remember anything about this person?"

"Yes, I will, but they aren't all here today."

"Mr. Nelson, take this card and call me as soon as you get done talking to every one of your clerks. The sheriff's department would really appreciate it."

27

THOR TOSSED AND TURNED MOST OF THE NIGHT. It was the second day after he torched the fishing house. Earlier, he felt gratified because the burn wound didn't hurt. But now an unbearable, intense pain didn't let up for a moment. Finally morning came and he paced around his house anxiously waiting for time to pass. The clinic opened at nine. He gently rubbed more salve over his burns and inserted his fingers and wrist into a paper bag.

He opened the garage door. Clumsily, he manipulated the shift lever into reverse. Thor backed out onto the street, leaving the door open. He almost fainted when he bumped his right hand against the shift lever. He got to the stop sign on Main Street and made a wide turn left, almost colliding with a yellow truck. The lettering on the truck placed the impression of the letter Z on his mind. He headed out of New Dresden on County 17, struggling with the numerous curves in the road.

Thor turned onto Highway 59, following it for a few miles before turning off onto County 6. The drive along the shore of Little Big Lake normally interested him…seeing all the fishing houses… not today. Instead beads of perspiration built up on his forehead thinking of what might happen at the clinic.

He pulled into the MeritCare Clinic parking lot, nearly colliding with a black sedan. His eyes locked on the senior driver whose mouth hung agape. Thor jerked the steering wheel with his left hand, narrowly missing the vehicle. Thor parked and hastened into the clinic. He fidgeted nervously answering a series of questions at the registration window.

Thor sat down next to a young woman and child, using a napkin to wipe the beads of perspiration off his forehead. The young girl's eyes stared at his head, then at the bag covering his hand. She frowned and snuggled closer to her mother.

Thor sat and had the jitters for close to an hour before a nurse called his name. Rising from his seat, he almost fell. Grabbing his injured arm by the elbow, Thor followed her up a corridor. She stopped and pointed. "Take a seat, please."

He walked into a small examination room and sat down on one of two chairs—next to a desk.

Thor waited some more. Finally, a woman doctor walked in. She greeted him and carefully removed the paper bag. She voiced instructions to a nurse standing in the doorway. Moments later, the nurse returned with a package of bottles, gauze and tape. The doctor treated and bandaged his hand as Thor squirmed in the chair. Then, she wrote out a prescription for a combination of codeine and Tylenol.

"Would you excuse me for a moment?" the doctor asked.

Thor nodded.

Dr. Ferguson walked rapidly to the control room. "Did someone say something this morning about watching out for new burns?"

"Yeah," the white-garbed young man said, and handed her a small sheet from a notepad.

"Bill, call the sheriff's office right away."

The doctor returned to the examining room. The man had left. She hurried out to the waiting room and didn't see him. Glancing through the glass panes, she couldn't spot him in the pharmacy either. She walked outside into the parking lot. The patient had totally disappeared.

THE PIERCING STARE IN THE DOCTOR'S FACE sent Thor a message. *She's going to call the cops.*

He rushed out of the clinic, quickly crossing the parking lot and jumping into his vehicle. He backed out of his slot and drove to the exit. *My burned hand is a reminder that I, too, need to suffer,* he thought. Thor signaled a left. Just then, he saw a Big Lakes sheriff's car turn into the parking lot. *Just as I thought.* Thor forced a smile.

His eyes fell on a woman officer sitting in the passenger seat. I've seen her before. I don't have anything to worry about, he said to himself. *The Lord will protect me. There is violence everywhere—one murder after another. Even the wild animals, the birds of the sky, and the fish of the sea are disappearing.*

Thor drove back onto Highway 59 and turned north. He desperately needed the painkiller prescription filled. Better now than later, he thought. He turned his vehicle west onto U.S. Highway 10 and headed for Kmart. His bandaged right hand rested against the steering wheel, helping him stay in his proper lane.

He entered the store and rushed down the aisle until he saw the Rx sign beyond parallel rows of shelves. He had the prescription ready in his left hand when a young woman approached the Prescriptions-In counter. She nodded. "It'll take about 15 minutes."

"Could you rush this, please?" Thor pleaded.

The woman frowned then nodded.

Thor checked his watch and retreated to the main aisle. A mother scolded a child who insisted on taking a candy bar from a cardboard box. "I want it!" the child screamed.

"No, you can't have it. Stop it!"

The child flopped down on the floor face down, kicked her feet and screamed.

"Oh, all right, but you've got to promise to be good."

Thor shook his head. The child needs a lesson from the Lord, he thought. The Bible would be a good start.

He wandered around the store, often checking his watch. Time to pick it up, he said to himself.

Oh no, Thor said to himself. He nervously waited behind a woman who dug into her purse. Her wrinkled hands had difficulty with a stack of green bills. She dropped one on the floor. "Here, let me help!" Thor exclaimed and reached down with his left hand.

The woman turned her head. "Thank you." Then she reached in

her purse and brought out a black pouch. She took forever to flip it open and count coins. Then she talked to the clerk about the weather. Thor fidgeted, trying to remain patient. "Oh, thank you, Lord," he muttered as she walked away.

He lay down a twenty-dollar bill. The clerk left for a moment and returned with a package. She made change and he grabbed the package with his left hand and stuffed it into his pocket. "Keep the change," he said and hurried away.

28

DEPUTIES IZZY FELTON AND KELLY MARTIN PULLED UP next to the rear door of Ace Hardware in New Dresden on Tuesday, two days after the fire. They entered. Izzy stopped at the checkout counter. "We're here to see Mr. Nelson."

"Just a second."

Matt Nelson peeked around the corner. "Come on up here. A little crowded but private."

"Thanks," Izzy said.

She made her way up the steps, Deputy Martin right behind her. "Do you have anything for us? Ya know—the gas can and bolt cutter."

"Yup. Excuse me for a moment, I'll go down and get Denise. She's the one who handled the sale."

The tall, smiling salesclerk entered the office space. "You wanted to see me?"

"Yes, Denise. How are things with you today?"

"Just fine."

"I'd like you tell us exactly what you observed when you checked out a small gas can and bolt cutter last week."

"The guy looked like a wacko. He had long, thin hair that stuck out in all directions." She laughed.

"Was he wearing a cap?"

"Yeah, he sure was. Different though—not what you normally see around these parts."

"What color was it?"

"Black. Sort of looked like something out of the past."

"Was he tall, short, medium height or what?"

"Ah short to medium—somewhere between."

"What type of clothes did he wear? Did he wear a coat?"

"I saw black. Not the usual blue jeans we see in here all day long."

"How about his voice? Deep? Shrill? What?"

"Right now, I'm thinking of Johnny Cash. Low and deep—sort of rumbled—like a train in the distance at night."

"How about his hands? Your boss said that he paid with cash. Did he have big fingers? Small fingers? What?"

"Small no, stubby yes. Sort of like someone cut a chunk from off each one."

Izzy placed a hand on Denise's arm. "You've been a great help. We really appreciate this. I want you to keep thinking about this person. If you remember anything else, please jot it down. I'll contact you within a week. Would you send up Tammy?"

Deputy Martin smiled when the second salesclerk arrived. "Hi, you must be Tammy?"

"Yes, I am."

"Come on up, we'd like to ask you a few questions regarding a certain customer."

"Okay."

Izzy shook her hand. "You probably already know who we are talking about, a man who purchased a bolt cutter and a gas can about a week ago. Your fellow employee Diane checked him out, but I understand that you were in the cubicle at that time. Can you tell us anything that you may have noticed about that specific customer—clothing, face, hands, or anything else?"

"Black—he seemed all black. Well, except for his face. It was close to white—sort of like a mummy. Never saw 'em before. Sort of weird. Not what we usually see here."

"How about the fingernails, clean or dirty?"

"Ah, clean I think—ah, big though. Stubby and big."

Izzy's phone rang. "Deputy Izzy Felton here."

She listened. "Okay, we'll check it out."

Deputy Martin eyed her quizzically. "Check what out?"

"The prescription that the doctor wrote out for the burn victim. It got filled at Kmart pharmacy in Big Lakes."

A STIFF WIND FROM THE NORTHWEST PUSHED slivers of snow across the highway as Tom drove toward New Dresden. The flock of blackbirds, which he had been watching all winter, bunched tightly together on the power lines near a dairy farm. He passed by the loon statue and glared at Paul Minton's house, the table-hopper.

The large storage shed next to the house had two vehicles parked in the approach. Two persons held open the rear door of a UPS truck as another wheeled a dolly up the ramp. Tom caught a glance of several corrugated boxes.

Tom parked in the Stillman's Super Market parking lot. He walked toward the post office and saw a light-colored Chrysler sedan parked the wrong way in the alley...a No Parking sign clearly visible on the outside wall of the building.

His eyes wandered up and down both sides of Main Street. It had become automatic to search for a white car. He saw one parked in front of the bank but it didn't appear to have any rust. What's the matter with me anyhow? he thought. The two men arrested for the robberies surely were being watched closely by the sheriff's department.

Tom picked up his mail and a newspaper, then drove his vehicle to the north side parking lot of Ace Hardware. He headed for the door. It opened and two sheriff's deputies emerged. He recognized both Izzy Felton and Kelly Martin.

The wide-shouldered deputy stopped. "Look who we have here, Izzy, one of our suspects."

Izzy pushed a hand against Martin's shoulder. "Ah come on, give it up. Give Hastings a break."

Tom chuckled. "When my brother finally returns back from Alaska, you'll have the answer to the Bible thing, Martin."

Deputy Martin scoffed. "Oh by the way, Hastings, do you own a bolt cutter?"

"Yeah, I do. Do you want to see it? It's in my garage."

Deputy Izzy laughed. "By the way, I understand that you were the first person at the scene of the fishing house fire on Sunday evening."

"Sure was. Pretty hard to miss it...and the explosion...the gas tank...the huge flare when the snowmobile gas tank ignited...quite the spectacle. I wish I had captured it on camera."

"Hastings, for the time being you're off the hook. We have a pretty good description of the *Ice Lord*...not you at all," Deputy Martin said.

"Geez, that's good news."

"Got one question for you before we leave," Izzy said.

"What's that?"

"Have you ever seen a guy who dressed like Johnny Cash, and has a pale face—and short stubby fingers?"

Tom rubbed his chin with two fingers. "Yeah, there was this guy at Spanky's one night. He sat all alone in a booth. As a matter of fact, I overheard someone mention Johnny Cash. Maybe it was me? Don't remember for sure."

"Look, if you see that man around again, give us a call," Izzy added.

"I will. I still have Deputy Jackson's phone thing. Now I have a question for you."

"What's that?"

"Did you people find any prints on the two beer cans or cigarette butts that I found?"

Deputy Martin scratched the back of his head. "According to Jackson, the prints on one of the beer cans match those of Tyke Carlson. He's one of the defendants in the gas station robberies."

"Wow. So the two thugs have been hanging around my place."

"Even if they have, they haven't broken any law—well, except for littering. It's not illegal to park on the shoulder of a township road."

"What would your people have done if I would have called you with your communication device when the car was next to my property?"

"We'd have checked it out," Martin said.

Tom shrugged his shoulders. He knew Deputy Izzy would have reacted to his call, but he wasn't so sure of anyone else.

Izzy smiled. "Have a good day."

29

TOM STARTED FIRES IN TWO OF HIS FIREPLACES. The bouquet of flowers he had bought earlier in Big Lakes was tucked neatly into a vase on the middle of the dining-room table. This is going to be my night, he said to himself. Nobody can stop me now. I'm going to ask her to marry me. This is it!

He showered, shaved and put on a pair of dress pants, a neat long-sleeve shirt and dark blue vest. The clock in the microwave showed 20 minutes of free time before Jolene was scheduled to arrive. Tom got a bottle of wine out of the refrigerator and filled a glass. He sat in the living room and listened to music, sipping wine and anxiously glancing out the window overlooking the driveway.

His breathing stiffened as the lights from a pair of headlights swept across the trunk of an oak tree. The brake lights came on as Jolene parked her vehicle in front of the garage door. He watched her get out of the Toyota. The long black dress she wore sparked a whistle. She looked great.

He rushed down the stairs, through the kitchen, and out to the door. Tom saw Jolene coming down the sidewalk and hurriedly opened the door. "Come on in!"

He grasped her coat as she wriggled free. Then Tom snuggled her into his arms, squeezing tightly.

Jolene coughed lightly. "Wow, what a greeting!"

"I'm so glad to see you."

Tom guided her to the love seat. He filled a glass and set it down on the table next to her.

They sipped wine and chatted to a background of soft music, featuring Al Martino. "Did you win the lottery or something? I've never seen you in such a good mood," Jolene said, her blue eyes glistening in the candlelight.

"Oh yeah, I thought I was like this all the time."

She grinned and shook her head. "Hah."

Tom opened the refrigerator door. He brought out the bottle and held it over his glass. "You're driving, aren't ya?"

She nodded.

Tom filled his glass. He sat down next to her and put his arm around her shoulder. "I love you," he said.

Jolene moved away an inch. "You've had too much wine."

Tom kissed her on the cheek and stood. He finished the wine and set it down. "Let's get rolling."

He assisted Jolene onto the seat of the driver's side. He opened the passenger door and got in. Geez, I wonder if I should take my pistol, he said to himself. Too late now, we're on our way.

THE HOSTESS AT SPANKY'S LED TOM AND JOLENE TO A BOOTH in the far corner, near the fireplace. "Thanks, Sherri," Tom said.

"I'll just have water," Jolene said to the waitress who set down two menus.

Tom keenly said, "Just water, huh?"

She nodded.

"Glass of Chardonnay for me."

They ordered dinner.

Jolene took a sip of water. "New Dresden has certainly been in the news lately. How about those robberies...and the fishing house fire?"

"I suppose you heard that I was the first person on the scene at the fire."

Jolene leaned forward. "No, you gotta be kidding."

"Well, it was right out front of my place. I punched in 911 soon as I saw the flames. By the time the fire-rescue crew arrived, the structure didn't exist—just a pile of charred boards covered with a sticky melt of insulation."

"What's the latest on the fishing guy?"

"Not sure, but he's in the hospital fighting for his life. I was surprised that he didn't die right on the ice. That little thing burned to the ground so fast."

The waitress brought their salads and they stopped talking for a few minutes.

Tom pushed away his plate. "Cigarettes are on everyone's mind in New Dresden. That's all they're talking about after the robberies at Quality Supply."

"Did they have another one?"

"No, not since the one I witnessed."

They stopped talking as the waitress set down two plates.

"Yum, looks good," Jolene said.

Tom wiped his lips and set the napkin down on his plate. The expression on his face darkened. His eyes narrowed as his head turned slightly to watch Paul Minton approach the bar. "Uh-oh, there's the table-hopper again. He better not come over here."

Jolene looked up. "Take it easy, Tom. He's just a forward type of guy."

"Just as long as his forwardness goes in another direction," Tom said, taking another sip of wine.

Paul Minton remained standing, talking to someone sitting on a stool. Then he turned. Tom shifted his head quickly. He heard the shuffling of footsteps. A shadow spread over the tabletop. Jolene flashed a smile.

"Hello, my two favorite people," Minton said, smiling from ear to ear.

"Good evening, how are you?" Jolene asked.

Tom felt the blood in his head heat up. I've got to stay cool, he said to himself. This is a special evening.

Minton, still standing, placed both palms on the table. Tom grabbed his steak knife with thoughts of sticking the blade through Paul's hand and pinning it to the table—just like the scene in the movie, *The Godfather.*

Tom didn't listen to a single word during the exchange of small talk between Minton and Jolene. He set the knife down. The guy better leave pretty soon or I'll lose my cool, he said to himself, taking another sip of wine.

Jolene laughed. Tom spread out his elbows. He felt the eyes of his tormenter staring down at him. "Time to go, Jolene," Tom said, his voice raspy.

"What's the matter, Hastings? Can't you handle a little competition?"

Tom looked up. "I don't consider you competition."

Tom stood and shoved Minton away with his elbow.

"Hey, watch it, old man."

Tom's brain exploded. "You get the hell away from us right now!"

Minton laughed. "Or what?"

"This!" Tom exclaimed and shoved him away with his right hand.

Minton stepped forward and slapped Tom across the face. Tom's entire life flashed across his brain. He remembered the fast balls, the tennis strokes, the tossing of hay bales—

Minton sneered at him. Tom clenched his right fist, pulled it back and drove an uppercut into Minton's chin. Tom felt better than he had ever felt watching Minton stagger backwards and fall, upsetting two chairs and a table. He groaned and didn't make any attempt to rise. Tom looked across the room. The owner, Jeremy, stood in the doorway of the kitchen staring at him.

"Let's go, Jolene," Tom said.

Jeremy rushed over. "What's going on?"

Tom pointed. "That bastard got what he deserved."

"Tom, you just can't leave him like that!" Jolene exclaimed.

"Figure out the damages, Jeremy, and I'll write you a check the next time I come," Tom said and grabbed both his and Jolene's coats.

Randy stood behind the bar, his mouth agape. Tom caught a glance of him applauding as they crossed the room.

Jolene parked her vehicle in Tom's driveway. He got out and approached the driver's door. She opened the window. "Tom, this evening has been very upsetting. Right now, I'd rather go home and we can discuss this later."

Tom stuck his head in and kissed her on the forehead. "You're right. It was upsetting for me, too. I'll give you a call."

30

"WE'RE GETTING CLOSE," IZZY TOLD THE SHERIFF. "Our people arrived at the clinic just a little too late—missed the *Ice Lord* by only minutes."

Deputy Martin pushed back a rope of thick brown hair that had moved onto his left cheek. "The trail gets wider. Half an hour later, a pharmacist from Kmart calls. The *Ice Lord* had his prescription filled there. Unfortunately the images the security camera produced were blurred."

"Are the descriptions accurate?" the sheriff asked.

Izzy's large sky-blue eyes widened. "To the tee. Unless he totally disappears, we'll get him soon."

"Do you think the fishing house murders and gas station robberies are related?" the sheriff asked.

"No…don't think so," Izzy said.

"What about you, Kelly?"

"I think Izzy is right except for…."

"Except for what?"

"Hastings. For cripes sakes, he's in on both of 'em."

The sheriff laughed. "Small town, Kelly."

"What's the latest on Mr. Sabolik?"

Izzy looked at Kelly. "He's hanging on by a thread, according to the info that came into the office this morning."

Kelly raised a finger. "You forgot something."

"What?" Izzy asked.

"Hastings got into a scuffle with someone at Spanky's last night. It's all rumor, but…he packs quite a punch apparently. Knocked a dude down with one blow," Kelly said, sneering.

Sheriff Johnson raised his eyebrows. "Hmmm, like you said it's all rumor. No one called our office. Much more importantly, I want one of you to arrange to have someone at the hospital in Fargo around the clock. If Sabolik wakes up, we need to be there."

Izzy said, "We've been checking every hour with the nurse in charge of the station. They are to call us if he starts waking up."

"Good. Keep doing it."

"What's your plan for today?" the sheriff asked.

"We're going to make some calls on people and businesses in New Dresden. The *Ice Lord* likely has been seen by many," Izzy said.

"Good luck. That's all for now."

Izzy and Kelly left the room.

PAUL MINTON HUNG UP THE PHONE. He smiled widely, despite the Band-Aid covering three stitches just under his chin. He brought a hand up to gently massage the wound. Hastings is going to get his, he said to himself, pounding his fist down on the desk… got to make just a little more money first.

Paul had successfully paid off his note. Deposits by eBay's Paypal into his Minneapolis bank account in just the past two days easily surpassed his debt. He turned his head and watched his workers package carton after carton of cigarettes. None of them could speak any English, except Pedro. The UPS truck should be here pretty soon, he said to himself, glancing at his watch.

I'll need Hub and Tyke more than ever, he thought. The demands on tobacco supplies by my eBay customers are growing through the roof. I like the way my pair of bandits hit their target and disappear into the night...long before the break-in is discovered. So far, they've been seen by only one person...Tom Hastings. Huh, I've got a score to settle with that old man myself for more than business reasons. Then I'll go to Indiana and get the Don.

The scare tactic we used the other night didn't seem to change his behavior. That was clever of Hub and Tyke to park their car next to his roadway. The intention was to give the guy a message. It doesn't seem to be working. Hastings has been seen talking to the police a little too often. Paul put his legs up on the desk. Blisters huh, if I get rid of him, I'll have a free run on that blonde friend of his, too—sweet Jolene.

BURNING DOWN THE SINNER'S LAIR WAS THE RIGHT THING TO DO, Thor said to himself, after hurriedly rushing out of Kmart. He anxiously waited for a break in the traffic so he could turn onto Highway 10. Finally a space...Thor drew a horn from a pickup truck as his vehicle barely missed getting hit. He turned onto Highway 59 and set the cruise to 57. The last thing I need right now is to get stopped by a trooper, he said to himself.

He took a right at the stop sign after arriving in New Dresden and drove into his garage. Thor had only one thing in mind—pain and a nap. The doctor's treatment of his hand had helped tremendously. Thor poured water into a glass and sloshed down two of the painkillers. Then he headed for his bedroom.

31

TOM CHECKED HIS GLOVE COMPARMENT to make sure the police communication device and his pistol didn't stay behind. I wonder how many years are going to pass before I quit looking for the white car next to my roadway, he said to himself as he drove onto the township road. He tensed, seeing a dark-colored sedan parked on the county highway. Oh, he thought, relieved, it's just one of my neighbors picking up mail.

I may as well head into New Dresden and get the ordeal over with, he said to himself, thinking about his fight with Minton the night before. Damn it anyhow. It turned Jolene off and she left right after dropping me off. Not sure what I should do now. Maybe she'll marry Minton. Lots of luck, lady. I can't imagine a worse fate than a life of table-hopping.

Tom approached Purgatory Curve. What, again? he asked himself. Another UPS truck...what the heck is that Minton guy up to besides making me miserable?

He crossed the railroad tracks and did a U-turn on Main Street, ending up next to the curb near the post office. I'm just like everyone else around here, he said to himself...make up my own driving rules. Tom removed the glove from his right hand, exposing three Band-Aids across the knuckles of his three middle fingers.

I better make this quick, he thought, entering the post office. The lone man inside held up a palm, grinning from ear to ear. Not funny, Tom thought, fishing out his mail and heading outside. He picked up two newspapers at Stillman's.

"Rocky, the second," Ellie uttered, and gave Tom three quarters in change. "Everyone's talkin', Tom. You're a hero. No one around these parts thinks much of that Minton guy anyhow."

"What do ya know about 'em? What kind of business does he have?"

Ellie shook her head. "Don't know."

"Whatever it is sure requires a lot of UPS traffic," Tom said.

"I'll ask around," she said. "Oh yeah, my boss has mentioned it, too…that he has seen a UPS truck parked in Minton's driveway more than once."

"Uh-huh," Tom said.

"You know, years ago everyone in this town knew anything and everything that was going on. Things have changed. So many new people have moved in the past few years that…."

"That what?" Tom asked.

"No one pays much attention anymore. There's so much irregular activity going on. Who cares?"

Tom stared at Ellie, thinking about what she said. Geez, we better all start caring. He nodded and said, "See you tomorrow."

He got into his vehicle and headed for home. Four vehicles were parked close to each other next to the big door of Minton's shed. He slowed and glanced in his rearview mirror. He didn't see anyone behind him and came to a stop, watching Minton's place. I wonder what the tyrant is up to, he said to himself.

Tom pushed down on the accelerator when he saw a vehicle approaching. He glanced at the cemetery as he passed. Geez, if my wife was here, I probably wouldn't get into any of these hassles, he thought. I wouldn't have met or at least gotten involved with all those women.

He drove down the township road toward his home. Geez, there it is again! He scooted over the last hill and spotted the rusty, white sedan. Tom stopped his vehicle and opened his glove compartment. He reached in and pulled out the pistol. Tom released the brake and his SUV began rolling ahead slowly. Suddenly, the car's lights came on and it took off, heading toward Rocky Point. Tom increased his speed, stopping at the beginning of his roadway. The taillights disappeared after passing over a rise in the Rocky Point road.

Tom pushed the gas pedal and drove his vehicle down his roadway at a brisk pace, scanning the areas on both sides of his road as he bounced over the small knolls. I've been through this kind of hocus pocus many times before, he said to himself. Just let those snakes show their faces and they'll pay. The face of a previous intruder entered his mind...the creep who tried to kill me to cover up the murder of his neighbor Maynard Cushing...three years had gone by since that happened.

Tom pushed the button and the garage door opened. He racked the slide on his automatic pistol before exiting his vehicle. Staying in the shadows, he worked his way out of the garage...quickly slipping across the parking area and into his house.

He bolted the door and shut off all the lights. Tom stared at the electronic device that he held in his left hand. Geez, all I have to do is push this button and the cops will come.

Tom sat down on the carpeted floor by the window in the living room that overlooked the driveway. His grip on the automatic loosened as waves of sleep gently flowed into his brain.

"HAND ME THE JUG," HUB SAID, reaching his hand out. "I bet we scared the pants off of him again, huh?"

He grasped the bottle from Tyke's outstretched hand and lifted it to his mouth. "Is he following us?" he asked and handed the bottle back.

Tyke turned his head. "Nuthin' comin' this way."

Hub released the gas pedal approaching the turn that would take them back to where they came in. "I was hopin' that he'd take the bait and come after us."

Tyke opened his window and heaved the empty bottle into the ditch. "I know that Garcia wants us to harass the guy...but I'm not convinced it's the right thing to do."

"What have we got to lose? The cops can't touch us. Sooner or later, we'll draw the old man into a trap...beat the hell out of 'em." Hub laughed.

"Ah hell, let's go home," Hub said and turned the vehicle onto County Highway 4 and headed toward Chilton Mills. "Garcia's gonna be callin' us…set up some more jobs. What do ya say, Tyke?" Hub slammed a fist against Tyke's shoulder. "Things are finally going our way."

32

PAUL MINTON POURED HIMSELF A WHISKEY. He walked to the window and watched the bobcat push snow off his driveway into huge piles. Must have snowed ten inches, he said to himself. Good thing I shipped out what I did during the week. I doubt my workers could have gotten here today.

The white snow covered the landscape for as far as he could see. The daylight had begun to shrink. Snow continued to fall. I've got plenty of time before heading over to Spanky's to meet Garcia, he thought.

The whiskey that lined the walls of his stomach removed most of the tension that had been building for weeks. I got the bucks now, he thought. Life will be different. What would I do without the Internet? He walked back into the kitchen and refilled his glass. Sales are huge. He laughed out loud. Imagine no taxes…very little risk.

His smile turned into a frown when he rubbed the side of his lower jaw. The stitches had been removed but tenderness remained. He felt his face flush as he thought about that night at Spanky's. He got a lucky punch in, Paul said to himself. It won't happen again. Hastings! You're going to have….He sneered and laughed…a misfortune. His woman will soon be up for grabs.

Paul carried his glass onto the porch that housed the spa. He set the drink on the ledge, took off his robe, and slid into the soothing hot water. The floor-to-ceiling windows in the three outside walls had fogged over totally. He dropped in to his chin and smiled, listening to modern rock music that flowed into the room from two speakers mounted on the inside wall.

He thought about his past...living in Chicago, working for the mob. I'm now the head hauncho. I call the shots. I've disappeared from the face of the earth. As far as the police and my bosses know, I'm feeding fish at the bottom of Lake Michigan.

Paul reached up and grabbed the glass. He sucked in a double, enjoying the warmth as the liquid bathed his esophagus and pooled at the bottom of his stomach. He closed his eyes. This is as good as it gets, he thought. Almost the greatest...Blisters, I need a woman....

Then suddenly his mood changed. His insides boiled over with rage thinking about his most recent confrontation with Hastings. He threw the empty glass across the room, shattering it into fragments. Then he stepped out of the spa.

THOR SAT IN A BOOTH THAT had a view of every person coming and going at Spanky's restaurant. He wore a red jacket and red cap, his right arm hanging at his side, hiding the gloved hand. He lifted the wine glass with the fingers of his good hand, bringing the delicate good-tasting Pinot Noir to his lips.

The treatment I got on Monday must be working, he thought. It better...I can't go back...can't get any more painkillers either. I'd be sitting in a jail cell within the hour. *The sinners would celebrate.*

Thor watched through his dark-framed plastic glasses as the tall, wavy-haired man entered. Thor had gotten his name, Paul Minton, from the waitress the last time he was at the restaurant. He knew the first moment he had laid eyes on him that he was a bad person. He harassed people. Thor thought about the man who had stood up to him and struck him down—*an angel striking the devil, crashing him to the floor.*

Minton stood at the bar until the bartender placed a drink down in front of him. Then he wandered to a far booth and sat across from a man sporting a very thick, bushy black mustache. Another devil, Thor thought. He watched the wavy-haired guy gesturing with his hands, one finger moving around like a housefly.

Thor got up from the booth, took along his slip and stopped at the check-out counter. He laid a twenty down and headed out the door.

The evening temperature had chilled considerably, causing him to pull up his collar and press the open ends of his jacket against his neck. Thor drove down the approach and headed toward New Dresden. He slowed and turned into the parking lot where the big loon towered over him. He got out of the car and studied the larger-than-average, luxurious fishing house not far from the beach. It had attractive decorative wood trim all around the upper outside wall.

The devil himself uses it, he said to himself. He had learned from Ellie at the supermarket that it was none other than Minton who put up that box of sin.

PAUL MINTON GRABBED HIS WHISKEY OFF THE BAR and headed for the booth where Garcia waited.

"I see you got my call."

"Sĩ."

"Garcia, I need more supply…by Monday. You take care of that, yes?"

"I can do that, but—"

"But what?"

"Has to be close…here in New Dresden."

"Why?"

"The Alex pair is gone."

"Gone?"

"Sĩ, they'll be back."

"Which place in New Dresden?"

"Buzz's and Nabor's. Should be easy."

Paul nodded. Then, he raised his glass to his lips. He sloshed whiskey down his throat and set it down. "There's one more thing."

"Yes?"

"I need someone to…to eliminate an obstruction. Do you get

what I mean?"

Garcia nodded. "Kill someone?"

Paul rubbed a finger across his lips. He nodded.

"I don't know. Risk...big risk." Garcia opened one of his palms "How much you pay?"

"Ten thousand."

Garcia shook his head. "Twenty thousand."

Paul stared at the man. "Great guns!" He puckered his lips. "Done!"

"Give me a week to arrange. I'll let you know."

33

"**H**OLY COW, HOW MANY BAGS DO YOU HAVE BACK THERE?" Tyke asked Hub.

"About a dozen should do it."

"Where are we goin' first?"

"Dent."

Tyke lit a cigarette and looked at his watch. "It's almost 1:00. Are you sure we can get all of 'em done in one night?"

"Get it together, you jerk. All you have to do is hold the bag open when I shovel 'em in."

The sign Dent, population 251 greeted them as Hub made a left turn off State Highway 108. He turned onto what looked like the main drag. "The bar is supposed to be here somewhere," he said and threw his butt out the window.

Tyke pointed. "Thar it is. Only a couple pickups left."

He made a U-turn at the end of the street. He stopped across the street from the building that had a huge Budweiser sign in the window. The door opened and a man staggered out. Tyke and Hub watched as the man got into a pickup. The rear wheels spun as the truck backed out onto the street, jerked and headed toward the highway.

Hub laughed. "It's perfect timing. Right now, this town's as dead as a fence post."

He pulled away from the curb, turned left and parked a short distance away from two pairs of gas pumps at the Dent Haven. Hub opened his window partially and lit a cigarette. Tyke did the same. "Put that fag down and try your keys," Hub muttered.

Tyke glared at his partner. He left the cigarette in his mouth as he opened the door and stepped out. He grabbed the key ring from his jacket pocket and kicked sludge off his boots approaching the single door. Tyke turned his head and grinned after the fourth try.

"Hah—we're in," Hub muttered.

"Grab four bags and let's go," he said when Tyke returned. Hub reached into the back and brought out a small crowbar in one hand a large shop dustpan in the other.

He used the crowbar to pry open the cabinet doors. He used the dustpan to scoop up carton after carton of cigarettes. Tyke dropped the first bag to the floor and held open the second. Minutes later all four bags had been filled.

"Let's get the hell out of 'ere!" Hub exclaimed.

They each carried two bags to the car and dropped them into the trunk. Hub glanced at his watch. "That went fast. I told ya...took only fifteen minutes."

Hub spun the front wheels as he turned onto the county highway and headed out of town. Tyke lit a cigarette and looked straight ahead.

THE RED LIGHTS ON THE WATER TOWER HIGH ABOVE THE TOWN of New Dresden blinked as Hub turned the white sedan off Highway 35 onto County 4. He sped past the New Dresden city sign, slowing down before reaching the first stop sign. The car lurched as he made a sharp right, pulling up to a food service store. A large white ice receptacle, partially covered with snow, sat next to a red door.

"Give it a shot," Hub said.

Tyke lowered his head and stepped out. He took a position in front the red door, turning his head to look around before grabbing the expansive key chain from his coat pocket. "God almighty, one of these gotta work!" he exclaimed, glancing back at Hub who remained behind the wheel.

Hub dashed out of the car. He stopped next to Tyke. "Get out of the way. We don't have the time for you to try all those keys." Hub sprung the door open with his crowbar. "Get the bags."

Hub entered and held the red door open as Tyke entered. They walked up the handicap ramp and stopped in front of a second door. Hub popped that one open in seconds. "We're in."

Hub led the way toward the front of the store. He turned and cussed when Tyke tripped on the corner of a display. "Watch it, for Christ sakes! People upstairs," he grumbled.

Hub opened all the cabinet doors below the counter. "We've hit the jackpot. Must be a thousand of 'em."

Tyke began to laugh as he held open the fourth bag.

"Shut up, you stupid idiot. We gotta be quiet, remember?" Hub whispered loudly.

Tyke held a hand over his mouth.

"That does it, let's go," Hub said.

They carried the four bags down the ramp and stopped at the door. Hub opened it slightly and peeked out. "All clear." He dumped his two bags and the crowbar on the pavement by the car, and quickly opened the door.

All four bags went onto the floor in front of the back seat. Hub banged the door shut still holding onto the crowbar. He hurried around the back toward his door.

He heard a yell. "Hey, what's going on down there?"

Startled, Hub dropped the car keys. He stared at a man in a housecoat, not more than ten feet away.

"We're fillin' a tire with air," Hub said.

"Why do you need a crowbar for that?" The man advanced and stood directly in front of Hub.

"Mind your own business!" Hub exclaimed.

"This is my business…."

Tyke swung the crowbar. The man dropped like a rock. Tyke stood over him, holding the tool in both hands. He raised, it readying to strike again.

"Don't, for Christ's sake. We don't need a dead man on our hands."

Tyke held the crowbar up and turned his head.

"Get in the car, you dope," Hub said.

Tyke dropped the tool on the blacktop and rushed to the passenger side door. The white car didn't even slow down for either stop sign as its wheels screeched, and it headed north toward the railroad tracks. Hub increased the speed.

"Aren't we going to do that one, too?" Tyke pointed.

"Hell no! Not now! Jesus, someone's called the cops by now."

TOM PULLED UP AT A PUMP AT NABOR'S. He swiped his card and pressed the *Yes* button for a receipt. He started the pump and saw two sheriff's cars parked next to the curb. The area next to the ice machine, including the red door, had been taped off. Two officers worked within it. Wonder what happened now, he thought.

He walked up the steps and entered the convenience store. "Hi, Kim, what's going on?" he asked after placing a newspaper on the counter.

"Somebody stole all our tobacco last night."

"Geez, not again. Well, not for you guys…first time."

Kim handed Tom a quarter. "Quality's been hit three times. This is our first."

"What are the deputies doing outside?"

"Our renter upstairs got into it. He must have heard the noise and came down. They hit him over the head with something."

"Ouch. It didn't kill 'em did it?"

"Not sure, he's in the hospital…doin' okay, last I heard."

"This is getting to be a dangerous place to live. Sabolik's in the hospital after almost getting burned alive. Now this."

Kim shook her head. "January's been a long month. First our dog got sick and now this."

"See ya," Tom said and headed outside.

He stopped next to the police tape. "Deputy Jackson, do you remember me?"

"Yeah, you're the guy that tipped us off about the other robbery in town. Hastings, right?"

Tom nodded. "Can I ask you a question?"

"Sure."

"Do you think this was done by the same people that are awaiting trial?"

"Different vehicle according to the tire tracks. So far no witness— there is Jorgenson, but he's still unconscious."

"Geez, is he hurt bad?"

"The perpetrators hit him over the head with a crowbar."

"A crowbar!"

The deputy nodded. He turned his head and looked at Tom. "That's right, you saw one that night, didn't you?"

"Sure as heck did. I bet the robbers used it to get into the station."

"No, they didn't, but they used it to gain access to the displays. Lots of thieves use crowbars. Handy tool."

Tom returned to his vehicle and drove onto Main Street to pick up the mail. They could've gotten a different car, he thought. Oh well, I'm sure the deputy is on top of it.

34

DEPUTY JACKSON LAID THE PLASTIC COVERED TOOL on the sheriff's desk. "We're shipping it off to Bemidji today, but I doubt we'll learn anything. The thieves used gloves in all their other heists."

The sheriff rubbed his chin. "Except this one could end up being a murder weapon."

"Last info we got is that Jorgenson is still out...but his vitals are stable," Jackson said.

"Good and bad...we need a break bad," the sheriff said. "No witnesses as to the vehicle?"

"None. New Dresden at two in the morning is pretty quiet, especially Sunday."

"Now we've got two victims and neither one can help us, at least until Jorgenson wakes up...if he does."

"You're sounding like the two are related. The fishing house incidents and the tobacco robberies, I mean," Jackson said.

The sheriff ran a palm over his forehead. "Same area is all. Yet gut feeling tells me that they are. Somehow...."

"Izzy told me this morning that they haven't gotten anywhere talking to people, showing them an artist's drawing. The killer's probably all done after the burn," Jackson said.

"Well, for now I'll double our patrols in the New Dresden area. Double...now that's a laugh. Even one car would be a double."

"You're doin' all you can, Todd. Don't worry, we'll get a break."

"Maybe we should put a shadow on that Hastings guy. He always seems to be close," the sheriff said.

Jackson laughed. "Yeah, he showed up at the Nabor's gas station this morning, and he came over and asked me some questions."

"What did he ask?"

"He wondered if the robbers were the same as the ones he's testifying against."

"He wasn't carrying a Bible, was he?"

"Humph, you're funny."

"Yeah I know, just joking."

PAUL MINTON GOT OUT OF HIS VEHICLE AND PUT ON HIS SUNGLASSES. He walked to the door, opened it and softly made the three steps down. Paul walked inside and looked around. I don't recognize anyone, he thought. That's what I like about this place. He took a table in the far corner with limited lighting. Paul ordered a Johnny Black on the rocks and lit a cigarette.

He gave the waitress with a short skirt a pat on the butt as she turned to walk away. She stopped. Paul stared at her, a crooked smile on his face. She looked down at him, anger in her eyes. Then she smiled and clicked her heels as she strode away.

Paul saw the mustache. The large man, his back slightly stooped, hesitated at the door. Garcia didn't show his usual smile as he approached. Paul sensed something had happened.

Paul waved to the waitress. "Sit, Garcia."

"Tequila," Garcia told the waitress. He sat down.

Paul waited.

"We've got a problem."

"We?" Paul asked.

Garcia cleared his throat. "Our two local messengers botched the job in New Dresden on Monday."

"What happened?"

"Someone…a man from upstairs caught them as they were leaving. Tyke hit him over the head with a crowbar."

"And?"

"The man…name of Jorgenson. He's in the hospital…still unconscious."

"Did they get the loot?"

"Sĩ...and in Dent, too."

"When ya gonna bring it over?"

"I'll send it with Gomez when they come over tomorrow."

Garcia took a drink. He set the glass down. "What should I do with...the two?"

"Kill 'em."

"Señor!"

"No, not now, but later...before the trial."

"As long as Jorgenson doesn't wake up, they will be fine?"

"What if Jorgenson can't wake up?"

"Señor!"

"It's going to have to be one or the other."

Garcia drank the last of his tequila and turned to get the waitress's attention.

Paul stared at the table top. "What about the other deal?"

"My contact in Minneapolis has agreed to do it, but...."

"But what?"

"He wants thirty thousand."

"Great guns...thirty! I thought we had a deal at twenty."

Garcia shrugged his shoulders.

THOR CAREFULLY SLIPPED THE GLOVE over his right hand. He walked out to the garage and pressed the button to open the door. He wore his red jacket and cap as he had since the fire. He backed out and drove slowly onto Main Street. Thor pulled his SUV up to the curb next to the post office. He watched a few people go in and out before getting out of his car.

Thor entered the mailbox room. He squatted down and opened his box. He fished out his mail. Thor closed the small door and locked it.

"Good morning," he heard someone behind him say.

Thor turned. He recognized the man he had seen at Spanky's

with the woman, the two who were harassed by the table-hopper.

"Nice day out," Thor said.

"Where have I seen you before?" Tom asked.

Thor shook his head slowly. "Not sure…don't go out much."

Tom raised a finger. "Sure. It was at Spanky's."

Thor looked out the window. "May have been."

"Yeah, you were the one sitting with your hands clasped next to a nifty-looking glass of red wine."

"Must have been someone else," Thor said, and headed for the door.

He looked back and saw Hastings shrug his shoulders.

Thor slipped back into his SUV and drove northward, slowing for the railroad tracks and the approach to Purgatory Curve. He watched the UPS driver loading boxes into the van. That's the devil's den, Thor said to himself. What is he shipping? Then he saw eight Latinos leave the storage building and pile into two vehicles.

Thor turned into the park area. The massive loon statue still had a cape of snow sticking to the back of its neck. He parked facing the lake. The large fishing house in front of Minton's place had no machines parked next to it. He watched the road toward New Dresden. The two vehicles that had been parked in Minton's driveway came down the road.

Thor backed up and turned toward the exit. He sped up the ramp and got behind the two cars. The sign Chilton Mills flashed by his window as he remained three car-lengths behind them. They crossed the tracks and kept going, turning left at the big school. He followed them until they turned into a drive that led to a large two-story house. A two-stall garage has obviously been added on, he said to himself.

I wonder how many people live in that house. I bet it's a bunch, he thought. Thor kept going and did a U-turn two blocks later. He slowed as he approached the house, his curiosity growing. *What are those little people doing at the devil's den?*

Thor drove back toward New Dresden. He slowed while passing Minton's fishing house, thinking about how he could catch the devil in his lair.

35

GARCIA CARRIED HIS SUITCASE across the street to short-term parking that fronted the Hector International Airport terminal in Fargo, North Dakota. He had arrived on a Northwest Airline flight from Minneapolis. Garcia breathed a sigh of relief when the motor in his car started. Then he spent considerable time brushing off the snow. Must of snowed a foot, he said to himself.

As he drove across the Red River Bridge into Moorhead, he had mixed feelings about his failure in Minneapolis. He didn't connect with the contact who he felt would do the job. On the other hand, if I do it myself, I'll get the whole amount…thirty thousand.

Garcia arrived in Big Lakes and parked in the lower level of the apartment high-rise where he lived. He checked his mailbox before going up the elevator. As he flipped through the envelopes, he feared the worst. Most of his payments were in arrears, including the rent on his apartment. My share of the tobacco sales just isn't enough.

He rode up the elevator thinking deeply: I can solve the problem by making a final deal with Minton, or I can get the heck out of here and move in with Carlita in Edina. Ah, she's so warm….

Garcia opened a bottle of beer and sat at the kitchen table. He opened the first envelope. Hell, it's worse than I thought, he said to himself, setting the bill down and banging his fist. So it's three months overdue. You'll get your money, you beggars.

He opened the last one and scoffed. Standing up, he dropped all the bills into a kitchen cabinet drawer. Garcia flipped open his cell phone and made a call.

PAUL MINTON LISTENED. "When will it happen?"

Pause.

"About a week, huh?"

Pause.

"If I can't come up with fifteen by then, you'll have to wait."

Pause.

"Good. Meanwhile you need to keep the heists going. When will your two local boys be ready again?"

Pause.

"Ah-huh…ah-huh…okay then…great guns. This weekend will work."

Paul set the phone down and looked at his watch.

He put on his long winter boots. Paul rummaged on the shelf of his backdoor closet. He found a knit beanie cap to wear with his black-hooded wool coat. He walked out his back door and looked at the deep snow. The first step is always the hardest, he thought. Paul broke trail down the slope and onto the lake, heading for his fishing house.

Man, I haven't been down there since Garcia and his boys hauled it out during the holidays, he said to himself. They put it right where I told 'em to, away from that cluster of five farther up. Blisters, I haven't even seen the inside, since it came with the house purchase. Paul found himself breathing heavily arriving at the fishing house. He walked around to the backside and opened the LP tank valve. The first key that he selected from the ring worked. "Hey, nice place," he muttered.

Thick insulation lined all four walls and the ceiling. Man, a sink and kitchen cabinets, he said to himself. "Wow, is that a fridge?" he said and pulled open the small brown door. By gads, it is. He spotted a broom in the corner and swept the snow off the carpet that he had carried in with his boots.

Paul flicked a switch on the thermostat and he heard a furnace light. He opened one of the upper cabinets. Paul smiled and fingered one of the three bottles: two whiskies and one brandy; and a whole bunch of glasses. Good place for a party with the right person, he thought.

Why not? Paul asked himself and got out a glass and poured himself a whiskey. He sat down and continued to look around. If I was ever going to kidnap someone, this is where I would keep 'em, he said to himself, laughing out loud.

His mood soured as he thought about Garcia. First ten, then twenty and now thirty thou. Next it will be fifty. Even if I would pay him and he got the job done, Garcia would have to go. He knows too much already…too much already.

Paul lifted the glass and swallowed. He cleared his throat and coughed. "I need a change in my plans," he muttered.

THOR PARKED HIS BLACK SUV NEXT TO THE LOON. He shut off the engine and slouched down in the seat. Suddenly, he saw someone trudging through the snow, coming down the hill from Minton's place. Could it be? he asked himself. It's the devil himself. He sat up straight and picked up his binoculars.

Thor patiently waited for the man to reach the house. Minutes later, he saw smoke coming out of the chimney. *Thieves are on the inside and bandits on the outside! People do not realize that I am watching them. Their sinful deeds are all around them and I see them all.* I wouldn't even need my snowmobile, he said to himself. He heard a sound behind him. A pickup rumbled past and turned onto the path leading down to the lake. It rolled past Minton's house and stopped near a cluster of five farther down.

He focused his binoculars on the exhaust pipe. It's different, he thought. An apple won't work…duct tape should do it. Thor had been working on an innovation that would prevent the door from opening. A two-by-four cross piece just under the doorknob. Then another two-by-four leaner with a metal sharp end that stuck in the ice. The crosspiece needed three penetrating claws.

"There he goes," Thor muttered, watching Minton walk back toward his home. *What sorrow awaits those who have deserted me! Let them die, for they have rebelled against me.*

36

HUB TURNED THE STEERING WHEEL, taking the Yorktown exit ramp shortly after 1:00 a.m. on Friday night. "What's it look like over there?" he asked, glancing at the first building: a service station and convenience store.

"Deserted," Tyke said.

"Good. We'll do the grocery first."

He parked his new acquisition—a brown Chevrolet station wagon from the sixties. "Go try the keys."

Tyke lumbered to the door. Hub watched him try one after another. Then the door opened.

Hub shut the engine off and jumped out. He opened the back door and grabbed the pan, then an armful of bags. Hub hurried toward the store. He heard glass breaking. Tyke had taken the new crowbar with him, and had already found the tobacco cabinets.

"Hit the jackpot!" Tyke exclaimed.

Ten minutes later, they carried the bulging bags toward the door. Hub pushed on the door. He stopped. The headlights from a vehicle flashed across the street. A pickup appeared. It slowed after coming abreast of their car. Then it continued down the street.

"Come on, let's git!" Hub exclaimed.

He led the way, partially dragging the bags on the pavement. He reached into his jacket and used a key to open the rear lid. "Look at all that space. We easily got room for the whole shebang."

Tyke dropped his load first. Then he picked up the other bags and heaved them into the truck. Hub slammed down the lid. It bounced back up. He slammed it again. It locked. Hub threw the dustpan over the back of his seat. Tyke held onto the crowbar.

Hub drove their vehicle to the service station and convenience store. He parked on the dark side of the building. They both got out. Tyke carried two empty bags and the ring of keys. Hub had bags in one hand and the crowbar in the other. "Move it, Tyke!"

The key turned. Tyke glared at his partner.

They found the cigarettes all stored exactly where they had seen them when they scouted the place. "Huh, it's not even locked up here," Tyke said, and used his arm to sweep the packages and cartons onto the floor.

"That's it," Hub said and stood. "It's all clear out there," he added and led the way out the front door. They dropped the bags down on the floor behind the back seat. Hub got behind the wheel. "We're off."

Hub drove the station wagon back onto Highway 10 and they headed west. Some time later, he exited the highway at the Highway 228 exit, heading for New Dresden. "This is going to do it for awhile," Hub said as he slowed the car on Purgatory Curve.

"Why do they call it Purgatory Curve?" Tyke asked.

"A couple of years ago, the cops caught a speeder who led them to a shootout at a hog farm. The sheriff got killed."

"Hmmm, was he the crooked one?"

"Yup," Hub said, turning off the county highway and pulling behind a building next to a woodpile. "This is it…should be a snap."

Tyke found a key that worked on the back door of Buzz's in moments.

"Only three bags, huh?" Hub muttered after loading the cigarettes.

They carried the loot out the back exit.

Hub opened the car door, and then suddenly heard, "Freeze!"

Flashing lights seemed to pop out of nowhere. Two white deputy-sheriff cars blocked the thieves' vehicle. Hub dropped the bag and dustpan. He put his hands up.

Tyke made a run for the trees on the other side of the car. He slipped and fell. Then he groaned as an officer knelt down on his back and pulled one of his arms back. A second officer pulled the other arm back. Tyke heard the terrifying click. He felt himself yanked up.

"We gotcha…this time for good," the deputy said.

The clock struck 4:00 a.m. at the county jail. Hub and Tyke were booked and placed into two separate cells.

GARCIA THREW HIS CELL PHONE ON THE TABLE. "*Culpar a alguien de algo*," he said in Spanish, blaming Hub. *Que no cunda el panico!* he said to himself, feeling his stomach churn.

He took another sip of tequila and sighed deeply. I don't give a crap what happens to those two guys, he thought. I was gonna dump 'em anyhow…right after the Buzz's heist. It's the loss of a whole car full of tobacco that bothers me. Minton's not going to be happy. Maybe I should pack up and get the hell out of here. Fortunately, the idiots don't know my name. The judge is going to throw the book at 'em. Jesus, I either have to get out of here or find another team.

Garcia lay down on the couch and watched soap operas all afternoon. He got his tequila bottle out after the 6:30 sitcom ended. He took a swig right out of the bottle. Garcia wiped his lips and headed for his bedroom to change clothes.

An hour later, he turned onto Spanky's approach. He found a vacant parking spot at the far end of the lot, near the big shed. Garcia got out and pulled the cap down low over his eyes. He felt a smudge of tension knowing that Minton was going to meet him.

Garcia pushed through the first door. He stopped and studied the bulletin board, waiting for the area in front of the hostess station to clear of people. Garcia moved ahead quickly, nodded as he passed the counter, and headed for the corner booth in the darkest corner of the bar area.

His tequila arrived. He took a drink and looked around, pulling the brim of his cap even lower. Through the spaces between the wooden runners, he could see anyone that entered.

TOM DROVE SLOWLY UP HIS ROADWAY. He had heard from Ellie at the grocery store that the two cigarette bandits had been caught. He couldn't believe that they were the same two that had accosted him earlier in the month. They were out on bail for God's sake, he said to himself. Their trial shouldn't last very long. The judge will throw a rock at 'em.

He left his pistol at home because of the good news. No more parked car out by my gate, he thought as he drove onto the township road. I wonder what Jolene is going to wear. I hope it's the black dress. She looks sexy in that slick getup. I can relax again. Hmmm, wonder where I should take the babe for dinner.

Tom parked close to the main entrance of the apartment building. He dashed in and pushed the button. "It's me. I'm here."

The door buzzed and Tom entered the foyer. He took the elevator up to the third floor. Moments later, he knocked on her door.

"Wow! I sure like that dress," Tom said and gave Jolene a big hug and a kiss on the lips.

"Come on in, Mr. Hastings. Have a seat and tell me about all the trouble you got into today."

"Hah. You're funny. I hope you're not jinxing me for the rest of the evening. The two bandits are in the jug. I'm off the hook."

"Wow, what happened?"

"The sheriff's guys captured 'em last night. They had just cleaned out Buzz's Stop & Shop of smokes."

"Well, we'll have to celebrate. Where are you taking me?"

"Anywhere you'd like to go?"

"How about Spanky's? However."

"However what?" Tom asked.

"You have to promise me you won't get into any fist fights... got it?"

Tom hesitated. "Yeah, I'll stay cool; however no more of this fraternizing with that Minton guy. I think I gave him a message the last time we were there."

Jolene's face remained stern.

THE ROADS COOPERATED ON THE FINAL SATURDAY in January as Tom turned his vehicle up the slope leading to the parking lot at Spanky's. No ice or snow. He got out and quickly moved around his vehicle to open Jolene's door. "Looks like a good crowd," he said.

He grabbed her by her elbow and steered her toward the door. "Watch the ice," he warned.

"Good evening," the hostess said.

"Howdy. How about a booth close to the fireplace?"

The hostess pointed. "There is one."

"Great."

GARCIA STIFFENED. Hastings and his friend Jolene walked past and stopped at the counter. Garcia took another long, deep drink. He turned his head toward the bar, his hand swinging slightly, knocking the drink to the floor. "*Distraccion!*" he exclaimed.

Heads turned as the glass shattered. The bartender came over with a small broom and dust pan. He swept up the pieces. "Accidents will happen," Randy said.

"*Tengo sed.*"

"What's that?" Randy asked.

"Thirsty—I'm thirsty."

"Another tequila comin' right up."

Garcia watched Hastings and his date sit down at a booth across the room. Hmmm, he doesn't sit across from her…always next, he said to himself. He won't be sittin' by her in a few days. "*Ten paciencia,*" he muttered. "I need to be patient."

TOM SUSPICIOUSLY GLANCED AROUND THE RESTAURANT as Jolene chatted with Carrie, their waitress. Geez, I'm sure glad that the table-hopper isn't here tonight, he said to himself. He watched as a man, slightly slumped in the shoulders, walked in and stopped at the hostess station. I've seen that pale face before...yeah, Johnny Cash. Hmmm, he's wearing red tonight. Tom watched him take off his red coat and sit in a booth next to the Hispanic guy with a bushy mustache. Right now, he's Johnny Red.

Their entrees arrived. Tom felt upbeat, especially since his tormenter hadn't shown up. He laid his fingers on Jolene's wrist, liking the warm feeling in his chest. "How's your dinner, sweetie?"

"Tremendous. Great food in this place."

Tom nodded. He lifted a hand to signal the bartender that they needed more wine. Moments later, Randy brought over a half-carafe. "Anything else?"

"Nope. Thanks. That'll do it for now."

"I talked to my brother yesterday. His fishing house is still available for us to use. Remember, we talked about having dinner in it?"

"Oh yeah. Well, it sounds like a lot of inconvenience. Dinner would be so much easier at my house."

"Oh come on, Tom. Don't be such a stick-in-the-mud."

"I'll give it some thought."

"We would have to do it soon. The fishing houses need to be off the lake by the end of February."

The sound of glass breaking interrupted their conversation. At the other corner of the room, Tom's head jerked to his right. The Hispanic man held his palms upward. Randy hurried over with a dustpan and small broom. He swept up broken glass and quickly returned to his position behind the bar.

"That guy looks pretty drunk," Tom said.

"Do you know him?" Jolene asked.

"No, I don't, but I've seen him around...maybe even here."

Tom finished his plate first. He wiped his lips and pushed it forward. "That was great. How are you doing?"

"I'm taking my time."

"Of course...no hurry."

His eyes caught movement across the way. The Hispanic guy stood. He staggered some as he made his way toward the exit. "Boy, that guy's sure had enough to drink," Tom said.

Then the other man, the pale-faced one, also got up and left.

Jolene finished her plate. "Oh my, that was good."

She looked up. "Did you hear that?"

"Hear what?"

"Sounded like two shots…oh well, maybe a car…some hot rod kid."

Suddenly, they heard a scream. A woman rushed from the exit door toward the hostess station. She yelled, "Someone got shot! Outside! Call for help!"

"What should we do?" Jolene asked, wringing her hands.

Tom's Adam's apple bounced as he swallowed. "If we don't leave now, it's going to be awhile. The sirens from police cars arriving are going to blare real soon."

Jolene pressed her hand against his shoulder. "So what do you think?"

Tom got up off the booth bench. "Let's go…take our chances in the parking lot."

Jolene scurried out of the booth. She turned her back toward Tom as he hurriedly helped her with her coat. He threw his leather jacket on and grabbed the ticket folder off the table. Jolene followed him to the check-out counter.

The woman who had yelled earlier had her face buried in Jeremy's chest. Tom wrote a check and put his wallet back into his coat. "What do you think, Jeremy? Do we dare leave now?"

"It's now or much later."

Tom considered the possibility that someone with a gun was still outside. He took a deep breath. "Come on, Jolene, let's go."

Tom pushed the front door open and vigilantly looked around. He grabbed Jolene by the arm and headed straight for his vehicle that was parked in the second row.

"Uh-oh, there he is!" Jolene exclaimed, pointing to her left.

Tom steered her in the other direction. "Listen—a siren!"

He reached into his jacket pocket and brought out his fob. Tom pressed the button and saw his vehicle's lights flash. He held on to Jolene's arm, guiding her between two vehicles. He jerked the passenger door open. Jolene bumped her head on the upper frame as he pushed her into the seat. "Take it easy!" she exclaimed.

Tom's eyes caught the dark bulk lying on the pavement farther down. He looked away and got into his vehicle.

Tom drove his SUV down the entrance ramp and took a right. He slowed and veered to the right side of the road as a sheriff's vehicle, lights flashing, approached. "This is just the beginning," Tom said.

37

THOR PARKED HIS VEHICLE IN HIS GARAGE. He moved quickly into his house and changed to night clothes. Thor hurried to his special room and lit the candles. He got down on one knee. The room grew so quiet that he could hear his own shallow breathing. "I witnessed the devil commit murder," he whispered.

Am I committing a sin by not calling the police? he asked himself. Thor bowed before the candles, his hands clasped tightly together. His voice cracked as he forced his words, "My Master, give me the strength to do the right thing."

Thor's mind drifted into a trance. He saw riders, their backs bent over to avoid the wind as the camels plodded along in the desert. They headed toward a bright light that had dropped down from the sky. Suddenly, Thor heard a loud thumping noise outside. No more camels, no more riders. The bright light disappeared, too. He heard the sound again. Thor stiffened.

He stood and walked into the dark kitchen. Thor stopped to listen. He heard nothing. Cautiously, he made his way over to the window overlooking his driveway and garage. Suddenly, he saw moving shadows. Someone is out there! His insides churned. *They've come for me. The Lord is angry and sent an agent.*

Thor turned. He rushed to the kitchen counter. He fingered the top of a block of knives. Thor pulled out one at a time, settling for a large butcher knife.

He returned to the window and waited in the darkness. There it is again, he said to himself, jerking his head upward. His breathing quickened. His heart thumped. His cold, clammy hand tightened its grip on the handle. He pointed the blade at the door. Then he heard the clatter of a garbage can cover. Heavens! I forgot to close the garage door. Dogs have found it, he said to himself, relieved.

He set the knife down and walked outside. "Git—git otta here!" he yelled waving a broom at the intruders. He hit the button to close the garage door and reentered his house.

PAUL MINTON STOOD OVER THE BODY. He heard footsteps. For a moment, his eyes locked with a pale-faced man's. Blisters, he saw me! Paul exclaimed to himself. He ran to his car. Paul saw the headlights of the vehicle that just left the parking lot splash out on the county highway below. He quickly jumped in and squealed onto the highway, following in the same direction. He pressed down the accelerator after the taillights disappeared. Paul's tires screeched as he rounded a curve. Again, he saw the taillights. Again, they disappeared. He almost lost control of his vehicle after hitting heavy bumps in the road just past the dairy farm.

The dark SUV came into full view. It didn't signal or stop for the state highway as it headed toward New Dresden. Paul followed at a safe distance, slowing dramatically after crossing the railroad tracks. The SUV did a rolling stop at the stop sign and continued straight ahead. Paul did the same, slowing to watch the SUV turn into a driveway. He drove past slowly, craning his neck. He saw a light-green house and a separate garage.

Paul turned his vehicle around at the next intersection and drove back up the street, rolling slowly by the green house—watching.

He stopped his car a block farther down. He shut it off and waited for a few minutes. He checked the gun in his jacket pocket and exited. Paul pulled his collar tight around his neck and walked upward toward the target—the garage with the black SUV. No traffic around here, he said to himself. This should be easy.

Satisfied that the street was empty, he cautiously walked up the driveway. Huh, the nut doesn't have a light on out here. He saw a dim light come on in one of the rooms. Paul stopped…he waited and listened.

Suddenly, he heard a noise. Two large dogs raced towards him. Paul panicked and retreated toward his vehicle, tightening his grip on the pistol. He turned. The dogs did not pursue him, instead headed right for the garbage can just inside the garage door.

Paul got into his vehicle breathing heavily. Christ, those two mutts scared the pants off me, he said to himself, gently grasping his throat as he waited for his heart and lungs return to normal. He heard a siren and then another one. A police car, lights flashing, made a fast turn at the main intersection and headed north out of town. Moments later, another vehicle with flashing lights blasted through the intersection.

Paul started his vehicle and drove slowly. He passed through town and turned onto his roadway, coming to a stop in his attached garage. He closed the door and went inside. Grabbing a whiskey bottle, he poured some in a glass.

Where have I seen the pale-faced man before? he asked himself. "Spanky's!" he exclaimed.

There's something sinister about that pale-faced guy, he said to himself.

38

TOM'S EVENING WITH JOLENE again lost its spark after the shooting incident at Spanky's. That's all he could think or talk about as he drove his date back to Big Lakes. "What do you think really happened?" he asked her.

"You've got some kind of nut on the loose out there, Tom."

"Or more than one nut," Tom said. "The fishing house fire and robberies may not be connected."

"Maybe not, but I'll bet whatever we just saw in the parking lot is tied to one or the other."

"Right now, I'd give a lot to know who it was that got shot—the Spanish-looking guy, or the pale-faced man," Tom said.

Jolene turned to look at him. "Or—it could've been someone else altogether. Maybe—"

"Maybe what?"

"Someone simply going in."

Tom sighed. "How about the woman who came in and yelled? Did you notice that she was alone?"

"No, how did you know that?"

"Well, there was no guy around after she came in. If there was one, I didn't see 'em. We didn't see anyone outside either did we?" Tom said.

"Hey, you're right."

Tom slowed his vehicle. The sign at the city limits of Big Lakes read *Speed Limit 50.*

"We were the only ones out there, unless—"

Tom glanced at her. "Unless what?"

"Unless someone was hiding—could've been, you know."

"I'll learn all about it in New Dresden tomorrow."

Jolene chuckled. "I think the police should dump the whole thing in the laps of the people that hang around Border's Café. They probably have it all figured out."

Tom pulled up his SUV into the parking lot at Jolene's apartment complex.

"Tom, I'm beat and have three showings tomorrow. I would love to have you come up, but…."

Tom felt pain. He looked forward to snuggling with her on this night.

"I'm sorry, Tom. Another time?" Jolene said and grasped his hand.

Tom took Highway 10 on his way back. He wanted to drive by Spanky's Restaurant to see if the police had left. Several minutes later, he had his answer. The blinking lights reminded him of Christmas as he drove by.

Again, his mind fixed on a scene that occurred just before the shooting. Two booths across from the bar. A drunken Hispanic-looking guy in one of them. The pale-faced man in the other. Both men had left just before the gun shots. It had to be one of them.

THOR AWOKE WITH A START on Sunday morning. He put on his robe and walked into his small living room. He stood next to the window and looked out over Main Street. There'll be plenty of buzz at the grocery store this morning, he said to himself.

In the kitchen, he dumped the ugly, used coffee-filter into the wastebasket and prepared for a fresh pot. Thor thought about the nightmares that he had experienced the past few nights. *Slimy devils armed with forks came right through my wall. I jumped out of bed and ran for the door. More devils blocked my way. They crowded around me, gradually leaving no space for me to move. Then I fell through a hole into a bottomless pit of fire, flames lashing at me.*

One of the devils looked different, Thor said to himself. He was the only one who smiled—blond, wavy hair kept blocking out other scenes in his dream.

Thor dressed and focused on his mission: *Destroy the smiling devil.* He walked toward his sacred room. *Lord, I have one more assignment.* The *Ice Lord* drifted into the room, lighting candle after candle. He knelt and closed his eyes. He saw blond, wavy hair again. The evil one! He opened his eyes and stared at the flicking lights. *The Lord has given me permission to destroy the devil.*

39

IZZY LAY DOWN A STACK OF PAPERS ON THE SHERIFF'S DESK. She took a seat directly across. Deputies Kelly Martin and Todd Jackson occupied the other two chairs. Dave Johnson removed the paper clip and picked up the first sheet. "Ernesto Manual Garcia; Address Big Lakes, Minnesota; Age 46…occupation unknown; Cause of Death: two bullets in the brain, both entered via his forehead; .44-caliber."

The sheriff set the paper down. "What have we got on this guy's past?"

Izzy looked at Kelly, raising her arms and opening her palms.

Kelly swept aside the hair from his left eye that normally dangled over his ear. "Nothing…dead end!"

The sheriff scratched his chin. "You mean the driver's license is phony?"

"Hot tomato!" Kelly exclaimed.

"What about his personal effects? Find anything interesting?"

"A .38-caliber revolver…could be interesting," Izzy said. She shook her head. "Nothing else—no bank accounts. Oh yeah, close to a couple thousand in cash."

"What kind of vehicle did he drive? How about the license and other things?" the sheriff asked.

Kelly leaned forward. "The plates were stolen in Minneapolis a couple of months ago. We traced the 2004 Chrysler to a used car dealer in St. Louis Park. They sold it to a woman who doesn't exist."

"What about the people at the restaurant? Anything?"

Todd Jackson's left eye squinted. "The bartender reported that Garcia got pretty drunk on tequila. He broke at least one glass."

"Was he alone?"

"Yes, quite alone."

"Anything else from the bartender?"

"Yeah, he mentioned that a couple left right after the shooting."

"And?"

Todd laughed. "You're not going to believe this. The man was Tom Hastings. The woman was Jolene Hunt, his girlfriend."

The sheriff chuckled. "I might have expected that. He's usually right in the middle of the action. We better check them out."

Kelly made a notation in his notebook.

The sheriff licked his lips. He looked directly at Izzy. "Okay, Izz, what do you think? Is there a connection? Garcia and the cigarette heists—to the fishing house murders?"

"My gut feeling is overwhelming. It insists that there is too much crime going on in too small an area for them not to be related."

"What do you plan on doing next?"

She threw up her hands. "Dave, I suppose we could talk to Hastings...or hang around New Dresden and look for a pale-faced guy."

PAUL MINTON WOKE UP WITH A HANGOVER on Sunday morning. He stared at a frame on the wall—a picture of his two children whom he hadn't seen in over ten years. I miss them, he thought.

Paul sipped coffee and wondered about the pale-faced man. Not only is he weird, but he didn't call the cops, he thought. They'd of been after me hours ago if he had. *So why didn't he call the cops?* He scratched the itchy area just under his ear. Suddenly he knew. *He's the fishing house killer!* Sure, he's always alone...got that yearning look...deep within. *The hands clasped together. The Bible.* It all fits. That's why he'll never call the cops.

His thoughts drifted to Jolene. She is one nice-looking babe. I've got to figure out a way to take out that Hastings guy. Hmmm, maybe an accident. He does live alone. Shouldn't be too difficult. I wonder if he has a fishing house. The cops would blame it on the fishing house killer. Now wouldn't that be a brainy move on my part, he asked himself. How could I get him to fish on a Sunday?

Suddenly, he raised his head. Blisters, what if he—the pale-faced one—gets caught? He'll blow the whistle on me.

Paul placed his fingers on his forehead. Oh, damn this headache. Hell, I'm goin' back to bed until it goes away. The aspirin is sure takin' its time.

JOLENE SIPPED FROM HER TEACUP IN HER APARTMENT. I feel totally confused, she said to herself. I have made such a mess of my life. Tom is a great guy but....I cannot go on like this. I do like my job. It's exciting. This Minton guy is terribly good looking. Younger than Tom, too.

Yet, Tom risked his life to help me when my father was killed by that train—cold-blooded murder it was. That creep of a nephew was out after the money. Oh my, but Tom saved me. But I can't help it if I don't have the right kind of feelings for him.

She walked to the counter and poured more tea into her cup. Her watch read 8:15. Still plenty of time before readying for church, she thought. That's my main problem with Tom. He doesn't think much of the organized church. Yet he sometimes thinks and talks spiritually. Oh my, what am I to do?

Maybe I should take a week off and go somewhere and think. I wonder what would happen if I would marry Tom. But then he's never asked me. Maybe he doesn't want to get married...never will. I could go on like this for the rest of my life...going nowhere, just a night out now and then.

"I think what I will do is talk Tom into the dinner at Steve's fishing house," she whispered. Then I will take it from there, she thought. Yes. Yes. That's what I'll do.

Jolene picked up her phone and punched in a number. "Hi, Tom.

How about some breakfast this morning?"

She listened.

"Okay, I'll see you about 11:30 then." She hung up the phone. I'll shoot for next Friday, she thought. Better call Steve today.

She headed to her bathroom and prepared for church.

40

TOM STEPPED OUT OF THE SHOWER. He bounced up his steps and headed into the bedroom. I can't wear jeans when I go out with this girl, he thought.

He backed his vehicle out of the garage and headed up his roadway, blasting through a series of snowdrifts that built up during the night. He kicked the brake pedal to slow down for a cluster of turkeys pecking away at the grasses next to his road. "Geez, why doesn't that bird get off the road," he muttered as he slowed. The bird ran up the roadway directly ahead.

Fifteen minutes later, he pulled up in front of Jolene's apartment house.

Tom punched the white button on the panel that had the names of the tenants. He heard a phone ring and Jolene said, "Come on up." He heard the door latch click. He took the elevator to the third floor, walked up the corridor and knocked on Jolene's door. Tom hugged her warmly. "How are you this morning, sweetie?"

"Just fine, Mr. Hastings."

Tom took a seat on the sectional and watched her pour him a cup of coffee. He felt warm inside as she strode around in her kitchen. I'm gonna do it, he thought. I'm going to ask her to marry me and soon…maybe not right now, but soon.

Jolene sat down next to him. She reached out and they clinked their cups. Tom looked deep into her blue eyes. A section of her blonde hair drooped down over one eye. She smiled and leaned her head toward him. They kissed. Tom's heart rate increased and he felt his face flushing. He took a sip of coffee and said to himself, I've got to cool it.

"Shall we get going?" Jolene asked and stood.

Tom touched the hem of her dress with one hand and pushed the armrest with the other. He stood. "Okay, let's do it."

Tom opened the passenger door and gently grasped her shoulder as she sat on the seat and swung her legs over the running board. He got in and drove the vehicle to the parking lot at Perkins restaurant in Big Lakes.

He quickly got out of his vehicle and opened the passenger door. Tom guided Jolene as they made their way down three steps and passed an icy patch on the sidewalk. They sat down at a booth next to a window. Thin drifts of snow, coming from the northwest, swept across the parking lot.

Jolene ordered first. Tom followed. When the coffee and tea arrived, Jolene took a sip. "Tom, how about doing dinner with me in Steve's fishing house this Friday? I'm cookin'."

Tom smiled. "Let's do it. I read in the paper that the *Ice Lord* has attacked only on Sundays."

"Yeah, I read that, too. Also, Steve's fishing house is pretty modern. I heard that the *Ice Lord* has attacked only older ones."

Tom frowned. "Nevertheless, I'm packin' a pistol."

Jolene looked up at the ceiling and chuckled. "Hmmm, maybe I should pack one, too. My cousin's husband has a bunch of 'em."

"What ya gonna do this afternoon?" Tom asked.

"Nothing special, just sit around, I guess. Would you like to come over and watch a game? It's about Super Bowl time, isn't it?"

Tom smiled. "Yes, I would like that."

"As a matter of fact, I've got a pork loin in the fridge. I've also got some wine. What do you think?"

Tom smiled widely. "It's a deal—but, I've got to go home first for a bit."

THE *ICE LORD* TURNED HIS HEAD AND WATCHED THE SUN as it touched the tops of the trees shortly after 4:45 p.m. He shivered and tightened his coat around his chest. Thor had been sitting in this vehicle in the parking lot of Loon Park for over an hour. Then he sat up. A lone figure emerged, moving slowly away from the south shoreline toward Minton's fishing house.

Moments later, he focused his binoculars on the approaching person. "It's him," he muttered. *The devil himself!*

Thor leaned forward anxiously and watched as his adversary reached the fishing house and entered. Then he saw the small window light up. Minutes later a plume of smoked emerged from the smokestack. The *Ice Lord* jumped to his feet, no longer able to contain himself. The light went out. *The Lord has delivered him to me,* he said to himself. *I must obey.*

He opened the vehicle door and gently clicked it shut. Thor then walked around to the rear and opened the hatch. He slipped on a pair of asbestos gloves that stretched all the way to his elbows. Then he placed a hooded cloak over his body, partially fastening the open front with two large buttons.

Thor lifted the small gasoline can and set it on the ground. Then he grasped a stovetop lighting tool. Thor closed the hatch. Headlights from a vehicle coming down the state highway filtered through the trees. He crouched down and waited for it to pass. Then two snowmobiles worked their way toward town on the other side of the road. He hated the noise and stood still until they were out of sight.

It's quiet at last, he thought, and edged his way down the slope, skirting the lighted area of the parking lot. He made two steps onto the snow-covered ice and stopped. A police car approached from the direction of New Dresden. He stepped back toward the bank and waited. The car slowed as it passed by the approach. The car was nearly out of sight when it stopped and the overhead flashing lights came on.

Thor felt his heart jump into his throat as the police car made a U-turn and headed toward the approach. It turned in and pulled up behind his vehicle. Thor slumped down in the snow, ducking behind the trunk of a tree.

He heard voices. A car door slammed shut. The lights still blinked, brushing the snow with red and blue. “What do you think, Jeff? Should we call a tow?”

“Dunno, the registration appears confusing. Let’s put a mark on it and check it out when we return from Pine Lakes.”

“Yup, sounds good to me.”

Two car doors slammed and the blinking lights went out. Thor peeked up from behind the tree and saw the police car turn around and drive onto the highway. He waited until it rounded the curve toward Pine Lakes before climbing up the slope. He quickly unlocked his vehicle, got in and exited.

The perspiration on Thor’s forehead had dried by the time he entered his house. He went directly to his special room, lit six candles and knelt. “Next time, Lord,” he muttered.

JOLENE AND TOM STRETCHED OUT ON THE COUCH TO RELAX. It wasn’t what he had planned to do, but somehow the turn of events led to spending the night.

Tom left Jolene’s apartment at 7:30 a.m. Driving home, he scolded himself for not popping the question. Damn, what am I waiting for? he asked himself. I could easily spend the rest of my life with that woman. But, there’s something—something mysterious in her actions and what she talks about. I think that she’s holding something back from me.

He parked in his garage and walked toward his house with his keys dangling from his fingers. The answering machine beeped. Tom pressed a button. “Hi, Tom, this is Julie. I’m going to be in the area and would like to have lunch with you.”

41

IZZY FINGERED THE TIP OF HER CHIN AS SHE LISTENED to deputies Jeff and Andy tell her about the abandoned vehicle they marked at Loon Park. "We didn't make much if it," Deputy Jeff said. "I've seen lots of vehicles parked there in the past. I'm really sorry that we didn't record the plate number."

"No one's perfect," Izzy said, smiling.

"But it was black, a Dodge SUV," Deputy Andy said. "Yeah, no one around—not a darn soul."

The sheriff stood up from behind his desk. "Boys, anything that looks irregular within twenty miles of the New Dresden area—consider it suspicious—no exceptions. Ya both understand?"

"Gotcha," Jeff said.

"Okay, boys, you can both go now," Sheriff Dave Johnson said, brushing the top of his desk with his knuckles.

The door closed.

Deputy Martin got up off his chair, stifling a yawn. "What do you think, Izz? Should we give Hastings a call before we head to New Dresden tomorrow?"

She hesitated and tightened her lips together. "I almost forgot. We haven't interviewed him and his girlfriend yet. Thanks for reminding me. I'll call 'em today and set up a time for tomorrow."

"Would you make it early in the day? We could coordinate it with another visit to New Dresden. There's no doubt that the key to all these crimes likely is buried deep somewhere, right in that small town—Little Chicago."

Izzy chuckled. "Are you comparing New Dresden to Chicago,

Kell?"

"I've been reading some about Al Capone days lately. He had a home here on a lake near Brainerd, you know."

Sheriff Johnson squeezed his lower lip with his upper teeth. "Remember, a black Dodge SUV…and a pale-faced man. That's what we are looking for."

Izzy nodded. She looked at her watch. "We'll head over there first thing tomorrow morning."

TOM TURNED ONTO THE COUNTY HIGHWAY deep in thought, wondering why Julie had called and requested a face-to-face meeting. He knew why the deputy called. Someone in Spanky's must have told the cops that he was there the night of the shooting. He wondered if they would want to talk to Jolene, too. The deputy had requested a meeting mid-morning, but Tom had a dental appointment then. They settled for early afternoon.

Slivers of snowdrifts angled across the asphalt road as he approached the dairy farm. The driver of a tractor plunged the front-end loader into a stack of silage. Two snowmobiles dashed across the road a short distance ahead.

He crossed the railroad tracks and parked at the curb next to his barber, Kelly's place. Tom took two steps toward the post office across the street. He looked at his watch and realized that he had to meet with Julie first.

Tom pulled open the door of William's Pub and saw her smiling face. She sat in a booth next to the wall. The light from the window and overhead light splashed across her hand as she swept a tuft of hair from her face. She stood as Tom approached. He hugged her tightly, feeling his heart racing.

Tom and Julie sat down across from each other. "What brings you into town?" Tom asked.

"You do."

Tom jerked his head back. "Me! What did I do now?"

Julie laughed. She frowned, and then looked at her watch. "It's past noon, so we can have a glass of wine. Okay with you?"

Tom shrugged his shoulders. "You're funny. Of course it's okay with me. Have I ever turned one down before?"

"I've quit my job with the congressman," Julie said softly.

Tom puckered his lips. "Whoa. You did what?"

"I mean it, Tom. I need something different in my life. I have been thinking about you and us for some time. I really miss our times together. I'm getting tired of traveling and would like to settle down."

The waitress placed a glass of white wine down in front of each of them. Tom picked his up and brought it up to his lips. He took a big sip and swallowed, staring at her eyes, feeling warmer by the moment. "I don't know what to say, Julie—heck, I feel very flattered." He felt his cheeks redden.

"I would like to take you out to dinner this evening and we can talk more," Julie said.

"Not too many restaurants open this time of the year. Hmmm, wonder about the Locomotive in Pine Lakes," Tom said.

"I got a better idea. Why don't I come up with ingredients and we can have dinner at your house. You still have my skis, don't you?"

Tom nodded. "Hey, I bought those from you—remember?"

"Oh, so you did. They still work, don't they?"

Tom looked at his watch. "I better get home. A couple of deputies are stopping out."

"What did you do now?"

"Do? Not much. Just went out for dinner at Spanky's the other night. You heard about the shooting in the parking lot, didn't ya?"

"No, can't say that I have. I don't read the local papers and don't watch the news."

"A man was shot in the head and killed in the parking lot. I happened to see the victim leave the restaurant. I saw someone else leave, too…a man…and about the same time."

"Were you alone?"

Tom looked across the room. "Well, not exactly. I had company."

"That Hunt lady, huh?"
Tom nodded.

TOM TOOK A CHAIR AT HIS DINING-ROOM TABLE. The two deputies sat side by side on the love seat. Because of their previous encounters and visits, they communicated on a first-name basis.

"Tell us about the evening you and your friend spent at Spanky's on the night of the shooting. You know what I'm talking about, don't you?" Izzy said.

"Yup, sure do. I was with my friend Jolene Hunt…just a casual dinner. I noticed two men, each sitting alone in a booth across from the bar.

"One looked Hispanic. He got pretty drunk…spilled a drink. The glass fell on the floor and shattered. The other was the pale-faced man. I've seen him around before. Usually he dresses in black. That night he wore red."

The deputies asked several more questions. They also wanted the name, address and phone number of his friend Jolene Hunt.

Deputy Martin stood. "Thanks for your time, Hastings."

Izzy followed him to the door. "Stay warm." She smiled. "And out of trouble." She held the door partially open and turned her head. "Oh, by the way, Tom, one of the witnesses at Spanky's told us that you had an altercation with one of their customers a few days ago."

Tom shrugged his shoulders. He followed with a wry smile. "Yeah, I got in a lucky punch…knocked the guy down…hurt my hand but it felt good."

"Why?" Kelly asked.

"This guy Minton is the mother of all table-hoppers. He's been buggin' the heck out of me and my date. He had it comin', that's for sure."

"Minton?" Izzy said.

"Paul Minton. He's moved here recently…bought a house in New Dresden. Don't know what he does but he sure has a lot of people hanging around at his place at times."

"Hanging around?" Deputy Kelly said.

"One time I saw four cars and a truck in his driveway…the one in front of the storage building."

The two deputies looked at each other. "Thanks, Tom," Izzy said and closed the door behind her.

42

TERRY PENDLETON LOCKED THE DOOR TO HIS SHOP. He shivered stepping outside to get into his black SUV. It's still January, he said to himself—a Tuesday, I think. He drove across Washington Avenue and headed for Bates Motors. One of his shoe customers had told him recently that they had the best deals. After the sheriff's deputy checked out his vehicle at Loon Lake, the *Ice Lord* decided he needed a change.

Thor turned off the highway and parked in a narrow space between a red pickup and a green Grand Prix. Terry got out and stood by his open door, studying the car dealer's parking lot. Satisfied, he walked toward the front door.

His stocky frame filled the doorway as he stood, eyeing two men talking. One of them opened the door of a Buick Regal.

A voice behind him startled him. "Can I help you, sir?"

"Ah…yes. I would like to trade in my vehicle."

The man wearing a dark-blue, long-sleeved shirt stuck out his hand. Terry grasped it lightly, shook it quickly and released. "I'm Kevin Kloster, sales manager. Welcome to Bates Motors. What type of vehicle are you driving?"

Terry cleared his throat. "Ah, it's that one out there…the black Dodge."

"Let's go take a look," the salesman said.

Terry followed Kevin toward his vehicle. The salesman opened a folder, leaned over the windshield and wrote down some numbers.

He opened the driver's side door, sat down on the seat and continued writing. "Well now, Mr.…ah…."

"Terry. Terry Pendleton."

"What kind of vehicle do you have in mind?"

"Something with better gas mileage…lots of space inside for hauling things. I have a shoe store in town…the one on Washington."

"Follow me."

They walked toward the other end of the lot. Kevin stopped next to a light-blue van. "This is something new. It can seat seven people. All the rear seats fold down giving you lots of space. Gas mileage will double what you have right now."

They took the vehicle for a test drive. An hour later, they shook hands in Kevin's office. "We'll have it ready for you by four this afternoon."

Terry pulled the front door open and stumbled as he stepped down. He recovered and felt a hand grasp his arm. He glanced up and locked eyes with a uniformed police officer.

"Are you okay?" the officer asked.

"Fine…I'm fine." Terry walked hurriedly toward his vehicle. He stopped short, reaching out and placing a hand on the hood of a red pickup. He turned his head. The police officer hadn't moved. Terry tensed, feeling the officer's eyes studying him. Then Terry walked away from the pickup and beyond his own vehicle. Moments later he glanced back. The police officer had left. Terry rushed to back his SUV and hurriedly left the parking lot.

DEPUTY MARTIN TURNED THE WHEEL AND THE SHERIFF'S car headed up the Hastings's roadway after the interview. He slowed approaching Rocky Point Road, visibility limited because of a dense stand of trees near the intersection. He headed up a township road with bare fields on both sides. The deputy respected the stop sign at the bottom of the small hill. He took a left, and Izzy opened the notebook that lay on her lap.

Martin made a right onto the county highway toward New Dresden. Izzy waited until the car finished rounding a wide curve before lifting the notebook to her eyes. "Number one target: black, Dodge SUV."

Kelly Martin nodded.

"Number two target: pale-faced man who looks like a ghost."

"What did you think of the interview?" Kelly asked.

"It pretty much summarized my thinking that the solution to both sets of crimes is right here…in and around New Dresden."

Kelly turned his head. "Maybe so, but one of these days we're gonna get that Hastings guy."

Izzy laughed. "I doubt it. So far, Hastings has been totally innocent of anything illegal. Sooner or later, you're gonna have to accept that."

"Hmmph," Kelly snorted. "One of these times, it's going to be more than just getting in over his head," he added.

"Oh, come on now. He's just one of those guys whose curiosity gets him into trouble. He's not the criminal type."

Kelly sighed and slowly shook his head.

He slowed for the first curve approaching New Dresden. "Look, someone defaced that loon."

"I'll be darned," Izzy said. "Vandals strike again. Not our problem, though."

They waited for two freight trains to pass through town. Kelly glanced at his watch. "Well, blow me over…it took almost fifteen minutes for those ugly boxes to get through town."

Izzy chuckled.

Kelly parked the sheriff's vehicle across from the post office.

"So you think this Wendy will help us?" he said.

"Yup, I've known her for some time and she probably knows what's going on in this town more than anyone else."

The two officers got out and stood on the sidewalk.

A small blue car came hurtling over the railroad tracks. It didn't slow down rolling down Main Street. Deputy Kelly raised his arm and pointed his fingers toward the ground. "Take it easy, you idiot," he said under his breath.

"It's a young lady," Izzy said. "She's going to have to learn to slow down…lucky for her we're not in our car. She's ripe for a speeding and careless driving ticket."

"Gads, she can hardly see above the steering wheel," Kelly said.

The two deputies attracted several sets of eyes as they walked slowly toward the bank on the corner.

Kelly pulled on the bank's front door and opened it, allowing Izzy to enter the small entryway. She stepped up and opened the inner door. The woman behind the first teller window frowned as they entered the lobby. Izzy led the way to the farthest teller window, which was not busy. A woman with dark hair occupied the station. Izzy approached. "We need to talk to Wendy Sanderson."

The woman nodded and hurriedly left her station, disappearing around a corner. She returned moments later. "Miss Sanderson will be with you in a moment."

Izzy took a seat in the small sitting area connected to the lobby. Kelly walked over to a window. "Well, look at that. There's a cream-colored Chrysler parked right in the *No Parking* zone at the post office," Kelly said.

"Are you in the mood to issue a parking ticket?" Izzy asked.

Kelly laughed. "That woman would probably tell me where to go."

"Can I help you?"

Both Izzy and Kelly turned their heads toward a smiling, smartly dressed woman. "What can I do for you? I'm Wendy Sanderson."

"Hi, I'm Deputy Izzy Felton. This is Deputy Martin. We're investigating the recent fishing house murders."

"Ohh…." Her voice tailed off. "Please follow me."

The officers walked behind her down a corridor and into a small typical office room with a single window in the back wall. "Take a seat." She sat down behind a desk. "How can I help?"

"We're looking for a man. Pudgy sort of build…pale face. He drives a black SUV. Not sure if he lives in this town or not," Kelly said.

"Oh…that would be Terry…Terry Pendleton."

Izzy puckered her lips, and glanced at her partner. She wrote the name on her notebook page. "Do you have an address?"

Wendy nodded. "I suppose we could give you that." She fingered through the pages of a ledger. "It's 215 Main Avenue."

Izzy asked, "Do you know where he works? Does he have an account here?"

"No to both questions. I know very little about him. I see him very little. He sure doesn't hang around Main Street."

Kelly stood. "We would appreciate you keeping our conversation private."

Wendy nodded. Her eyes narrowed. "I can do that."

"Thanks a lot." Izzy got up off her chair.

The bank officer escorted the two deputies to the lobby. They smiled and nodded at the tellers as they walked toward the exit door. Outside, they stood on the sidewalk as a dark-blue pickup spun its wheels and parked across the street in front of Stillman's Super Market. The driver's door opened and a man got out. He wore a striped black-on-gray cap that resembled a railroad engineer's cap from years back. The cap matched his overalls, also striped—dark lines on a whitish background. The man moved jerkily and quickly. Suddenly he stopped and saluted.

Kelly shook his head. "We've seen this nut before, haven't we? Wasn't he a suspect in the death of a farmer from a train crash a couple of years back?"

Izzy broke out in loud laughter. "He saluted you, Kell! Salute back!"

Kelly sighed deeply. "Get with it, Deputy."

THE TWO DEPUTIES GOT INTO THEIR CAR and drove through the four-way-stop sign intersection. They continued forward slowly. Deputy Kelly brought the car to a stop. "There it is…215 Main." He took a sudden left and pulled up in the driveway.

The small light-green house had a latticed front door. The single-door garage had a lateral extension that doubled its size. A single, small window overlooked the parking lot.

"Suppose you could get a snowmobile trailer into that space next to the door?" Kelly asked.

"It's probably a shop and full of junk," Izzy said.

The deputies got out of the car. Kelly stepped over to the front door and pressed the doorbell. No one answered. He cupped his hands over his eyes and attempted to look in past the curtain. "Can't see a darn thing. Doesn't look like he's home."

"What do you think, Izz? Do we have enough for a court order? I'd kill to see what's in the other part of that garage."

"It would be a tough sell to the judge. All we really have on him is the fact that he was in Spanky's the night Garcia got it."

Izzy grimaced. She stepped toward the street and glanced in all directions. "Not a soul in sight." She leaned over and picked up a piece of snow-covered paper. Blowing the flakes off, she added, "What have we got here? Hey, Kell, we may have gotten lucky. Look, it's a sales slip from a bookstore."

Kelly turned his head.

Izzy held up the slip. "Kelly! It's for over a hundred dollars. Get this...a bookstore in Little Falls...*Bookin' It*."

Kelly stepped over to his partner and handed her a small plastic bag. She placed the slip in the bag. "Little Falls is out of our territory, but we need to follow up on this slip as soon as possible—could be Bible sales—the break we need so bad."

43

THOR PULLED HIS SLEEVE BACK OVER HIS WATCH. He decided to leave work early. January sales are slower than ever, he said to himself. Thor flipped the latch on the front door lock and reversed the sign he had hanging in the window. *Closed.* He felt anxious to pick up his new vehicle.

He slid into the front seat of his black SUV for the last time and turned onto Frazee Street. Moments later, he turned into the parking lot of Bates Motors.

"Hi, Mr. Pendleton," Kevin, the sales manager, said. "We've got your new Pontiac van ready. However, we need you to sign some additional papers. Kathy will help you out."

Terry followed Kevin into an office. He took a seat, anxiously glancing back toward the showroom.

"Now there, Mr. Pendleton, you've already paid for your new vehicle, but we need some other signatures...purely routine."

Terry's hand shook as he grabbed the pen. He steadied it with his other hand and brought the tip down to the line on the sheet of paper.

"One more...there, that'll do it," Kathy said. "Thanks for coming in."

Terry stood and left the room, his hands still shaking. Kevin was waiting for him, and they stepped outside and got into the new Pontiac with Terry behind the wheel. Kevin spent 10 minutes explaining the features to his new client. Terry drove the vehicle out of the parking lot with the salesman next to him. He followed the highway east for a bit and then returned to the dealership.

Terry felt much more relaxed when at last he was alone in his new vehicle. The mileage gauge on his speedometer read 41. He smiled after getting out on Highway 10 east of town. He set the cruise button at 69. I don't need a speeding ticket, especially right now, he said to himself.

Approaching New Dresden, Terry slowed for the railroad tracks and hit the brake. An elderly woman, struggling with a cane, edged her way across the street. Terry came to a full stop. At the intersection, he drove up Main toward his home. The police car in his driveway froze him. Terry gasped. Somehow he managed to keep his vehicle from jumping the curb. He kept his new van rolling, coming to a stop at the next intersection. Slowly, he took a left with his new Pontiac and glanced back toward his house. Two uniformed cops stood next to the police car. Thor's breathing returned to normal after driving around three blocks and parking at the curb in front of Border's Café.

Terry placed his right palm over his heart. Thanks to the Lord, I traded vehicles yesterday, he said to himself. He protects me. He destroys evil. Good will prevail.

Thor slouched down in the seat and peered under the bottom edge of his visor. The police car moved. It backed out of his driveway and headed toward him, stopping at the stop sign. Thor pulled the visor of his cap down and looked straight ahead as the police car passed.

TOM'S HEART FLUTTERED WHEN A PAIR OF HEADLIGHTS sprayed light across his driveway. I'm afraid that I still have strong feelings for that woman, he said to himself. I wonder what Jolene would think if she knew that Julie and I have a date tonight. She would likely ditch me in a moment.

He hurried down the steps and headed for the front door. Julie had left her vehicle and approached the sidewalk. Tom opened the door and felt his heart rate increase as a smiling Julie walked toward him. He grabbed her hand, then closed the door behind her and hugged her tightly.

She gasped. "Tom, you're breaking my ribs."

Tom released her. "Come on in, I'll get you a glass of wine."

Julie sat down on the love seat in the dining area. "Remember when I talked you into bringing that down from the loft?" she said, pointing.

"Yup sure do—your mind works different than mine—I would have never thought of that. It's a great place to sit and see what's going on."

Tom set down the glass of wine on the table next to the love seat. She picked it up and stood. "Let's toast," she said.

He felt his insides heat up as they looked into each other's eyes and clinked their glasses.

"Oh, I better get back to my car. I have a surprise for you." Julie put on her jacket and rushed outside. Moments later she returned with a box. Tom watched as she opened the refrigerator door and placed it inside.

"So what's for dinner?" Tom asked.

Julie smiled.

WEDNESDAY MORNING TOM WATCHED AS JULIE'S CAR backed away from the garage. Her brake lights blinked as the back end of her vehicle turned to the left. The car stopped. Julie got out. She stood alongside her open car door and waved. Tom returned her smile and raised an arm. She got back inside and slammed the door. Moments later her vehicle disappeared.

Tom returned inside his house and placed a half-full cup of coffee into the microwave. He pushed two buttons and waited. The dinger went off and he carried his cup to his computer corner. His eyes wandered to the curve in his drive where Julie had passed just minutes ago. I wonder where she is going to take me, he thought. So far it's been all talk. Do I have the guts to say no? Probably not....

He thought about Jolene and their upcoming dinner date on Friday. There's no way someone could be nicer to me than she was the other night. Geez, I should ask her to marry me and then it would be all over. Julie would be sad and disappointed, but what the heck... we've split before. Or maybe I should say good-bye to Jolene and go for Julie. Tom slammed his palms against the side of his head. He looked up at the ceiling and asked himself, how do I get into these impossible predicaments?

44

PAUL MINTON SCRIBBLED HIS SIGNATURE on the check at Stillman's Super Market. He tore it away from his checkbook and handed it to Ellie. A sheriff's car pulled up at the stop sign in the intersection. He turned his head and the paper slipped out of his fingers. The next person in line at the checkout reached down and picked up the check. Paul grabbed it and handed it to Ellie. Staring blankly down at the woman next to him, he said, "Sorry…thanks."

A semi truck blocked his view as it made a wide turn, heading toward the railroad tracks. The police car moved ahead and continued down Main. Paul walked out onto the sidewalk and pulled his coat collar up. Blisters, they're pulling into Pendleton's driveway, he said to himself. Then he saw a gray van pull up at the stop sign. He knew in an instant that the driver was Terry Pendleton.

Paul thought about the gun he had hidden in a shoebox in his bedroom closet. I wonder what the sheriff would do if they found it in Pendleton's house. Then the pale-faced eccentric could point at me all he wants. The cops would have the evidence to arrest him for murder.

TERRY PENDLETON NERVOUSLY GLANCED AT HIS WATCH. Only ten minutes left, he said to himself. He had the package ready—a pair of winter boots he had repaired. The customer said she would return by 4:00 p.m. The image of the police car in his driveway kept cropping up in his mind.

The Lord requires I do one more deed of justice…and then…and then I can disappear. My mission will be ended. Thor smiled thinking about the warm sun in southern Texas.

He heard the door open. The woman had a wool cap pulled down over her eyebrows, the dark brown eyes barely showing. She smiled and walked to the counter. "Oh, it's ready. Thank you."

"That'll be twelve-fifty," Thor said.

"See this scarf. I made it myself. My mother used to sew for the first lady and the governor of Wisconsin. The governor always wore a red vest…forty of 'em, my mother made in her lifetime. And…." She pressed a finger into Thor's chest. "The governor's wife, Joyce, had a gown made by Mom that she wore at the inauguration."

Thor nervously grabbed the package off the counter and handed it forward toward her fingers. She took it.

"My husband used to say, 'When you get something new, you have to get rid of something old.'"

"Thank you and good day, ma'am."

Thor locked the back door of his shop and anxiously entered his vehicle. He turned onto U.S. Highway 59 and headed south. His heart fluttered spotting a state patrol car parked at an approach. His right foot tapped the brake and he looked straight ahead while passing by the trooper. His rearview mirror exposed only a semi truck. Thank thee, Lord, for not sending him after me, he said to himself.

Thor slowed his vehicle to 58 miles per hour and set it on cruise. He had a difficult time focusing his mind on driving as all he could think about was the police and Paul Minton. Finally, he arrived in New Dresden, slowing to 35 and making a full stop at the main intersection. He took a right and felt relieved. There weren't any vehicles parked in his driveway.

SHERIFF DAVE JOHNSON STOOD. "Okay, I'm calling the state police. You guys remember Perry and Ben?"

Deputy Kelly nodded. "Aw, come on, Dave. We're only an hour and a half from Little Falls. We'd be back before you know it."

Johnson smiled. "I want you two to continue your surveillance of New Dresden. From what I've seen and heard so far, you're close to a solution. The media won't leave me alone, and they won't until we solve this case...both cases actually."

45

PAUL MINTON HUNG UP THE PHONE. He threw his empty glass across the room—it shattered, spreading fragments across the floor. "That one's for Clara," he muttered, thinking about his cleaning lady. "Two hundred thou missin'! Someone besides Garcia has been dippin' into the moola."

Money is one problem, spending the rest of my life in a prison is a bigger one, he said to himself, the image of a pale face flashing across his mind. The clock on the wall read 1:12 a.m. Paul pulled on a black turtleneck shirt. Spreading his fingers over his waist, he slicked down the shirt ends over his black warm-up pants.

He put on a black stocking cap and jacket. His hand padded the bulging pistol in his left pocket. Paul visualized the rear basement window in Pendleton's house. He guessed that it would not be locked. All I have to do is to remove the screen, he said to himself. In case of unexpected problems, he placed a heavy-duty flat screwdriver into his other pocket.

Paul opened the outside door and winced. Huge snowflakes streamed down from the low-hanging clouds. He closed the door and headed for his garage. Paul drove speedily toward the county highway, going through the stop sign—there wasn't a single vehicle on the road. He gunned the engine and headed for Main Street. Two vehicles remained at William's Pub, which usually stayed open until 2:00 a.m.

Minton drove through the intersection and took a left on the next street, parking his vehicle in the community center parking lot. He pulled his keys partially out of the ignition and left them in his vehicle. He walked quickly back toward Main, turning toward Pendleton's house when he reached the intersection. He saw two streetlights between the lot and Main. In moments he reached the driveway. The yard light at Pendleton's place wasn't on. Minton glanced in all directions, seeing no one. Then he quickly walked around to the back of the house, amazed that his boot tracks were being erased by the snowflakes.

He knelt down by the basement window, pressing the spring locks of the screen. It removed easily. Then he pushed on the window. Nothing happened. He pushed harder. The window opened upward. Minton grasped the frame and raised it high until he heard a click, which signaled that the window would stay open.

The beam from his flashlight showed him a table setting directly under the window. He slid his legs into the room, grasping the sides to make certain he didn't fall. The bottom of his feet felt the top of the table, and in moments he was inside. He closed the window but not tightly. Minton found an old, abandoned towel hanging over the back of a chair. He wiped the bottom of his boots.

He shined his flashlight around the room and saw a wooden stairway heading upward. Minton climbed the steps quietly, placing each boot down gently. He reached the door and stopped. Grabbing a small WD-40 can from his pocket, he sprayed the three hinges and the latch mechanism.

Minton smiled when the door opened without a sound. The flashlight beam exposed a closet near a door next to the kitchen. He tiptoed over to the door and again used the WD-40 to spray the hinges and latch. The door opened. He reached into his pocket and brought out the gun, sliding it under a blanket in the far corner of the shelf.

Minton felt satisfied and hurried back to the basement. He set open the basement window again and attempted to lift himself up and through. After several tries, he realized that it was futile. Then he closed the window and headed back up the stairs. One of his knees caught the edge of a table as he crossed the kitchen—the noise froze him in his tracks. He stopped and listened—nothing.

Minton opened the door leading outside and grasped the latch on the storm door. He slipped outside, carefully re-locking them. The heavy snow fell as he made his way down the three steps onto the driveway. He stopped. A pair of headlights approached from the direction of the Main Street intersection. Minton stopped, breathlessly waiting. The pickup drove by.

He returned to his vehicle and drove around the block, avoiding the main block of Main Street. He crossed the railroad tracks and thought of the screen. He had failed to re-attach it. Damn, he thought. Oh well, who in the heck is ever going to notice that?

THOR DREAMPT ABOUT AN ANGEL WHO hovered above Loon Lake on a Sunday night. Fishing houses that had been active during the evening were destroyed. He saw a flash of light and a plume of smoke—an entire structure disappeared. A crackling noise awakened him. He raised his body, supporting it with an arm. Then he heard the light footsteps. Thor sat up, listening. The front door opened and then closed.

He rushed into the kitchen and looked out the window. A dark shadow, partially masked by falling snow, dashed toward the main intersection. "Minton!" Thor muttered. He flicked on a light switch. His eyes locked on small streaks of wetness that extended from the basement door to the front door. Thor noticed the additional wet spots in front of the closet door. He opened the door and stood still for a moment.

"Lord have mercy," he whispered after grabbing the pistol barrel between two fingers. Thor walked to the table and lay it down. "Minton!" he exclaimed. "That devil is trying to frame me."

Thor tossed and turned for hours after returning to his bed. Morning can't come soon enough, he said to himself. Restless, he jumped up to examine the basement again. The wet areas on the floor had disappeared but left smudges. He filled his coffeemaker with water and flicked the switch. Thor pulled the front curtain back and saw a sea of white. He took a deep breath and felt sudden pain in his leg. Thor limped to his holy room. He lit the candles and thought about the police car that he had seen in his driveway. The pain disappeared. *I've got to make some changes...the police will be back*, he said to himself, dropping to his knees.

He returned the pistol that had been planted in his closet. Then he reached his knife block and pulled out his largest butcher knife. I have to get this out of the house, he said to himself.

46

THE SOUND OF CRUNCHING SNOW REVERBERATED off the trees as Tom and Jolene trudged down the hill, loaded with dinner supplies. Tom slid the strap off his shoulder. He lay down the other bag that he carried and pulled the strap completely over his head. "There, that's a lot better. How's your load?"

"We should have brought a sled."

"Hey, I've got one in the garage." Tom glanced at the hillside that fronted his lake home. "Oh well, I think we can make it as we are."

A snowmobile approached from the east and roared by them, moving well past the fishing houses. They stood and watched until Tom pointed. "It's that big one over there, isn't it?"

"Must be."

The lower rim of the sun had reached the horizon, lighting up the snow for most of the length of the bay.

"That's pretty," Jolene said.

They had trudged for about half the distance. Tom stopped and lifted the strap from around his neck. "Darn thing gets heavier and heavier."

"Oh, we're almost there."

"Yeah—we are—we are."

He hung the strap around the other side of his neck. "Guess I'll make it."

An ATV ran up the middle of the bay, crossing in front of Tom and Jolene. It stopped at one of the other fishing houses. A man got off the machine and entered. "Well, at least we won't be out here alone," Tom said.

"Just a few more steps."

Tom set his two containers on the ice next to the small building. Jolene walked forward with a key in one hand and opened the door.

"I'll open the valve to the gas tank," she said, and walked around to the other side of the house.

The snowmobile that had passed by earlier made a turn at the end of the bay. It headed back toward the cluster of fishing houses. Tom watched as it sped by. He felt glad to see the red taillights getting smaller and smaller. Tom opened a new bag of coals and he filled the grill.

"Wow, sure doesn't take long to warm this thing up," Tom said. "I'll get the coals started," he added.

The lower rim of the sun had reached the horizon. The snow on the bay brightened. Each passing minute, bigger shadows reduced the size of the glare. He felt a chill as the top rim dropped below the wall of trees in the west.

Tom opened the door and entered. Jolene sat on a chair, her head between her hands. "Something the matter?" Tom asked.

"A lot's been on my mind lately," Jolene said and rubbed her right cheek with her thumb.

"Nothing serious, I hope."

Jolene looked up, her face somber. "I'll talk about it after dinner. How are the coals doing?"

"Should be ready to go," Tom said, and sprinkled a heavy layer of sage on a porcelain plate. He rubbed both sides of each steak onto the herb and made a step toward the door. His mind drifted to Julie and how quickly she had gotten back into his life. There's something different going on with Jolene, he thought, and passed through the door.

Jolene and Tom ate in silence. He poured himself another glass of wine, noticing that Jolene hadn't touched hers.

Jolene picked up the empty plates from the table and dropped one on the floor. It shattered. "Oh my!"

Tom opened a long narrow door. "Ah-ha, a broom and dust-pan."

He swept up the glass pieces into the pan and dumped them into a wastebasket.

"Let's head back," Jolene said.

Tom turned off the heater and walked around to close the valve on the gas tank. Jolene turned the latch inside the door and pulled it shut. They walked toward Tom's house in silence. Suddenly, the headlights of a snowmobile appeared.

"Geez, where did that come from?" Tom asked. He felt Jolene's fingers tighten on his. They stood still and watched the driver's bulk lean as he curved away from them.

"That was scary!" Jolene exclaimed.

"Some nut of a person looking for something to do," Tom said. "Let's get the heck out of 'ere." He stepped forward quickly, pulling on Jolene's arm.

Tom tightened his hand on hers and held it as they climbed the slope to his house. He opened the door and they entered.

Jolene looked up into his eyes. She said, "Tom, I'm not going to be able to see you any more."

Tom's insides turned to butter. He let go her hand and stared at her face. "Not see me any more! I don't get it—what's going on?"

Her eyes became moist. "I've joined this religion. That makes us not right."

"Religion!" Tom exclaimed. "It's something to do with your family, isn't it?"

Jolene nodded and grasped Tom's hand. "I know that you're not going to understand. I don't expect you to." She pulled away. "I have to go."

Tom hugged Jolene tightly. His forehead furrowed as he looked into her eyes, seeing—distance. Tom released his grip and followed her out the door. He felt stunned as she got into her vehicle, backed it out of the driveway and drove up the roadway. Tom stood on his sidewalk for several minutes wondering if what just happened was a dream.

FINGERS OF SNOW STREAMING ACROSS TOM'S ROADWAY caused his vehicle to lurch as he accelerated. Tom blasted through the drift at the end of his roadway and sped up the township gravel road. A half a mile later, he touched his brakes and barely stopped short of a deep ditch. Gotta get my mind back on driving, he said to himself.

Tom yawned as he stopped his vehicle at the county highway and waited for a pickup to pass. He had awakened at close to 2:00 a.m. and had difficulty falling asleep again. His thoughts had jumped back and forth between the two women for close to three hours before he got up to visit the bathroom and grab a drink of water.

A flock of blackbirds that had avoided migration for some unexplained reason tucked close to each other as they perched on a power line next. Tom touched the brakes as an ATV vehicle crossed the road directly in front of him. No wonder so many of them die every year in Minnesota, he said to himself.

He came up behind a car going very slow as he approached Purgatory Curve. If that lady was going any slower, she'd be going backwards, Tom said to himself. Geez, those wheels are barely turning. His frustration worsened as the flashing lights on the gates at the railroad crossing came on. Damn, he thought.

Ten minutes later, Tom dropped three quarters on the checkout station at Stillman's Super Market. "Anything new on the gas station robberies, Ellie?"

Her head moved slowly from side to side. She reached out for the next item on the checkout conveyer.

Tom pulled the outside door open, meeting a cold gust of wind. He flinched. He placed a gloved hand over his face as he walked toward his vehicle. He stopped. A light-blue van pulling a trailer drove through the intersection from the south. The snowmobile looked normal, Tom thought, but the strange-looking long table next to it is out of place. He caught a glimpse of a pale-faced man behind the wheel. Tom placed his gloved hands over his ears. Geez, it's cold out here. He watched the van and trailer cross the railroad tracks. Then it made a right turn toward a long narrow storage building.

He placed the grocery bag on the passenger seat and entered his vehicle. Tom had an eerie feeling as he crossed the tracks. He saw the pale-faced man unhooking the trailer that he had just backed into a storage unit. It's none of my business, but there's something weird going on here, he said to himself.

Tom's thoughts changed as he turned onto the township road. The house that his old friend Maynard Cushing had lived in had a different color. Must have new owners, Tom thought. He cringed, remembering the cryptic artwork that had outlined a dead body on the hallway floor.

The *Fargo Forum* had an article regarding a recent issue concerning the rejection of an appeal by the murderer of Cushing. I'm sure glad the judge turned him down, Tom thought. I don't need the likes of someone like that hanging around. There are enough weird characters living around here as it is.

The phone answering machine beeped as Tom opened his house door. He stepped over and pushed the button. "Tom, this is Julie. Would you be able to have dinner with me at Spanky's this evening? I have some important things to tell you."

Tom stared out the window, focusing on the waving tops of the tall oaks behind his garage. Julie! It's like a miracle, he said to himself.

TOM'S INSIDES WARMED WATCHING JULIE WALKING down his sidewalk. He opened the door and grasped her hand, gently pulling her into the room. He hugged her tightly, feeling her arm tighten against his back. "I'm really glad that you're here," Tom said.

"And why is that?"

"Ahh...I'll tell you later. Come on in and sit down. She lifted up the two rear pillows of the love seat next to the corner windows. Julie used her knee to push the bottom cushions back into place. She sat down. Tom handed her a glass of wine. "Thanks."

Tom sat down on the antique rocking chair nearby and took a sip from his glass. I wonder what this woman has in mind, he thought. Does she have any idea that I've just lost Jolene?

"What are you having for dinner, Tom?"

He shook his head. "Have to look at the menu."

"I would think that you would have it…."

"Have it what?"

"Have it memorized by now."

"It's changed a lot lately. The new owner has created a whole bunch of different entrees…very good, too."

"Who's the new owner?" Julie asked.

"Jeremy Hanson. Used to be a cook…'bout ten years I think."

Julie nodded. "Does he have salmon on the menu?"

"Don't know about that one. It's not one of my favorites, ya' know."

"You're missing on the great Vitamin D," Julie said, taking another sip of wine.

"Would you like another?" Tom asked.

"Best not. I'm going to drive."

"Oh, fine. Then I can have another."

"Why don't you have it at the restaurant? I'm hungry."

"Okay. Let's get going then."

Tom lurched forward as Julie hit the brakes, stopping for the county highway. He took a deep breath as she spun her vehicle onto the paved highway and sped toward Spanky's. "Watch it, it's a 30 zone. Deputies like to hang around here."

Julie tapped her brake pedal. "I'm not used to the country."

Tom laughed.

"Wow, the parking lot is darn near full," Tom said. He always admired Julie's ability to find a parking place in a crowded lot.

"There's a *Julie spot*!" Tom exclaimed as she drove down the first aisle.

"Darn, didn't see that one."

"Ah-ha, another one." She rolled her vehicle into the space and hit the brakes. Tom jolted forward again, placing a bracing hand against the dash.

Tom exited quickly and dashed around to the other side of Julie's car. He opened the door.

"Thank you, sir."

He grasped her hand and they walked toward the door. Inside, Tom continued to hold her hand. He stopped at the hostess station.

"We'll have a booth right around the corner in a minute. Gotta clear it first."

Tom nodded.

A minute later, the hostess led them to a booth. A wave of uneasiness spread through his body as he spotted Paul Minton sitting on a stool. I wonder what that goofball is going to think…seeing me with another woman…not Jolene, he thought.

Tom ordered a half-carafe of Chardonnay. "I don't think you have to be too concerned about having more wine. Dinner will use it up…besides, we're only two miles from home."

Julie nodded. She smiled widely. "You always have everything figured out, don't you?"

"This is my turf, Julie."

"Yeah! I'm out for dinner with King Thomas."

Tom laughed and held up his glass. They clinked. "Here's to a nice evening."

Julie ordered her salmon and Tom followed with an oriental chicken platter. Tom glanced toward the bar after hearing Minton's voice become louder and louder. Tom's nemesis slapped the guy next to him on the back. Suddenly, Minton turned his head, fixing his eyes on Tom's. The men's gazes locked together. Minton's smile disappeared. His brain cells are churning big time right now, Tom thought.

"What's the matter, Tom?" Julie asked.

"Just saw someone I know…an obnoxious nuisance."

"He's a nice-looking man."

"Stay away from him. Take my word for it."

Julie turned her head and looked at Tom. "So, Hastings, why are you glad that I'm here? Remember what you said at the door?"

"Oh, yeah...I did say something like that, didn't I?"

"So what's the deal?"

"Okay, I'll spit it out. The woman that I had been seeing recently and I have split."

Julie set her glass down and smacked her lips. "How long have you been going with her?"

"Off and on for a couple of years."

"How can I be sure that you won't go back?"

"Julie! Julie, there's no chance in hell. What's done is done. It's over."

Julie frowned and lifted the wine glass to her lips.

Tom felt his cheeks redden. "I mean it, Julie." He heard footsteps approaching.

"Well, well, if it isn't Romeo...yeah, Romeo...with another blonde yet."

Tom's heart thumped against his chest. He looked up and hated what he saw—the sneering face of Paul Minton.

"Aren't you going to introduce me to your new dish?"

"Minton! Do you want me to call the manager right now or are you going to leave us alone?"

Minton placed a hand on Julie's shoulder. "You watch out for this guy. He'll get you into trouble."

Tom slammed his palms down on the table and began to rise.

"Save your strength, old fella. I'm leaving."

Paul Minton laughed loudly as he strutted back toward the bar.

"Friend of yours?" Julie asked.

"Are you kidding? He's the biggest pain I've ever met."

They quietly finished their dinners. Tom assisted Julie out of the booth and grasped her hand. He quickly led her to the checkout station, glancing at the bar before rounding the corner. He saw Minton turn and crudely clap his hands together.

He set the slip and his hastily written check down on the counter and hustled Julie into the parking lot. Tom opened the passenger door for Julie and scampered to the other side. He put the fan button on high. "Cold night, huh?"

Within three minutes, he pulled into his garage. Tom stretched his arm around Julie's shoulder as they walked down the sidewalk and into his house.

They sat on the loveseat and talked for a few minutes. "I've got to go, Tom," Julie said.

Tom frowned. "How about coming over for dinner tomorrow? I'm cooking."

TOM LEFT THE KITCHEN AND ENTERED THE DINING ROOM. "Should I fill up your glass, Julie?" She sat on a flowered love seat in front of a bay window. He reacted to her wide smile with one of his own. "Ah dumb question, huh?"

He walked back into the kitchen and opened the refrigerator door. Filling her glass and his own, he returned the bottle where he had gotten it. "Geez, Julie, I've dodged so many bullets out here... wonder if another is coming...all those robberies and murders...so close by."

Julie set her glass down after taking a big sip. "Thinking about the past, I'm probably safer sitting right here than anyplace else."

"I hope you're right." Tom took another sip. He gazed around the room. "I wouldn't be a bit surprised if this Minton guy isn't involved in some of it...the robberies and the killings."

"You really hate that guy, don't you?"

"Hate is a tough word. Despise would probably work better," Tom said and returned into the kitchen. He turned and took two steps toward Julie. "If that so-and-so bothers me one more time, I'm gonna—"

"Gonna what?" Julie asked, her smile turning into a frown.

"I'll kill the bastard."

"Tom, you're way out...no way you would do that. Get real."

Tom walked over to the stove, grabbed a spoon and stirred the pot. "Potatoes are doin' nicely. Better get those steaks ready."

He left the room and returned with a spotlight strapped around the top of his head. Tom opened a spice bottle and splashed a bunch of leaves over the top of a plate. Then he rubbed the side of a steak into the spice, then the other side. He repeated the same process with a second steak. "Here they go, for better or worse," he said, and smiled at Julie as he opened the door to the deck.

Tom gasped after closing the outside deck door. "It's colder than heck outside." He rubbed his hands together. "I saw something odd in town his morning."

"What was that?" Julie asked, and lifted the wine glass to her lips.

"That pale-faced guy moved his snowmobile from his home and parked it in a storage place, the one by the tracks."

"What's so odd about that?"

"He also had a long narrow table on the trailer…looked like some kind of church thing."

"Church thing?"

"Well, sort of an altar."

"Don't lots of people store furniture and stuff in that building?" Julie asked.

"Yeah, but…."

"But what?"

"Oh never mind. Every time I see that guy, he gives me the creeps."

The early evening passed. Tom and Julie had finished the dishes. He walked to the front door and looked out. "Not nice out there, Julie…I don't think you should go home."

"Oh darn," she said.

47

SHERIFF JOHNSON REACHED FOR THE PHONE. "Thanks for calling back, Perry. Have you heard about the fishing house murders over here?"

The sheriff nodded several times and listened. "We have reason to believe that our suspect purchased some Bibles at a book store in Little Falls."

He nodded again and listened. "That would be great…morning would work good. So you'll get here early tomorrow afternoon, huh?"

He smiled and hung up the phone. "We don't have to go to Little Falls, guys. Perry Layton and Ben Perkins are coming down. They're going to make the stop. Do you two remember them?"

Both deputies nodded.

"Izz, I want you to take the sales slip and fax it to the Bureau of Criminal Apprehension, attention of Perry Layton," the sheriff said.

"Sure, Dave," Izzy said and left the room.

"Kelly, if the purchases on that slip are what I think they are, we need an immediate court order for a search warrant. Can you take care of that?"

"Got it boss. I'll make out a report and go see the judge immediately."

Sheriff Dave Johnson smiled and sat down, settling deep into his chair. We're gonna have the *Ice Lord* in a cell…and soon, he said to himself.

THOR PULLED THE STORAGE DOOR DOWN. He made sure it was locked and returned to his vehicle. *The Lord has guided me to this place,* he said to himself. *What does he think that I should do with the gun?* He sat in his van with the motor running for a few minutes watching the traffic. There goes that Hastings guy—never misses a day. He watched the gray SUV until it disappeared around Purgatory Curve.

He drove back onto Main Street and parked in the Stillman's Super Market lot. Thor pulled the brim of his gray winter hat down and headed for the post office. Inside, he got his mail and sorted it on the bench by the window. He tossed unwanted pieces into the wastebasket. Perhaps I should toss the gun in there, too, he thought.

On the other hand, I could mail it back to Minton. I wonder what the devil would think about that. Or I could use UPS over at the hardware store. Suddenly, Thor's mind locked on an idea. *I've got it....I've got it….*

"SHERIFF'S OFFICE."

"Hello, this is Terry Pendleton of New Dresden. I would like to report a burglary."

"GADS, THERE'S A MILLION TRUCKS ON THIS ROAD," Ben Perkins said to Perry Layton. The two state police agents' first stop was scheduled for a bookstore in Little Falls. Both men didn't wear hats. Ben's chin tilted upward to allow his eyes to see the road over the dash. "Look at that idiot ahead of us…did you see that?"

Perry rarely smiled and didn't spare one now. "That was one of the tightest cutoffs that I've ever seen, inches away from the other guy's bumper."

The traffic eased after they passed by the city of Rogers and continued on I-94 toward the northwest. Ben's grip on the steering wheel relaxed a little as they passed over the bridge spanning two railroad tracks just east of Monticello.

They exited I-94 at Clearwater and headed north toward Clear Lake. Ben turned the wheels onto U.S. Highway 10 that they would use the rest of the trip to Big Lakes. "Ugly-looking place," Perry said. The gray rock walls of St. Cloud Reformatory dominated the western landscape.

"I hear that it's one of the crudest prisons in Minnesota," Ben said.

"Being inside is like dancing with the devil," Perry said.

A few miles later, they stopped for a red light in Rice. Perry reached into his shirt pocket and brought out a piece of paper, glancing at its bleary figures. "Over a hundred bucks for books. Seems like a lot to me."

Ben nodded. "If it's for Bibles and we get a decent description of the buyer, we're gonna hit the place early morning, Sheriff Johnson said."

Ben slowed for the light in Royalton but slipped through the intersection swiftly on a changeover to green. "Do you know what exit we get off at Little Falls?"

"Yup, Highway 76, a couple miles or so south of town, should be coming up in minutes."

They exited Highway 10 and re-crossed the highway to continue on into the city of Little Falls. "Were you ever taught by nuns?" Ben asked as they passed by a convent and church.

"Can't say that I have, but I hear that for the most part they are great teachers," Perry said.

"My parents sent me and my brother to a Catholic school for a couple of years in spite of the fact that we weren't Catholics," Ben said. "My older brother, Emil, got in trouble with one of the teachers in the public school."

"So how did that go?"

"Great."

"Hey, turn right at the next intersection. The bookstore is the next right, first block."

They parked. Ben entered the bookstore followed by his partner. Two women, standing behind a counter, turned their heads toward them.

"Hi folks, I'm state agent Ben Perkins and this is my partner Perry Layton. I believe that you've been expecting us."

"Welcome to Little Falls," the smiling woman said. "I'm Laura, the owner of this bookstore. This is Maryjude. She's my assistant."

Ben looked around the room. "Ah…do you have an office?"

The owner's eyes widened. "I'm sorry, but I don't. All my business is out here."

"Okay." Agent Ben pulled the copy of the receipt from his shirt pocket. "Our request is simple. We need to know what products were included in this receipt, and also we need to know who made the purchase or get a description."

Laura adjusted her glasses. She looked at the receipt. Her assistant's mouth opened slightly. "Laura, I sold six Bibles to a man. I don't have his name but he had a strange look about him."

"Strange look, huh?" Perry said.

"Yeah, he had a face that looked like a ghost...as white as snow."

Ben opened the folder that he had brought in with him. "Miss... ah, Miss...."

"Maryjude," the clerk said.

"Miss Maryjude, could you write down in your own words what you just told us, your description of the man, and the type of Bibles purchased...and how many?"

"He bought six. I remember it well because that many sales are rare. I'll get one for you."

Maryjude disappeared into the next room. Moments later she returned. "This was it. All six were exactly like this one."

"Thank you very much, ladies. It is possible that you may be called as witnesses down the road. Would that be a problem?"

Both women shook their heads.

"Thanks again," Perry said. The two officers headed out the door. Ben directed the state police car back onto Highway 10 as Perry talked on the phone. He hung up. "They're going to wait for us, Ben. We should be there within a couple of hours."

48

SHERIFF JOHNSON STOOD AT THE DISPATCHER'S COUNTER and waited for the door to open. He expected the two state BCA agents to come through the door at any moment. Deputy Izzy Felton walked toward him. "Dave, we've got all four cars ready to go."

"Good, the agents should be here any time."

The sheriff yawned. "By the way, what's the latest on Jorgenson and Garth Sabolik?"

Izzy brought out her notebook. "Jorgenson can help identify the two men who robbed the station, but we already know who they are. It'll help in court, though, help a lot. Garth remembers only a shadow...no face. A long way from a positive ID."

Then the front door opened and two plainclothesmen entered. The sheriff advanced a step toward the door. "Hi, guys," he said.

The three men shook hands. "Welcome back to Big Lakes County. You probably know your way around here."

"Sure do," Ben said.

"Come into my office. We've got a team ready to go to hit the suspect's house."

The two agents followed the sheriff into his office. "Boys, do you remember my two deputies, Kelly Martin and Izzy Felton?"

"Sure do," Ben Perkins said. The agents and deputies shook hands.

"All right!" the sheriff exclaimed, and sat down in his chair behind the desk.

They discussed the upcoming strike for fifteen minutes. The sheriff stood. "There's no doubt in my mind that we have the right man. Let's go."

Just as one of the deputies opened the outside door, one of the dispatchers left her station and hastened over to the sheriff. "Mr. Johnson...Mr. Johnson."

"What?" the sheriff turned.

"I didn't get this message to you earlier. We got a call from a Terry Pendleton of New Dresden. He said that his home had been broken into last night."

"Here, let me see that," the sheriff said.

No one else said a word. Dave Johnson shrugged his shoulders. "This doesn't change anything. Come on fellas, let's go."

ELLIE LOOKED AT THE WALL CLOCK. Her work day at Still-man's Super Market usually ended at 5:00. The clock read 4:45. She pressed a key on the terminal. "Twenty-four fifty, please," she said, and handed the receipt to a customer. "Thank you, Bob." Out of the corner of her eye, Ellie saw a police car stop at the intersection. Then she saw another one do the same coming from the west. Suddenly, they lit up like Christmas trees.

The customer, an elderly man next in the checkout line, pointed. "Wonder what's going on outside. A drug bust maybe."

The man and Ellie both stepped toward the window. They watched as the police cars both headed south, still on Main Street.

Two other employees and owner Ron joined them at the window. They all walked outside to watch. A third police car rushed through the intersection. "Look, another one!" Ron Stillman exclaimed.

Several spectators had gathered at the service station corner of the intersection. They slowly walked toward the array of police cars. "I've got to see what's going on," Mr. Stillman said. He put on a coat and crossed the street. Then he waited for two pickups to go through. His white apron stuck out well below his jacket. He didn't wear a hat or gloves. As the intersection cleared, he hurried toward the crowd of people who had gathered across from the house that appeared to be the target of the police.

DEPUTY KELLY MARTIN MOVED UP THE THREE METAL STEPS and used his gloved hand to push snow off the wrought iron railings. He waited for his followers to catch up. Then he pressed the doorbell. Martin stomped his feet and did a little dance before pressing the doorbell again. Another minute went by. He turned his head and waved at a man carrying a brown bag. "Okay, Felix, open the door."

The locksmith swept a finger across a row of keys hanging from a metal ring. He grabbed one of the keys and inserted it into the door lock. It didn't work. His second choice did.

The deputy stepped inside, cupped his mouth with his palms and yelled. "Police! Anyone home?"

Sheriff Johnson, who stood directly behind him, turned his head and waved his hand. Six other deputies entered the house. He placed a hand on Ben Perkins's shoulder. "Come on in. Let's have a seat and watch the fun…see what they find."

Sounds of hurrying footsteps, banging cabinet doors, and sliding drawers dominated for the next half an hour. Deputy Kelly approached the men in the living room. "Look what we found in the front closet." He held up a gun with a pen pushed through the trigger guard. Kelly carried it over to the two state officers and the sheriff. They all nodded and he placed it into a plastic container.

Sheriff Johnson said, "Off to Bemidji with that as soon as possible, Kelly."

The front door opened. "Ah…Dave we have a visitor. The resident of this house, Mr. Terry Pendleton."

The sheriff stood. "Mr. Pendleton, this here paper is a legal document signed by a judge which gave me and my staff the right to search your house."

"But…but why?" the stunned, pale-faced man said. His eyes rolled with anxiety.

"You are a suspect in at least one murder case…a man by the name of Garcia…shot and killed in Spanky's parking lot within the past month. Do you know anything about that?"

"Lord, no."

The sheriff grabbed the bag with the gun in it. He held it up in front of Pendleton. "Do you know who this gun belongs to? It was found in your front closet."

"I certainly do not." The man's face reddened. "Didn't you get my call? My house was burglarized night before last. Go down in the basement. You can see the foot tracks, and the…the screen on the basement window. It's been removed."

The sheriff's voice stuttered slightly. "Kelly, would you check that out…the screen?"

"Sure."

Another deputy followed Kelly down the basement steps.

"So, Mr. Pendleton, tell me about the burglary. What did he or she take? Did you see the person? What time did it happen?"

Terry's voice crackled and then tightened to just above a whisper as he told the officers of being awakened at about 2:00 a.m. by the sound of someone crashing into a table.

"Did you get up?" the sheriff asked.

"No, I waited and heard the front door close. Then I went into my kitchen and put the lights on. I saw wet tracks across the floor coming from the basement door. The tracks led to the front closet door. Then the tracks led to the front door." He placed his hands over his chest, took a deep breath and lost his balance. One of the deputies grabbed him by the shoulders to prevent him from falling.

Kelly returned into the room. He grasped the edge of a rectangular window screen with his plastic glove. "We found this out back next to the basement window."

"Mr. Pendleton, you're going to have to come with us to Big Lakes. I'm arresting you as a suspect and you will be officially questioned. You have the right to an attorney...."

49

THE SMALL INTEROGATION ROOM at the Big Lakes Sheriff's Department had a small table and six chairs. Terry Pendleton sat on a chair at one end. Sheriff Johnson sat across from him. State agents Perkins and Layton sat on one side. Deputies Kelly Martin and Izzy Felton sat across from them.

Pendleton had lowered his head, nestling it between his two hands. A knock on the door stopped all talking. The sheriff loudly said, "Yes."

The door opened. An officer stuck his head in. "A lawyer...name of William Sherman here to see his client."

Kelly Martin stood and walked to the door. "Okay, Mr. Sherman, you can come in."

Izzy, who had been sitting next to Pendleton, also stood. "You can have my chair, sir."

"Sheriff, I need some time alone with my client."

Dave Johnson scratched the top of his forehead with a finger. "I'll give you five minutes." He stood and led the officers and agents out the door.

The sheriff led them into his office. They all sat down. "What do you think, Ben?" he asked.

"That basement screen and discernable bootprints in the basement give him an edge. If someone did plant the gun, why couldn't they also plant the sales slip?"

Perry shook his head. "Yeah, Ben, but what about the description those bookstore women gave us? It sure looks like the guy in the next room."

Izzy said, "When's the last time we did an ID lineup here?"

"Never did one," the sheriff said. "Sounds as if it's time."

Izzy looked down at the floor. "I think we need one, even if it means driving down to Little Falls to get the women…then take them back."

"What do you think, Kelly?" the sheriff said.

A deputy walked over. "They're ready for you, Dave."

The sheriff curled his lower lip over his upper and stepped toward the door. The other officers followed him in. Attorney William Sherman stood by the table. "Please be seated."

"Sheriff, Deputies, Minnesota Bureau Agents, I will read you this statement, and then unless my client is charged with a crime, I will expect him to be released.

"Mr. Terry Pendleton had his house broken into two nights ago. The intruder came in through the basement window. Your evidence supports that. He has never in his life owned or possessed a weapon. The gun that your search found in his closet was planted by the intruder.

"Furthermore, the intruder had previously intentionally dropped a sales slip in the driveway, expecting the police to find it. You are after the wrong man.

"I request an immediate release of my client." The attorney sat down.

"Mr. Sherman, I'm going to discuss your request with my staff. Give us a few minutes." The sheriff stood and walked hastily toward the door. The others followed.

Minutes later, the sheriff returned alone. "Pendleton, you're free to go for now. I advise you not to leave the area."

Pendleton stood, his eyes flooded with tears. He opened his mouth as if to speak.

Sherman put a hand on Pendleton's shoulder. "Thank you, Sheriff, for doing the right thing," the attorney said.

"Kelly, would you get the gun from the judge?"

The deputy nodded and walked away.

PAUL MINTON WATCHED FROM HIS HOUSE WINDOW. Four police cars passed, all headed north. "They've got the pale-faced wimp," he said, laughing out loud. I wonder how…the gun…." He laughed louder. Minton grasped the glass on his counter and brought it to his lips. He swallowed deeply and burped. Good stuff, he said to himself.

I bet the wimp stuttered trying to explain the gun. Wait until they get the ballistics. Goodbye Garcia. Goodbye Pendleton. Hello Minton.

The cigarette market is getting ready to roll again, and soon, he said to himself. He laughed again. At last I got rid of one of my adversaries. Not done, though. That Hastings guy is a stupid pain in the butt. I'd like to make out with that chick of his…she's a beauty.

It's Wednesday. Spanky's is open tonight. Bet the old man will be there with her, he thought.

Minton spent the next half hour in his spa. He slipped while exiting, coming down on his right knee real hard. "Ouch!" he exclaimed. "Damn, that's all I need is a broken knee."

He limped to his bedroom and got dressed.

TOM HASTINGS FLICKED THE SWITCH ON HIS COFFEE POT. He checked the outside thermometer. It read -4 degrees. Not bad for January, he thought. Should be a nice day. He watched the sun work its way through a haze, the upper rim spreading a light glow over the snow-covered bay.

The coffee cup sitting on the countertop had been removed from the cupboard the previous evening. Tom grabbed the pot and filled it. Darn good thing it wasn't behind those doors last night, he said to himself. It would've been ice cold.

He carried the filled cup and sat down in his computer corner. Tom clicked the Internet icon and checked the news. The market is going up today, he said to himself. I wonder what Julie is doing. Tom checked the weather and grimaced. Gonna be cold as heck the next couple days. I wonder if she'd like to come over for a session in the hot tub.

He thought of Jolene. Then he quickly switched his mind to focus on Julie. Jolene is gone…gone for good. I have to quit thinking about her…as if she never existed.

The cold northwest breeze swept across Tom's cheek as he opened his front door and headed for the garage. One of these years, I'm gonna head south for the winter, he said to himself. Southern Texas would be great. I gotta do it. Minton couldn't follow me that far.

He approached the railroad tracks in New Dresden. Tom slowed his SUV for a van and trailer. It came from the storage area. Well, I'll be damned, he thought. The pale-faced guy is taking his table back…maybe back…or maybe he sold it to someone. Tom followed the trailer to the main intersection. It crossed and continued. He stayed behind and watched it take a left and turn into a driveway.

Tom drove around the block and parked in front of the post office. After getting his mail, he walked to the grocery store. "Tom, did you hear about the sheriff's raid?" Ellie asked.

"No, what raid?"

"Four cars, all lights flashing, surrounded the Pendleton house. They must have been after drugs."

"Who's Pendleton?"

"Some guy who lives alone in one of those houses down the street. It's about the third one on the left."

"Do you know what this Pendleton guy looks like?"

She nodded. "He is short and stocky...has a pale face and beady eyes."

Tom picked up a newspaper from the rack. "Geez, I wonder if it was...."

"Wonder if it was who?" Ellie asked.

"The trailer with a snowmobile and a strange-looking table."

Ellie shook her head. "Tom, you need a rest. Better go home and take a break."

π

50

DEPUTY IZZY FELTON OPENED AN ENVELOPE. "We have a positive ID, guys. The gun found in Pendleton's closet is the one that was used to kill Garcia."

The sheriff stood in front of his desk, his back end perched on the edge. "We have the murder weapon. Now the big question... who fired it?"

He walked around to the back of his desk and sat down. "Kelly, what do you think? Was it Pendleton?"

"The guy can't be that dumb...knowing already that the police had been at his house...then leaving the gun for someone to find. Naw...."

"Izzy?" The sheriff looked at her.

"I agree with Kelly. Pendleton couldn't be that dumb. But then, who planted it...the gun...who? Why?"

She looked around the room. "If Pendleton didn't pull the trigger, then someone was out in the parking lot waiting for Garcia to come out. You know what, guys?"

The sheriff leaned forward.

Izzy pointed her finger. "I think that the fishing house murders, the gas station robberies and Garcia's killing are all related somehow. I'm not saying that one person is behind everything...but...."

"But what?" the sheriff said, his eyes narrowing.

"I think there's an overlap."

"What do you mean by overlap?" the sheriff asked.

"Whoever did the killings...one or more...is also involved in the robberies. And you know what else?"

Deputy Martin narrowed his eyes and sighed. "Okay, Izzy, what else?"

"I think that Pendleton is definitely involved. I also think there is another major player. I think that if we look and listen in New Dresden, we will be led to that other person. I think we start with Hastings. He goes to town every single day. He goes to Spanky's restaurant a lot. We need to listen to him carefully...and...."

"And what?"

"Did anyone notice that one of Pendleton's hands looked different?"

"Different?"

"Yes, the skin looked reddish, as if it was recovering from a rash...or a burn."

TERRY PENDLETON'S FOREHEAD BROKE OUT with beads of perspiration as he laboriously stitched a brown leather boot. "Yow!" he muttered. The needle had scraped his finger and a small bubble of dark red blood oozed out. He placed the finger in his mouth, gently caressing the wound with his lips. "Lord, heal thy servant."

He felt vindicated after the police had released him and he was allowed to return to his home. Thor had wasted no time before restoring his altar in the spare bedroom of his house. He appreciated the honesty of Sheriff Johnson and his deputies. They examined the evidence carefully and agreed that the gun had been planted.

Thor felt strongly that it would not have been in his best interest to expose Minton—to tell the police that he had seen him shoot and kill the man in the parking lot. *The Lord will take care of that devil,* he said to himself. *My job is to do the Lord's work and keep the Sabbath day holy.*

The door to his shop opened and a tall, skinny man entered. "My boots done?" he asked.

Terry continued to hold his injured finger against his lips. He murmured, "They are…."

He reached up to a shelf and took down two items. He carried them over to the counter and set them down.

The man picked one of them up and examined the seam. "Looks good, Mr. Pendleton. How much do I owe ya?"

"Twelve-fifty."

The man slipped a hand into an inside jacket pocket and brought out his billfold. Terry took the twenty-dollar bill and opened his cash register. He picked out a five, three ones and two quarters. He handed the changed to the customer.

"Thanks."

Terry nodded. He followed the man to the door and then closed it. Then he flicked the deadbolt switch and listened to the bolt plunge into the door frame. "Time to go home and pray," he muttered.

He waited for a semi truck to pass before swinging onto U.S. Highway 59, heading south. Terry smiled passing by a golf course, the fairways and greens covered with snow. The golfers have all stayed home today, he thought.

His mind drifted to his nemesis Minton as he turned onto the country highway leading into New Dresden. I should write an anonymous note to the sheriff's department explaining what I saw in Spanky's parking lot the night Garcia got shot. But then, Minton knows what I have done to the devil's agents who dare to break the Lord's rules by fishing on Sunday.

Terry slowed his vehicle to 30 before passing by the New Dresden sign. He was aware that county deputies aggressively patrolled the highways leading into town. He came to a full stop at the main intersection. Then he turned right toward his home.

He entered his house and immediately headed for his holy room. Thor lit the candles and knelt in front of the altar. "Lord, help me dispose of Minton. He represents the devil and must be removed from the earth that you created."

Thor closed his eyes. He visualized the new bike trail that ran from the railroad tracks to the park on Loon Lake. The last time that he had driven by that area, plows had cleared the trail. I could park my vehicle uptown and walk the trail, going by Minton's house plus his fishing house, he said to himself.

TOM HASTINGS HUNG UP THE PHONE. Those deputies are never going to leave me alone, he thought. He checked his watch. Julie was expected to arrive in an hour. They had planned on going cross-country skiing. Oh well, what the heck, if the deputies are here at the same time, no big deal.

He sat down on the love seat and closed his eyes. He saw Jolene, down on her knees in a church, her hands clasped together. I wish that woman well, he said to himself. She's a very good person and deserves to be happy and at peace.

Tom bunched three pillows up on one end. He stretched out on the two-seat couch, his legs stretching out over the other armrest. In minutes, he fell asleep. He dreamed that he was a small boy and he walked up a series of wooden steps that led to the front door of his church. The bell in the tower clanged loudly. Suddenly he woke, startled. The doorbell dinged. Tom jumped up off the love seat. He saw a police car through the window.

He opened the door. Two deputies and Julie stood on the small porch, all smiling. "Sorry to bother you, Mr. Hastings, but we have some questions for you," the woman deputy said. "You remember us, don't you?"

"Sure, Martin and Izzy. How could I forget? Hi, Julie. Hey come on in, it's cold outside."

Julie removed her boots. The two deputies stomped on the entry carpet. Izzy looked across the room at Tom and smiled. He gestured for them to sit at the dining-room table. He and Julie sat down on the love seat.

Izzy opened her notepad and laid it on the table. "Tom, I want you to think hard and give us any names of any people who have acted vigorously or strangely toward you…whatever…over the past couple of months."

Tom raised his hand up partially. "That's easy. There's this guy by the name of Minton. He's been in my face over at Spanky's. Heck, Julie here can remember. Right?"

Julie nodded.

"Go on, Tom," Izzy said.

Deputy Martin leaned forward, his eyes narrowing.

"This guy…he's been after me…well, not exactly me…more after my date."

Julie lifted her chin, looking troubled.

Tom looked into her eyes. "Look, Julie, you know that I dated this other girl before you came around."

Julie forced a smile and nodded.

"Minton! He'd come over to my booth and deliberately hustled my date. He did it more than once. Why…why?"

"Why what, Tom?" Izzy asked.

Tom cleared his throat. "We came to blows. I knocked the bastard down. He piled into a bunch of chairs."

"Yeah, we talked about that earlier, remember? Anyone else?" Deputy Martin asked.

"No, that's about it. What's unusual is that as soon as I brought a date into Spanky's, most always he would come over and give me a bad time. He did it so many times." Tom grimaced. "I…."

"Tom," Izzy said. "Did you see Minton the night that Garcia got shot in the parking lot? You told us earlier that you did see Terry Pendleton leave shortly after Garcia did."

Tom shook his head slowly from side to side. "No I didn't… hmmm, amazing that he wasn't at Spanky's that night."

A few minutes later, Izzy snapped her notebook shut. She stood. "We appreciate this, Tom…you, too, Julie."

Deputy Martin stood. They left the house. Tom watched the sheriff's car turn northward and disappear against a bank of trees.

Tom led the way on his skis, gliding up a trail toward the northern part of his property. Julie followed. She wore light-blue ski clothes and a pink scarf neatly wrapped around her neck. A large, white bun, the size of a baseball, perched atop her knitted, bluish stocking cap. He reached the top of a hill and looked back. The warm smile on her face melted his heart.

They reached the northernmost trail in fifteen minutes. Tom decided to try a steep hill that tested his skills. He went down the southern slope first. His skis came to a stop and he looked back. Down she came, her body leaning forward. He quickly slid off the trail to prevent her from crashing into him. She turned and smiled widely. Tom looked back, pointed and said, "I'm going to call that *Julie's Hill.*"

They returned and placed the skis in his garage an hour later. Tom kept his arm around her shoulder as they walked toward his house. After they entered, he said, "Let's change. I'll make us a couple of hot brandies."

Julie smiled and pulled off her scarf.

51

TERRY PENDLETON WAITED UNTIL 11:00 P.M. He got up off his knees and stood for a moment with his head down. Then he walked to the altar and blew out the candles. Thor dressed in a black snowmobile suit, the sides of his pants lined with a narrow white stripe. He turned the knob on his front door and pushed the door open slightly.

Thor inhaled the cold air and took several deep breaths. He stood on the threshold for a time before locking the door behind him. He searched the surroundings for suspicious-looking vehicles. He closed his eyes and imagined a sheriff's car in his driveway. Both eyes snapped open. The frightening scene of a car topped with the bar of lights had disappeared. He could hear his own breathing and watched for movement. He saw no one and closed the door behind him.

The door in his garage rumbled upward. Thor drove up Main Street slowly, pulling up into an empty spot in front of the hardware store. He turned off the ignition. Thor sat and watched the traffic for a few minutes. Two people came out of William's Pub. He opened the driver's side window and listened to loud laughter and yelling. One of them, a woman, got in the passenger side of a pickup. The man staggered as he grasped the door handle. The motor roared. The pickup made a U-turn in the middle of the street and headed north toward the tracks. Downtown New Dresden became quiet.

Thor opened the door and stepped out. He slung the strap of a carrying bag over his left shoulder. Thor quickly got onto the sidewalk and walked toward the trail that began just past the tracks. He picked up the speed of his walk, going by a storage building and a food service station. The apartment complex had several lighted windows but no one was moving about the parking lot. He passed by the old tennis courts and an older house.

The house lights he could see in the distance belonged to Paul Minton. Thor passed by the assisted living center and crossed the Park View Road approach. His steps shortened as the trail sloped downward. He slowed even more approaching the lot where the Minton house stood, short of a cluster of trees that speckled the south shore of Loon Lake.

Thor walked the section of the trail that hugged the side of the county highway. He followed it all the way to the city park where a huge loon statue stood alone in the dark. Thor trudged along a snowmobile trail that led him to Minton's fishing house. Thor stared at the door, studying a modern conventional lock. On the outside of the back wall it had a 100-pound LP gas tank. Likely it has a modern gas heater inside, he thought.

The Lord isn't going to let me sacrifice Minton here…not in this house, he said to himself. Thor lightly thumped a gloved fist on an outside wall of the fishing house. He looked at the lights surrounding Minton's regular home on the far shore. "I have to dispose of him in his lair," he muttered, and walked back toward the trail.

Thor trudged onward, coming abreast of Minton's home at Purgatory Curve. Two vehicles passed by him, heading towards town. Thor walked southward toward the taillights. Suddenly he stopped. The two vehicles had both made a left turn off the county highway and headed toward Minton's place. They stopped in front of the storage shed. Then the vehicles disappeared.

They must have driven inside, Thor said to himself, his curiosity growing by the moment. The snow between the trail and the house appeared crusty and deep. He made three steps in and backed off. Each moment that he stood increased his desire to find out what was going on at Minton's place.

He walked rapidly toward town and his vehicle, his heart racing with excitement. Thor arrived at the railroad tracks and saw a vehicle parked next to William's Pub. He stood and waited a bit, then dashed to his van, getting in quickly. He shivered after taking his glove off and reaching into his coat pocket for the keys. Then he started the motor and allowed the vehicle to warm for a few minutes.

He drove across the tracks and took a right onto Park View Road, which led to Minton's house. Thor continued on the road, learning that it looped back to its origin. He drove around the loop three times before stopping a short distance away from Minton's driveway. There wasn't any sign of the vehicles that he had seen earlier.

His eyes scanned the surroundings and he decided to drive into the parking lot of the assisted living complex. He selected a spot off to the side, in front of a gondola and next to a high snow bank. No one can see my vehicle from the road, he thought. Thor shut off the engine and waited. He felt an urging within—got out and stood next to his vehicle for a short time watching for local traffic. His legs almost buckled when he made the first step toward the Minton place. Minutes later he walked up the edge of the driveway of the storage building, remaining in the shadows as much as he could. Then the *Ice Lord* walked on the dark side of the storage shed, quietly as possible. By standing on his tiptoes, he could see through one of the two windows.

Thor saw four people moving about. They appeared to be packing things into boxes and loading them into an enclosed truck box. None of them was Minton. Then a new figure appeared. "That's Minton," he muttered. His insides boiled as he watched the devil stacking boxes on a two-wheel dolly. Quickly, Thor moved around the back side of the storage shed and trudged through snow towards a door in the back of the garage attached to the house.

He didn't hesitate and entered, walking quickly across the concrete floor, pausing next to a gray metal door. The *Ice Lord* entered the house. A light coming from the kitchen exposed furniture that only the rich would own. That fancy lamp on the mahogany table is probably worth more than everything in my house, he thought. The *Ice Lord's* eyes darted around the room. The walls were painted white and dotted with framed art pieces.

The Lord has brought me here safely. He has bestowed on me the courage to destroy the devil. I cannot fail him. He saw several corrugated boxes on the kitchen table. He grabbed one and walked toward a stairwell. Then he went down the steps. When he reached the bottom, he set the box on the floor. Thor waited until his eyes adjusted to the darkness. At the base of the stairs, Thor opened a brown six panel door that exposed a large closet. He walked back and picked up the box he had brought down. Thor placed it in a dark corner, readjusting the coats that hung overhead. Then he checked out the third door, also brown. It opened into the furnace room. He put the light on and studied the layout—two-inch PVC pipes that ran from the furnace to an exterior wall.

Within moments he concluded which pipe removed the exhaust from the furnace. Then he held up a hand and touched the metal enclosure that began the ductwork to supply warm air to all the rooms in the house.

Satisfied, he returned to the sitting room, carefully adjusting the lock that controlled the rear door. He exited and made his way back around the storage shed and onto the roadway. In minutes, he was in his vehicle driving back to his home. He thought about his portable drill and other tools. They will work, but I need a flexible exhaust pipe.

PAUL MINTON'S WORKERS PLODDED between the storage shed, loading the last of the boxes they got from his kitchen table. He had recently hired two men who successfully robbed food service stations in Hawley and Lake Park, Minnesota. I need this shipment as a temporary fix. I can't believe the bills I got from Chicago yesterday. There must be about ten thou worth of cigarettes in those places, he said to himself.

He stood next to the big open door and saw a glimpse of a lone figure striding the curve in the roadway that connected with the county highway. That's unusual for someone to be walking on that roadway at this time of day, he said to himself—probably a hiker.

Paul watched the truck back out of the shed and turn around. Its engine roared as it turned onto the county highway and headed toward Chilton Mills. He pressed the button and the overhead door rumbled downward. He headed for the door that led into his house.

Paul locked the door behind him and walked into his kitchen. He froze. Something didn't feel just right. He inhaled. The room smells different, he thought. Hmmm. Oh, what the heck. He walked into his den and brought out a bottle of Scotch from the upper cabinet. Paul poured some into his glass. He added a touch of water from the faucet. He took a deep gulp and felt the pleasure as it slipped down his throat.

Paul felt good because he had another truckload of cigarettes to deliver to Minneapolis. Because Tyke and Hub got caught, he felt that he needed to temporarily delay any further robberies, even though it meant loss of income. He took another sip of Scotch and smiled. With Garcia gone, there's no way anyone can trace the robberies to me, he said to himself.

Paul's smile turned into a frown. He sniffed the air. What the heck is that smell? Could someone have gotten into my house when I was out in the garage? Paul set the glass down and walked into his bedroom. He came out with a Glock automatic pistol. He used the barrel of the gun to push in the doorways leading to the other two bedrooms. Then he opened the door to the lower level. He snapped on the light and eased his way down the steps, the gun grasped tightly in his right hand. Again he sniffed. Worse down here, he thought. He kicked open the door to the furnace room—empty. Then he opened the door to a storage room. Same result.

He tightened his lips together and shook his head. Could that pale-faced weasel have snuck in? Suddenly, he thought of the lonely figure that he had seen on the roadway while the storage shed door was closing. Paul walked to the rear lakeside door, the one that opened to the patio. He snapped on the light and opened the door. How come this door isn't locked? Paul stood there, breathing in short gasps. The snow outside the door had been ruffled as if someone had attempted to cover up tracks.

He's been here! The weasel is plotting against me! This should be easy, he thought. He plans on coming in through this door. It'll happen late at night when I'll be home. His thoughts raced from one idea to another in deciding what type of trap he should set. Should I call the cops? No way is the weasel coming back tonight. I can sleep.

Paul lifted his fourth glass of Scotch to his lips and drained it into his mouth. He swallowed and set it down. He placed his gun on his night table and locked his bedroom door. "Let the weasel try anything tonight and I'll blow his head off," he said.

TOM HASTINGS PARKED IN THE SIDESTREET LOT of the hardware store. He entered and filled a Styrofoam cup with coffee, thinking about the great time he had with Julie the day before. She had left mid-morning. He cracked open a few peanuts, munched them down, and headed for the aisle that was packed with electrical supplies. He picked up an outlet adapter and strode up the middle aisle. He froze in his tracks. Paul Minton stood at the counter where he had left his coffee cup. Tom stared at the rope and other supplies that lay before Minton on the counter.

Tom quickly stepped into a side aisle. He took a deep breath, sneaking a look around the corner of a display. He felt his face redden watching Minton reach out and grasp the top of the shoulder of one of the woman employees. Tom held his breath watching the long fingers work back and forth. You better watch your step, you misfit, Tom said to himself. The cops are going to come calling. Sooner or later, they're gonna click the cuffs on you, you table-hopper.

He waited until Minton left the store before returning to the counter. "All done, Tom?" the long-haired clerk asked.

"Yup, that's it."

"Need a bag?"

"Nope." Tom placed the adapter in his pocket. He walked over to the peanut barrel and picked up another peanut. He shelled it and dropped the shell into the wastebasket. Then he saw him. The pale-faced man had entered the store and briskly walked past the opposite counter. He made a turn and disappeared into an aisle. Tom remained at the peanut barrel. A short time later, the man returned with a box and some smaller items. One side of the box had a picture of a saber saw.

Tom watched the man check out. The clerk scanned the box and then the smaller item—a package of blades. The entire purchase was dropped into a large plastic bag. The pale-faced man quickly walked out of the store.

Tom ate two more peanuts and refilled his cup. He said, "See you later," and walked out the door, holding the cup.

As he rounded Purgatory Curve on his way home, Tom stared out the window—a police car was parked in Minton's driveway. He felt elated. The pest is finally getting some pressure, Tom thought. Just maybe he's the fishing house killer. I wouldn't be a bit surprised. Between him and the pale-faced guy, they are the oddest characters I've ever seen around here.

52

PAUL MINTON CAME UP THE STAIRWAY from his lower level. He took a last look at the door that led to the patio. "Just you dare and try get in here, you weasel. You'll never be the same."

I won't be calling the cops, he said to himself. Instead, I'll call the local fire guys. They'll take him away in a basket. Minton laughed out loud. Wonder when he's going to make his move. Soon I hope. He heard the doorbell ring. Quickly, he moved to the bedroom and grabbed his gun. Then he walked to the front window and looked outside. "Ugh! The cops!"

Paul slipped the Glock into a cabinet drawer. He took a deep breath and opened the door.

"Good morning. Are you Paul Minton?"

"That I am. What brings the law to my house?"

"I'm Deputy Investigator Martin. This is Izzy Felton, also a deputy investigator. We need to ask you a few questions."

"Ah, come on in. I guess I'll have to ask you some questions first before I can agree."

Kelly Martin nodded and motioned for Izzy to enter the house ahead of him.

"Have a seat," Paul said, pointing at a small couch in a crowded room next to the kitchen.

He remained standing and said, "What do the questions pertain to?"

"I'm not sure if you are aware that two people in this area have lost their lives recently. It's our job to interview as many people as possible. Someone in this community is a cold-blooded killer. It's our job to find this person."

Paul nodded and sat down. He lightly threw up his hands and said, "I'll help you all I can."

The deputies and Paul discussed people and places that he had connections with. The name Tom Hastings was brought up along with others such as Terry Pendleton. Paul thought that they intentionally did not ask him as to his whereabouts the nights of the murders because they thought he would clam up and call his attorney.

THOR PARKED THE VEHICLE IN HIS GARAGE. He carried his keys in his right bare hand, snuggling the bag from the hardware store between his left elbow and the side of his body. He set it down on the kitchen table. *I've got what I need to get the job done,* he thought. He visualized Minton in his bed, going to sleep—not having the faintest clue that he would never see another sunrise.

That night before retiring, Thor spent extra time at the altar, praying to the Lord that the devil would be removed from this earth. He lowered his head, clasping his arms. After returning to his bedroom and shutting off the light, he gently pulled the edge of the covers to the brim of his nose.

Before going to sleep, he mentally reviewed his plan. The door would be unlocked. He would use his new flashlight to make his way to the furnace room without stumbling. The new bits that he bought should drill through the sheet metal easily. Lord, what if Minton hears the drill, he asked himself, his head lifting off the pillow. Ah-ha. I'll wrap a cloth around the motor...should cut the sound down enough...new houses like this are insulated well.

His eyes were closed but he saw a series of holes arranged in a circle, at least the size of the flexible drain pipe. The side cutters would slither its way around the circle. Shouldn't take long, he thought—only a minute to cut through the PVC. I'll be long gone before the gas reaches his nostrils.

Tomorrow, he thought. Thor dropped into a deep sleep.

PAUL MINTON FELT A BIT UNEASY in spite of the fact that he had booby-trapped the lower level doors. He lay in bed but his one eye would open occasionally and glance at the small black device he had placed on his bed stand. It had two small lights. One shone green and other red. Any person or object that moved through the door and into the room would break an invisible beam. The object he was looking at would flash and beep. He had tried it earlier with one of his workers and it worked perfectly.

He took another sip of Scotch whiskey from his glass that he had brought up with him. His mind drifted into deep thought, attempting to derive a method of eliminating the pale-faced man. Suddenly, he sat up. I could knock off Hasting by myself and frame the man. He smiled and took another sip. That would be a fantastic accomplishment. The police would have their man. I would have it all.

53

THOR PRESSED THE BUTTON THAT OPENED HIS GARAGE DOOR. The time was close to 2:00 a.m. He covered his face with his glove, protecting it from the brisk air. The door rumbling stopped and it became deathly quiet. Feeling confident, Thor drove through Main Street slowly, noticing only one vehicle parked next to William's Pub. He made the turn onto Park View Road, the roadway that circled the new residences next to Loon Lake. Just as he had done earlier, he parked in the assisted living lot.

Thor grabbed his tool bag and left his vehicle. He briskly walked toward Minton's driveway. Thor used the same path that he had used during his previous visit, staying on the east side of the storage shed until he got into the backyard area. He relaxed seeing no light in the rear of the house.

His heart rate increased as he approached the rear entrance. Stopping in front of it, he stood in silence for a period of time, listening. Hearing nothing, he opened the storm door. Then he tried the knob of the main door. To his satisfaction it turned. Quietly, he pushed on the structure, allowing enough space for his head. His right hand tightly grasped a flashlight.

He splashed the light all around the room, paying special attention to the stairs leading upward. A small cabinet and chair drew his attention. They sat next to the opening of the stairwell across from each other. Thor entered the room and set the tool bag down. He focused the light on the stairwell and walked toward it. Then he saw it. Some type of electronic device had been attached to the wall directly behind each of the two small pieces of furniture. He spotted a tiny green light in each device. I'm just as smart as a squirrel, he thought. Thor smiled thinking about the gray rodents that continually worked their way around his bird feeder obstacles.

The devil doesn't want me up there, he said to himself, shining the light up the stairs. He turned and directed the light toward the furnace room door, noticing an irregularity near the floor. Thor advanced and saw a thin rope stretched across the opening near the bottom, both ends disappearing in a small, black device. He returned to the entry door and picked up his tool box. Then he opened the furnace room door, being careful not to touch the rope. He entered the room and flicked on the light switch after closing the door.

He set his tool bag down and quickly got to work. In minutes he had a series of holes drilled into the sheet metal duct. He smiled. The side cutting tool snipped through the metal tags easily. He pushed the metal flap away and pulled out his saw. Thor wrapped a towel around the motor and sliced through the PVC readily. Finally, he inserted the flexible tubing into the duct and around the PVC exhaust. He hurriedly grabbed the bag and carefully stepped over the rope in the doorway. Then he gently closed the door. In moments he stood out in the cold and headed for his vehicle.

PAUL MINTON AWAKENED. His head throbbed. Throwing the covers off, he sat up in bed. His clock read close to 4:00 a.m. Something smells, he thought. Then he knew what had happened. The weasel had gotten around his barriers. He opened a window in his bedroom and took several deep breaths. Then he dashed down the stairs to the main level and opened several windows. Then he stomped down the stairs to the lower level and opened the outside door. He stuck his head out and took several deep breaths.

As he expected, his furnace exhaust had been tampered with. Paul shut the furnace switch off and jerked the flexible tubing out. He reconnected the PVC pipe and turned the switch back on. His thoughts filled with rage as he went around the inside of his house closing the windows. The weasel isn't going to get away with this.

Paul got his coffee pot going and stood next to a kitchen window staring outside at the roadway. I could call the cops, he said to himself. There's no way I can do that. The less I see of them the better off I am. I'll have to deal with this problem in another way.

He backed his vehicle out of the garage and headed for Main Street. Paul made a full stop at the main intersection and drove on through. He swung his vehicle next to Terry Pendleton's driveway and opened his window. He thought of throwing the flexible tubing out. Instead he changed his mind. I've got to think this through and use the weasel to my advantage.

TOM HASTINGS PLACED HIS SKIS IN THE GARAGE and hurried to his house. He expected Julie within the hour. They had plans for dinner at Spanky's. He thought about Jolene and felt good because he didn't think about her very much any more. The shock of our breakup has almost vanished, he said to himself as he opened the front door and took off his outer clothes. Maybe it was never that strong.

He showered quickly and had just returned downstairs from his bedroom when he heard the front door open. Tom felt ecstatic entering the room where Julie had taken a seat. She stood and they hugged. "You look great this evening, love," Tom said.

"Wow, what's gotten into you?"

"I feel great. For once the local battles do not involve me. Heck, I saw two of the critters at the hardware store earlier. It appeared as if they were both supplying with tools and equipment...perhaps getting ready to do battle."

"Battle?"

"I had a visit from the sheriff's deputies the other day. They had a lead on a man by the name of Terry Pendleton. The evidence apparently showed that he, Pendleton, shot and killed that guy in the parking lot. But...they couldn't make it stick. So the pale-faced guy is back on the street...loose again. Then they questioned me further and I gave them Minton's name. This morning I saw a sheriff's car in the pest's driveway. It broke my heart." Tom forced a laugh.

"Yeah, I bet." Julie laughed with him.

Tom brought out the wine bottle from the refrigerator and walked over to Julie. "Only half a glass please, Tom."

"Okay."

They talked for a few minutes longer. Then Tom walked to the closet and brought out Julie's coat. "Let's get over to the restaurant. I'm hungry."

Tom sat in the passenger seat as Julie turned her car around and headed for the roadway. She pulled into Spanky's parking lot. Tom hastily walked around the car and opened her door. "You look sharp, Julie. Anyone that dresses like you do deserves special treatment."

Julie giggled. They walked to the restaurant hand in hand. Once inside they got seated at a table close to the fireplace. "Gosh, Tom, you're in such a great mood...nice to see. I was wondering if you saw Mr. Minton sitting in a booth down at the other end."

"Yup, I sure did, but you know what? I really don't care. I'm not afraid of him or...get this, anyone else."

Julie shook her head. "He could be dangerous, Tom."

"Big deal. He's had his chance. I let him know where he stands."

By the time they finished dinner, Paul Minton had left. As Tom opened the door for Julie out in the parking lot, he said, "See I told you, Julie. He's not going to mess with me anymore."

54

PAUL MINTON SAT ON A STOOL AT SPANKY'S BAR ON FRIDAY EVENING. He stole an occasional glance at his adversary and his date, Julie. They sat in a booth by the wall of windows. He fought against a growing impulse to go over and pay his respects. His other adversary, Terry Pendleton, played on his mind more than did Hastings. He lifted his glass and took a long draw, feeling the whiskey as it slid down his throat into his stomach.

I cannot go on much longer letting Pendleton harass me, Paul thought. I have to make my move soon—get rid of him and Hastings at the same time. Exactly how do I do it? Paul thought about his recent invasion of Pendleton's home and planting the murder weapon. That didn't work at all...but it did alert the cops. I need something more effective.

He glanced again at Hastings who appeared to be totally relaxed, talking and laughing. His date appeared even happier. Damn it, those two are having a good time, he thought. The old man is always one step ahead of me. He split off from his other broad, but she won't even talk to me.

His thoughts drifted to the recent robberies his new people had pulled off in the three small towns west of here. Then it came to him: One of his two robbers was a lock expert. Bernie could help him.

Paul downed two more whiskeys and waited patiently until he saw Hastings and his date leave. He paid his bill and drove straight to his home. He got himself comfortable on the couch and punched in some numbers on the phone. "Bernie, I need a special favor from you. You will be paid well."

Paul listened and nodded. "Okay, I'll find out tonight and call you in the morning."

He hung up.

Paul put his coat back on and backed his vehicle out of the garage. He drove to uptown New Dresden, making a full stop at the main intersection. He continued on and stopped across the street from Pendleton's house. He made sure no one was around and no active vehicle in sight. Quickly, he dashed across the street and headed for Pendleton's front door. He used the small beam of a flashlight to spotlight the two door locks on the front door.

In ten minutes he arrived back in his garage. Paul entered his house and jotted down one word on a notepad. He went to bed and fell asleep instantly.

SHERIFF JOHNSON SAT BEHIND HIS DESK. The two state police officers, Ben Perkins and Perry Leyton, had returned to the Cities with the understanding they would come back on special request. Dave Johnson ran his fingers through his hair. "Okay, what's the latest, guys?"

Izzy looked at her partner, Kelly Martin. He motioned with his hand. "Dave, I see two different crime perpetrators here. The fishing house killings on one hand and the shooting of Garcia and the tobacco robberies on the other," she said.

Dave nodded. "Go on."

"I think Paul Minton planted the gun in Pendleton's closet. If that's the case, Minton killed Garcia. But, we can't prove it at this moment. Also, we can't tie Minton to any of the robberies. Personally, I think that he's behind the whole thing. He shot Garcia to protect himself from us. The big problem: How can we prove it? The gun is untraceable. We have no witnesses."

Kelly interrupted. "Don't forget that people saw Pendleton leave the restaurant shortly before Garcia got shot."

The sheriff said softly, "Even though he doesn't admit it, I bet Pendleton saw the shooting."

Izzy raised a hand. “Pendleton. Minton. They’ve got something going that we don’t know about and....”

“And what?” Kelly said.

“They don’t want us to know about it...suggesting that they are covering each other’s tracks.”

Kelly sighed. “Maybe we’ll get lucky and they’ll bump each other off.”

“I wish it was that simple,” the sheriff said. “We just have to stay close and keep on top of things until we get the big break.

“Meanwhile, here’s the scoop on the recent tobacco robberies in Clay County. One in Lake Park, two in Hawley and one in Audubon. All done in one night. Looks like the same MO as our other robberies except for one thing.”

“What’s that?” Izzy asked.

“There was no break-in. The bandits appear to have used a key to get in the rear door.”

“So have we checked out the local smiths?” Izzy said.

“Yes, we have. I had Bruns check them all out. Seven of them within a hundred miles. None of them reported anything stolen or anything unusual,” the sheriff said. “Guess that’s it for now, guys. Like I said earlier, we need a break.”

PAUL MINTON DOWNED HIS FIFTH CUP OF COFFEE. Saturday morning had arrived and the plan he had developed the night before was only minutes away from execution.

He got into his vehicle and drove onto the county highway, heading for Chilton Mills. Paul took a left turn on County 29 and crossed U.S. Highway 10. He continued on, passing by a huge statue of a turkey. Hmmm, a town full of loons back there and a bunch of turkeys over here, he thought as he approached the railroad tracks. He took a left on Main Street and, two blocks later, he saw the van across the street. Minton watched for a police car. He didn’t see one and made a U-turn to come up directly behind the white van.

He got out and tried the driver’s door on the van. It wasn’t locked and he saw the key in the ignition. On the floor, in front of the passenger seat, he noticed the ring of keys. My man Bernie has come through, he thought. He pressed a button on his fob and his vehicle gave out a short honk.

Paul sat down in the van and started the engine. He heard the blast of a train's horn and waited for the 100-car freight train to pass. A man and woman crossed the street on foot in front of him. He shielded his face with a hand.

He drove the van across the tracks and headed for the exit that would lead him toward New Dresden. He felt excited thinking about his new plan. The road was clear of snow and he drove at exactly the speed limit. Don't need a deputy to stop me now, he thought. He slowed his van to 40 miles per hour and passed by Spanky's restaurant. He thought about Hastings and his plan to draw him into the plot as the van passed by Rocky Point Road.

Paul chuckled glancing into the rearview mirror. The cap that he was wearing had a red "Z" embossed above the brim. The name of an electric company showed between his shoulders on the back of his coveralls. He stopped at the stop sign and noticed a woman with blonde hair watching him from the window of Stillman's Super Market.

Anxiously, he pulled into Pendleton's driveway. He waited for a minute before getting out of the vehicle. Paul felt 99-percent sure that the owner was at work. He grabbed the ring of keys and stepped out. Quickly he walked to the front door, taking two steps at a time on the stoop. Paul began by trying each key in the ring. He tried a dozen different keys before feeling the lock give as it turned.

He stepped inside and closed the door. Not a sound. He wiped off the bottom of his boots and walked toward the basement door. He found a switch at the top and flicked on the lights. Closing the door, he walked down the steps, holding onto a two by four wooden railing. He reached the bottom and looked around. Paul spotted a door in the far corner. He guessed it led to a small room.

He opened the door and knew immediately that he had found what he was looking for. "Perfect," he whispered. "Just the ticket." The room had a small sink and a toilet. Both of them were vinyl. The light bulb in the ceiling did not come on when he flicked a switch. Don't need it, he thought.

He worked for an hour, using the tools that he had in his bag. The tightening of the large lag screws frustrated him. He used a crescent wrench, and it frequently slipped from his grasp and fell to the concrete floor. He finally finished installing four heavy-duty brackets and threw the wrench down—it clattered as it slid across the floor.

Paul slipped one of the four-foot two by sixes into the top bracket. It works perfectly, he thought. Then he tried the lower one. "Success," he hissed. Inside he found two old blankets parked on a wooden shelf. He spread them out on top of each other on the floor. Paul tried the flushing apparatus on the toilet. It worked. He smiled. Hastings, you're gonna love this room, he said to himself, laughing hoarsely.

55

TOM HASTINGS GLIDED ACROSS THE GREENWAY, the final run, ending a long bout with his skis. He became aware of perspiration under his t-shirt, a sign of a good workout. He slipped past the remains of his woodpile. Two more tractor bucketfuls and my wood supply is history for this season, he thought. Tom put his skis away and walked to his house.

He heard the answering machine beeping after entering the foyer. He took off his ski clothes and shoes before pressing the message button on the phone. Tom couldn't believe his ears. The caller was none other than the table-hopper Paul Minton.

"I would like to apologize for messing with you and your date at the restaurant. It was totally rude of me."

Tom sighed. "Does that mean you won't do it anymore?"

"Absolutely! Just to show you that I mean it, I would like to take you out for lunch at William's Pub tomorrow."

Tom said, "Okay, I'll do it. What time?"

"How about 11:30?"

"See you then, Paul." Tom hung up.

I better call Julie and see what she thinks, he thought. "Julie, you won't believe this but I got a call from Paul Minton. He wants to meet me and make up." Tom laughed. "Make up! That's what I said."

He listened and laughed again. "Sure, come on over soon as you can. The hot tub awaits us."

Tom hung up the phone. Things are really going my way recently, he thought. First, I get back with Julie and then…and then, my local nemesis wants to make peace.

Tom showered, dressed in his swim trunks and opened a fresh bottle of wine. He sat down next to his computers and saw Julie's car pull up. He took a sip from his glass and smiled as Julie made her way down the sidewalk. He got up and opened the door. "Come on in, sweetie. Got the tub ready for us."

They hugged and Tom hung up her coat. She removed her boots. Tom followed her into the kitchen. She moved past and headed for a washroom with a bag in hand. Julie turned and placed a hand on the corner cabinet. Tom smiled and watched her.

Tom lifted the cover off the hot tub and got in. He looked up the bay and saw thin, shimmering drifts of snow lift from the icy surface and skid across, piling up eventually into a larger drift. Tom admired how nature could be so perfect. The drift had a perfect knife-edged top. He turned his head when the house door opened.

"Gotta get in there quick…it's cold out here…freezing."

Julie dropped into the water. Tom smiled and watched her sink in up to her chin. "Feels good, huh?"

"Yeah…real good." Julie sat on a bench and reached for her glass of wine. "So Paul Minton called you. What's on his mind?"

Tom lifted the glass to his lips. "Hmmm, mighty good. He wants to make peace. No more irritating me or you over at Spanky's."

"How do you know he's not up to something?"

"Why? I don't see what he would gain either way. I think he was getting on me because of his ego."

"That could be, but I still wouldn't trust him."

"I plan on meeting him for lunch at William's Pub tomorrow."

"Well, have it your way, but don't ever say that I didn't warn you."

TOM CHECKED THE OUTDOOR TEMPERATURE before walking out to the garage. He thought about Julie's warning about meeting Minton. Ah, what the heck have I got to lose? He made a U-turn in the middle of Main Street and parked in front of the post office. Tom got his mail and headed for the supermarket.

"Hi, Ellie," he said as he grabbed a *Forum* from the rack. "Any robberies around here lately?"

"No, bet you're disappointed, huh?"

Tom laughed and shook his head. "I don't think so."

"Say, Tom, I saw Paul Minton drive by here a couple of times. One time he was driving his own vehicle. The second time he was driving an electrical service van."

Tom stopped his advance toward the door. "What are you suggesting?"

"Nothing. Nothing…just roused my curiosity."

"What do you think of Paul Minton?" Tom asked.

"It's not my place to comment on our customers."

Tom watched her eyes. They narrowed and a row of furrows formed on her forehead. She's tryin' to tell me somethin', he thought. Julie is tryin' the same thing. Soon I'll find out.

Tom dropped off his mail and the newspaper in his vehicle. He checked his watch and walked across the street. He waved at a dark, long-haired woman who carried a Styrofoam cup of coffee from one gift shop to another.

He walked into William's Pub and immediately saw the smiling Paul Minton waving at him. Tom returned the smile and sat down across from Minton. Paul reached out a hand and Tom felt a firm grasp and held on for a moment. He has a firm, friendly grasp, Tom thought.

"What would you like to drink?" Paul asked.

"Ah…MD draft would be fine."

Paul stood and walked to the bar. He returned with two mugs of beer.

Tom said, "Thanks." He raised the beer to his lips and swallowed twice.

"Tom, I'm sorry about our differences over at Spanky's. I apologize." He extended his hand.

Tom accepted it, shaking it a second time, and nodded.

"Life is too short to hold grudges against your neighbors," Paul said.

"I agree," Tom said, smiling.

"Hey, I'd like to show you my shop. How about tomorrow?" Paul said.

"Yeah, I could stop by."

They ate lunch and each had a second beer. Paul insisted on taking care of the entire tab. After shaking hands on the sidewalk, Tom returned to his vehicle and headed for his home.

JULIE NARROWED HER EYES. She shook her head slowly. "I think what's happened between you and Paul Minton is good, but I wouldn't trust that bastard across the street. He gives me the creeps."

"Julie, I've spent a lifetime doing my darnedest to get along with anyone and everyone in the community. This is a chance for me to mend the fence between me and Paul."

"Okay, but you haven't told me all of it, have you?"

Tom inhaled, smiling as he held his breath for a moment. "I can't hide anything, can I? Alright, he invited me to his place to look at his shop. What harm can there be in that?"

Julie frowned. "Why would he invite you to do that…to see his shop?"

"Because he knows that I am interested in woodworking and

such. His eyes lit up yesterday when I told him about my shop."

"Hastings, you're gonna do what you want to no matter what. Let's drop the subject and I'll start dinner."

"Yum, what do you have in mind?"

"I brought along a couple of pork loins. They're out in the car. Do you have some potatoes?"

"Sure do. Hey, I'll open up some wine."

56

TOM LISTENED AFTER PICKING UP THE PHONE. "Sure, I'll stop by after I get the mail."

Paul Minton hung up and hustled into his garage. He backed his vehicle out of the driveway and drove toward the county highway. He took a right and headed for Chilton Mills. He stopped at the main intersection and turned left, his eyes searching for the same van that he had used earlier. There it was…in the same spot.

Then he saw a police car, cruising toward him in the other lane. Instead of doing a U-turn, he circled around the block, pulling in right behind the van. The police car was nowhere in sight. Paul locked his vehicle and got into the van. The keys were in the ignition as he expected. The motor roared into action. He pulled out into the street. Suddenly, large snowflakes began dropping from the low-hanging clouds.

Paul experimented and found the switch that turned on the windshield wipers. He crossed the tracks and headed out of town, losing the markings on the highway. He drove slowly, attentively watching for markings that outlined the road. He met only four vehicles before arriving at Purgatory Curve where he turned onto the roadway leading to his house.

He parked in front of the storage building and exited. Pulling his collar up, he trudged to the side door and entered. Minutes later he had the van parked inside. Paul looked at his watch. Hastings should be in town, right about now, he thought. Paul glanced at the dolly cart that he had recently purchased. A black metal ramp sat on the floor right next to the cart, leaning against a wall.

Paul grabbed a scoop shovel and walked outside. He cleared the snow from the sidewalk between his storage shed and the side door in his house. Paul placed the shovel back into his storage shed and saw a vehicle leave the county highway and turn onto his roadway. Hastings is about to arrive. He watched for a moment and entered his house.

He stopped next to his dining-room table and looked down at two small bottles. He picked them up, looked at the labels. The frown on his face turned into a grin. My buddy in Chicago better know what he's talking about, he said to himself.

TOM PICKED UP HIS MAIL AND STOPPED AT THE SUPERMARKET. "Anything new today?" he asked Ellie.

"Paul Minton was in here this morning."

"Why are you telling me that?"

"Word around town is that you two are becoming the best of buddies."

Tom jerked his head back slightly and frowned. "I wouldn't go as far as to say that. Who passed that on to you?"

"Oh, just some local talk up and down Main Street."

"Okay, if you and the others must know, we have made up. As a matter of fact, I'm stopping at his house on my way home."

"Hi, how are you?" Ellie asked the next person in line.

Tom got into his vehicle and headed out of town. He signaled and took a right at the roadway that served a cluster of new homes along Loon Lake. He drove up Minton's driveway and stopped. A storage door opened and Paul Minton stepped out onto the driveway. "Hi, Tom, come on in."

Tom followed him into the building. He saw a white van parked to his right. Minton led him through a door to his left that opened into a shop. "Here it is. What do you think of it, Tom?"

Tom saw newly constructed benches hugging the lower part of three of the walls. Above them, neat shelves and Peg-Boards with a variety of accessories organized the tools.

"It's a lot neater than mine…that's for sure. Looks like it has all the tools one needs to fix about anything."

The two men spent the next fifteen minutes talking about equipment and tools. Then Paul opened a refrigerator door and brought out a quart of beer. He set two mugs down on a bench and filled them. "Have another one on me," he said.

Tom smiled and accepted the mug that Paul handed him. He took a long drag.

"So, when are you getting married?"

Tom laughed. "Could be tomorrow…but then, it could be never."

Paul placed a fist against his waist and said, "I've been thinking about starting a new business and I would be honored if you would consider helping me with the bookwork. Someone told me you do that type of work."

Tom licked his lips and tilted his chin. "Oh yeah, what type of business are you talking about?"

"Internet marketing. I've got a connection with a firm in Chicago. They are all set to send me the products. I have some people in Chilton Mills who are expert at packing and shipping. It could all be done right here, right in New Dresden."

"Let me think about it. My first feeling is that I would be interested."

"Good. Say, I'm expecting an important call and I appreciate you stopping by."

"No problem," Tom said, and drank the last of his beer.

He shook Paul's hand and walked back to his vehicle.

His thoughts were on Julie as he drove onto the county highway and headed for home. She isn't going to believe this, he thought. He approached the large dairy farm, hitting his brake to slow for a pickup that jumped out onto the road. Geez, that vehicle came out of nowhere. I could've piled right into him. Tom rubbed his fingers across his brow and blinked his eyes.

PAUL MINTON WATCHED HASTINGS DRIVE AWAY. He waited until the vehicle drove onto the county highway. Then he hurried into the house, heading for his bedroom. He changed into a dark jumpsuit and walked to his front closet. He put on a dark cap, also pulling it tight down to his ears. He slipped into his boots and walked out the door.

In a minute he drove the van onto the county highway and headed northward. He followed the same route that Hastings had taken. He almost hit a deer on Hastings's roadway. "Whew, that was close," he muttered.

He drove the van into Tom's driveway, stopping it just past the sidewalk. Paul opened the rear gate, pushing the two doors outward. He slid out the grated ramp and secured it to the back edge of the van floor. Stepping into the van, he carried out a stretcher with wheels. He brought it with him as he made his way down the sidewalk. Paul took a deep breath and opened the door.

His spirits rocketed seeing Hastings lying peacefully on a couch, sound asleep. Paul chuckled. The drug worked like a charm, he thought. Paul carried the stretcher forward and set it down on the floor next to the love seat. He carefully tugged on Hastings's body and laid him down stomach up. He moved quickly, using a quarter-inch vinyl rope to tie Tom's feet together. Then he pulled the wrists around to Hastings's back and tied them together. Paul stood and looked down. You look like an angel, Hastings. He reached into his pocket and brought out a roll of duct tape. He stretched it twice around Tom's mouth and tore it off. Paul used the basic straps to secure Hastings to the stretcher.

Paul squeezed the frame of the stretcher around a firewood storage cabinet near the door. He stepped ahead and pulled the stretcher through the door and onto the deck. Paul pushed the stretcher up the sidewalk. His heart rate increased as he bent and pushed Hastings into the van. He returned the ramp and closed the rear doors. Paul returned to the house and closed the door. He looked at his watch. I've still got another hour or so, he thought. Then he heard a vehicle approaching.

Paul quickly stepped inside and waited. A FedEx truck pulled into the driveway. He quickly removed his coveralls and waited. The doorbell rang. He counted to three and opened the door. "Sign here, please," the woman said. Paul scribbled Hastings's name. "Thank you." Paul waited until the truck left. Then he stepped outside and hurried to his van. Blisters, that was dumb of me to sign that paper, he thought. Ah what the hell, no cops are ever going to ever see that paper.

Paul felt relieved passing the beginning of Hastings's roadway and getting on the township road. Then he saw a vehicle come over the hill ahead. He saw blue. He caught a glimpse of blonde hair as they met and passed. It's her, he thought. I got out of the house just in time. Whew, that was close.

He pulled his cap brim down low as he entered Main Street in New Dresden. His heart stopped. A sheriff's car arrived at the intersection just before he did. It turned toward him. Paul didn't look at the driver. He cruised across the intersection and stopped on Main Street just past Pendleton's house. He backed the van into the driveway and angled it toward the house door.

Paul looked through the windows in all directions and made sure he saw nobody about. Paul smiled after connecting the ramp successfully from the rear of the van to the floor at the doorway. He pushed the stretcher quickly into the house. In a minute, he closed the front door and placed the ramp back into the van.

Everybody around here minds their own business, he thought as he glanced around before reentering the house—not the typical small town. His measurement of the width of the door turned out accurate. He had two inches to spare as he lined up the stretcher with the stairwell. Paul braced himself on the steps and began lowering Hastings down the steps. The wheels bumped and clunked as he eased the stretcher down.

Paul placed his hand on his heart after getting to the bottom.

He waited for some time to catch his breath. The stretcher easily rolled into the corner room. Paul rolled Hastings off the stretcher and wheeled it out the door. He dashed up the steps with one thought in mind—a Bible. He found them stacked in a cabinet in the church-like room. Quickly, he carried one down the stairs. Hastings slept like a baby. Paul set the Bible down on the floor next to his victim.

Paul sneered, looking at Hastings for the last time. Then he closed the door of the windowless room and placed both the top bar and lower bar into slots. "Tom would be proud of my creations," he muttered and picked up the stretcher. Whoops, almost forgot, he thought. He used a sealant dispenser to fill in the spaces all around the door. "No more oxygen for you, buddy," he muttered.

Ah, what the heck, he thought, and placed the stretcher on the floor under the stairway. I won't need that any more. He made his way up the stairs, using a rag to carefully wipe any tracks off the floor leading to the front door. I'm a genius, he thought as he backed the van out of the driveway and headed back up Main Street.

57

JULIE SWUNG HER CAR SLIGHTLY TO THE RIGHT to allow space for a vehicle that she approached on the township road. In her rearview mirror, she saw the van disappear over a hill. Julie watched for deer as she drove down Tom's roadway. She pulled into his driveway, parking her car in front of the garage door.

She got out and looked around. The popcorn-shaped clouds in the sky moved slowly, coming from the northwest. The blue spaces in between appeared brighter than usual. Spring is on its way, she thought, and walked toward the house.

She knocked twice and entered. Sure seems quiet, she thought as she took off her coat and boots. She walked into the kitchen wondering what Tom was doing. He usually met her at the door. She walked into the den. His laptop was in its usual place, the screen dark in its sleep phase.

"Tom," she said loudly.

She walked up into the great room, hearing nothing. Julie peeked into his bedroom. The bed was made but no Tom. Julie opened the door to the lower level and saw that the area was dark. She walked back into the kitchen area and peeked into his bathroom. Holy smokes, he's nowhere around. Julie put her jacket on and walked to the garage. She stopped in her tracks seeing Tom's skis in the usual spot, lying on the top of the golf cart.

Julie walked up the trail toward the snow-covered tennis court. Where the devil is the guy? she asked herself. Maybe he went for a walk…but if he does that, he usually walks to the township road and around the Rocky Point loop.

She reentered the house and sat down in front of his computer. She got online and checked her e-mail. Julie kept glancing out the window as she used the keyboard. The gauge next to the window read 21 degrees above zero—the outdoor temperature. Her watch showed 1:30. Julie felt a stab of fear as she walked back into Tom's den.

She stared at the phone sitting on the small table by the sectional. Julie reached down and picked it up. She looked out the window overlooking the bay. Six fishing houses dotted the snowy landscape. One of them had a snowmobile parked next to it. She set the phone back into its cradle. Moving quickly, she passed through the kitchen and the dining-room table, stopping in front of the computers next to the front door.

Julie saw Tom's gray SUV sitting peacefully in its place in the garage. Something is wrong, she thought, dreadfully wrong. She grabbed the phone next to the computer and punched 911.

She explained her problem to the female dispatcher at the sheriff's office. Her face turned dark after listening to the response. "But something is really wrong here."

She listened.

"Look, would you ring Deputy Izzy Felton?"

She waited.

Julie cleared her throat. "Deputy Felton, Tom Hastings is missing. His car is here. He was supposed to be home when I got here. He's not out on the trails. He's not out for a walk."

Julie listened. "Okay, I'll stay right here until you arrive. Hopefully, in the meantime he will show up." She set the phone down and wrung her hands together.

TOM HASTINGS'S BRAIN BEGAN TO AWAKEN IN SPURTS. Lousy dream, he thought. Then he attempted to jerk his hand around. Then he knew. This was no dream. My hands are tied behind my back. He jiggled his feet. They're together, too. Tom projected his tongue between his lips. He felt a fuzzy barrier. Where the hell am I? he said to himself.

He saw a bare wall. Swinging his neck over a little, he saw a toilet and a small sink. Rolling over he saw two more walls and a door. A small light came from something plugged into an outlet near the toilet. He stared at it for a time. Then he rolled and contorted his body to set his butt on the toilet. His head began to clear…the headache totally gone.

At least a toilet, he said to himself. That's about it…about it. Who? How? Then he thought of Minton. I drank a beer at his place. Then I went home and fell asleep on the couch….I remember nothing else…what happened?

He crawled toward the door, turned his body around, and gave it a push with his legs, gasping from the pain that he felt in his hips. Whew, I'm in tough shape, he said to himself, licking his lips. He lay still for a short time and then crawled back toward the toilet. What's this, he thought, one of his hands scraping an object. It's a book. He grasped it and made his way toward the small light.

It's a Bible! Geez, I'm positive that it's Minton who got me here…but he's not the Bible eccentric. I don't get it. His brain cleared more as sat and thought. He scanned the room, estimating it to be eight by eight feet. No windows, a wooden ceiling…probably tongue and groove pine, he thought. As his eyes began to focus more, he decided the ceiling and walls were surfaced with the same material. He studied two long wooden shelves on one of the walls. They were held up with four metal angular braces.

Tom crawled around the room, searching the dark corners and shadowed areas for any type of tool to work with. He found nothing. Then he thought of an intern with U.S. Senator McDougal. Tom couldn't remember his name, but he, too, was imprisoned in a room with a toilet. If I remember right, the guy lifted off the tank cover and cut his bindings with something sharp inside.

He stood and grasped the edge of the toilet tank with his fingers. Dang, it's plastic, he thought. It lifted off and dropped to the floor. Tom reached into the cold water with his still-bound hands. He probed in the wetness and did find two moving parts that had relatively sharp edges.

Tom pulled out his hands to rest. He felt his heart thumping against his chest. I've got to settle down, he thought. There's always a solution....He closed his eyes. I have to think my way out of this.

IZZY SHIFTED UNEASILY IN THE PASSENGER SEAT. Kelly was behind the wheel and they had just turned off of Highway 10 toward New Dresden. "You know what, Kelly? I think this case is coming to a head. Someone is pulling off a desperate move. They'll make a mistake...leave behind some clues."

"Well, depends if Hastings drove off with someone and will probably be back home by the time we get to his house."

"Possible, but...."

"But what?"

"But, unlikely. He is a creature of habit. If he did that, he would have left a message for his woman...plus his vehicle is in the garage."

"Julie Huffman, you mean?"

"Yes, Julie Huffman."

Izzy turned her head slightly and read the sign next to the road:

Spanky's Stonehearth. Open Wednesday through Sunday.

She watched the road ahead anxiously as they approached the Hastings roadway. Martin drove the sheriff's vehicle faster than usual, causing it to heave three or four times. She opened her door immediately when the car came to a stop in Tom's driveway. Kelly followed her down the sidewalk to the front door.

Julie Huffman stood in the doorway, anxiety radiating from her face. Izzy held out her hand.

"Come on in," Julie said, her voice harsh, and cleared her throat.

The three of them sat at chairs next to the dining-room table as Julie told her story.

"We'll have a look around, if that's okay with you," Izzy said.

"Yes, of course. Look all you want."

Izzy stood next to the love seat for a few moments. "That's been used recently. Look how the pillows are."

Kelly nodded.

The two officers looked around for ten minutes. Julie sat on the corner computer chair. "Did you find anything?"

Izzy shook her head. "Look, Julie. We want you to stay right here. We're going into town and pay Mr. Paul Minton a visit. I have your number and will call if anything happens."

Julie nodded, tears streaming down her cheek.

Izzy walked over to her and hugged her around the shoulders. "We'll do everything we can do to bring Tom home safely."

Deputy Kelly Martin turned off the county highway onto the Park View Road in New Dresden. He pulled up in Paul Minton's driveway.

Paul invited the two deputies into his house. "Would you mind if we have a look around?" Kelly said.

"Not at all. Help yourself."

Izzy remained with Minton as Paul quickly strolled around the main floor, eventually taking the stairs down to the lower level. She remained standing looking out the window. "Mr. Minton, have you seen Tom Hastings lately? You do know him, don't you?"

"Yeah, sure do. Let's see, when did I see him last? Oh yeah, we had lunch at William's Pub…couple of days ago."

"Do you consider him a friend?" the deputy asked.

"Yup, sure do."

"Did Hastings seem normal to you? What I mean is, did he seem troubled in any way?"

"No, he appeared to be his normal self."

Izzy nodded. She turned when the lower-level door opened and Kelly reappeared.

"Thanks, Mr. Minton," Kelly said. "Can we have a look at the building next door?"

"Sure, but it's sort of a mess."

Paul led the two deputies through the side door and they wandered around as Paul waited by the door. Kelly returned. "My shop is behind that door." Paul pointed.

Kelly opened it and peeked in. "Okay, Mr. Minton. Thanks a lot for the cooperation. We'll stay in touch. If you hear from Hastings, give us a ring." He handed him a card.

Kelly stared at Izzy as she approached. "Seen enough, Izz?"

She nodded. "I'm ready. Let's go."

"Thanks, Mr. Minton. Your assistance is appreciated," Kelly said.

JULIE PACED AROUND TOM'S HOUSE. She continually looked for a clue as to where he could have gone. She walked out onto the deck. The hot tub heater and fan caused the water to gurgle underneath the top. I could sure use some of that later today, she thought. Do I dare go into it alone? She slowly shook her head and reentered the house. She checked her e-mail and stared out the window at the garage. Her car and Tom's sat outside in the cold.

Her chin lifted sharply. Suddenly, she remembered meeting a large white van on the township road. Why the heck didn't I tell that to the cops, she thought? I'm losing it. Her mind flooded with anxiety. I've got to do something.

She put on her coat and boots and headed outside. She backed her car out of the driveway and sped up the roadway, her vehicle bouncing so much, her head touched the roof. In minutes she entered the New Dresden city limits. She saw the sheriff's car parked in a driveway near the road. I wonder if that's where Minton lives, she thought.

She continued into town and parked across the street from Stillman's Super Market. Julie strode quickly across the street and entered. She waited until Ellie finished with a customer. "Hi, Ellie. How are you today?"

"Just fine."

"Could I ask you a couple of questions?"

"Sure."

"Did Tom Hastings come in today?"

"Yeah, about his usual time, between 10 and 11."

"You see out that window pretty good, don't you?" Julie pointed.

"Did you be any chance see a large white van go by?"

Ellie nodded. "Yeah, same one as the other day."

"The other day?"

"Yes, it was either yesterday or the day before. I haven't seen it around before…has some different logo on the door. No one around here."

"What kind of logo?"

"Some electric company."

"Ellie!"

The clerk's expression froze.

"Ellie, did you recognize the driver? In either case?"

"Not positive, but it looked like Paul Minton."

Julie gasped. She grabbed Ellie's hands. "Thanks, Ellie. Thank you so much!"

She rushed out the door and got into her car. She sped across the tracks, hoping the sheriff's car would still be at Minton's place. Julie turned onto Park View Road. "The sheriff's car is gone," she muttered.

58

TOM HAD ADJUSTED TO THE AGGRAVATING DISCOMFORT IN his wrists. They throbbed and ached, but at times he forgot about it. He had examined the underside edges of the toilet tank cover. They were rounded and would serve no purpose.

The toilet paper dispenser was made of plastic, so was the sink. He didn't feel any sharpness when he ran his fingers over the faucet and the two valves. Tom thought about smashing the dispenser and hopefully producing a sharp edge. He used a wall to lean against and finally got up on his feet. Tom hopped over to the shelves. Both of them were empty. Tom stared at two screw heads that fastened the frame to the wood. It's a Phillips, he said to himself. He pressed his forehead against the lower edge of the shelf. Dipping down, he worked his way underneath. Pushing his head upward, he felt the shelf give.

Tom hopped to his makeshift bed and doubled up a blanket over his head. He went back to the shelf and got his head underneath again, this time with some padding. He pushed hard as he dared, lunging intermittently. Suddenly the wood broke away from the frame. Tom set himself underneath the frame on the other side. In minutes, his head thrusts broke the wood away on that one, too.

Using his head he nudged one of the wood shelves until it clattered to the floor. Feeling with his fingers, he found one of the screws. He searched for the other one and found it, too. Moving on his knees he successfully laid the board down on the floor and with his fingers worked a screw in one of the holes, screwing it as tight as he could.

He sat on the board, scuttling his way backward until he felt the screw head with his fingers. Tom experimented and positioned himself so he could pull the rope back and forth across the screw. He moved into endless positions trying to get as much force on the screw as possible.

Back and forth. Back and forth. Minutes later, his back begin to ache. He rested for a bit and just as he adjusted to his aching wrists, he adjusted to the hurting back. Suddenly he heard a noise. He stopped. Tom heard the rumble of a garage door. Then he heard it again. He heard a door open and shut, and footsteps across the floor above. Tom sat quietly, not knowing what to expect. Should I yell, he thought? Should I pound on the wall?

He ran a thumb across the ropes. The area directly between his wrists had roughened. It's working, he thought. It's working…but will my wrists survive? Tom sat in silence and awaited further noise from up above. A few minutes passed—still no sound. Tom continued his efforts working the rope over the screw.

Tom made a decision: get loose first, then consider making noise.

JULIE GOT BACK IN HER CAR AND SPED BACK TO TOM'S HOUSE. She rushed through the front door and grabbed the phone. Julie punched 911. She listened. "I need to talk to Deputy Izzy Felton. It's an emergency…."

She listened some more. "It has to do with the missing Tom Hastings. Have her call me at the Hastings home soon as possible."

Julie grimaced. "Okay, I'll be right here."

She threw up her hands. "Damn, I don't have time for a bunch of questions from the dispatcher," she muttered.

"WHAT DO YOU THINK, IZZY. IS THE GUY ON THE LEVEL?"

"No, I don't. There's a liar behind that perpetual smile. He's obviously a very clever person. Not a single clue around that Hastings was there, but…but I bet he was."

Kelly turned his head for a moment after turning onto the country highway and into New Dresden. "Why do you say that?"

"It's those eyes…one slightly narrower than the other. Usually that's a sign that someone isn't telling the truth."

Kelly slowed for the railroad tracks. He drove on through Main Street, slowing down by Terry Pendleton's home. "What do you think, Izz, should we pay the pale-faced man a call?"

She looked at her watch. "Wouldn't do any good right now. He isn't home from work yet."

"How about if we pay the hardware store another call? I'd like to ask the owner some more questions before the pale-faced man gets home."

"Sure."

Kelly drove around two blocks and pulled up into the Ace Hardware parking lot. They entered and exchanged hellos. walking over to the owner's office. Izzy looked. "Hello, sir."

"Howdy. What's up?"

"Wonder if we could ask you some questions?"

"Sure, come on up. Sorry there's no place to sit."

"Mr. Nelson, have you seen much of Paul Minton or Terry Pendleton lately?"

"Matter of fact I have. Just today, I saw Minton come down Main Street in a white van…big one at that."

Izzy said excitedly, "A van…have you seen it before?"

"No, I haven't."

"You're certain it was Minton?"

"Yup, I caught that smile…none other like it around 'ere."

"How about Pendleton?"

"I haven't seen him, but one of the girls talked about him a few days ago…seems like he bought something."

"Which one of the girls? Can you tell us?"

"Yup. It was Tammy. She's on the floor today."

"Thanks, Mr. Nelson…thank you very much."

Izzy and Kelly walked over to the counter. "We're looking for

Tammy. Anyone here with that name?"

"Uh-oh, what's she done now? Oh my...to jail she goes."

Izzy laughed. "No, not quite. We need to ask her a question."

"I'm Tammy," a woman clerk said, emerging from a side aisle.

"Tammy, your boss said that you waited on a Terry Pendleton recently. Can you tell us what he bought?"

Tammy looked up at the ceiling. "Oh yeah, he bought some bits, all the same size…and also, a good pair of metal side cutters."

Izzy placed a hand on her shoulder. "Thank you, Tammy. You've been a big help."

The deputies got back into their car and the phone rang. "This is Izzy Felton." She listened.

"Kelly, we need to get back to Julie immediately."

59

TOM CONTINUED TO WORK THE SCREW HEAD with the rope around his wrists. His shoulders ached and his wrists felt like raw meat, but he worked the rope back and forth, over and over again. Suddenly, he stopped. His wrists had sprung apart. Tom shook the rope sections off and brought his hands out front. My God, he thought, I've lost so much skin.

He used both hands to remove the tape across his mouth. "Ouch," he muttered. Tom gasped as he tore the rest of the tape away from his head. Then he attempted to untie the rope around his ankles. His fingers felt numb and didn't have the dexterity to do the job. Painfully, he picked up the shelf board and sat down on the floor. Tom used toilet paper to protect his fingers as he once again tightened the screw into the wood. Then he began the tedious process of pulling the board and screw head across the rope.

I can see what I'm doing this time around, he said to himself…

shouldn't take nearly as long. Within an hour, he had the rope off his ankles. Tom stood by the door and pushed. Solid as a rock, he thought. The inner walls were surfaced with tongue and grove pine just as he had noticed earlier.

He tapped on all the walls, deciding that two of them had concrete backing. Then he twisted the shelf brackets out of the wall. Using the bottom of his feet and his weight, he stomped to get rid of most of the bend in both brackets. I'd much rather have a gun, but these are better than nothing.

Tom sat down on the toilet seat and rested. He thought about yelling, but then he concluded that his best chance for survival was to attack his captor or captors when they returned. If I make a lot of noise right now, whoever is up there will come down more prepared. I'm gonna surprise the devil. Maybe I can get lucky.

He picked up the Bible. Maybe this is my best bet right now, he thought. He held it open near the small light and began to read: *There is violence everywhere—one murder after another. That is why your land is in mourning, and everyone is wasting away. Even the wild animals, the birds of the sky, and the fish of the sea are disappearing.* Tom set the book down and slowly shook his head.

Geez, I wonder what Julie thinks. She showed up and I wasn't anywhere. The garage door was open. My car was home. My skis were on the golf cart. She must have had a fit. What would she do first? She'd call the cops sooner or later…hopefully sooner.

Tom felt drowsy. He spread the two blankets out of the floor and lay down. Hey, I can't go to sleep now, he thought anxiously, tightening his grip on one of the brackets. He whispered, "I'm so tired… tired…."

IZZY WRAPPED HER ARMS AROUND JULIE. She listened as Kelly urgently talked to Sheriff Johnson.

Kelly hung up the phone. "Izz, Dave is sending out eight cars! They'll have a court order to search both Paul Minton's place plus Terry Pendleton's again. They'll call us when they get close. The court orders will take a little time, though."

Izzy walked Julie over to the love seat and assisted her in sitting down. "I'll get you some water." She headed for the kitchen.

Izzy opened three cabinet doors before finding a glass. Then she filled it with ice and water from the refrigerator facility. She returned and handed it to Julie. "I've got a hunch that this whole thing is going to turn out fine. From past experiences, Hastings doesn't ever go down without a fight. He has a unique ability to survive. Believe me, we've been here before."

Julie smiled for the first time. She nodded, a tear sliding down her right cheek.

PAUL MINTON PACED AROUND IN HIS KITCHEN. How am I going to steer the cops over to Pendleton's place in a couple of days? he said to himself. Hastings can't last very long. That room is airtight. Paul thought about a similar situation in Chicago when his cohorts sealed up a guy in a room about that size. I give him two days at the most. I could just call the cops anonymously. That's probably my best bet.

He walked toward his bedroom. I could sure use a nap right now, he thought. Suddenly, he stopped. The siren he heard seemed to be coming closer and closer. He walked over to the front window. Then he saw them. Four police cars turned off the highway. They all came in his direction. Damn it, maybe I should make a run for it, he thought. Naw, they've got nothin' on me. They've been here before.

The sirens abated when the vehicles stopped in his driveway, but he could see the reflection of the flashing blue and red lights against the far wall. His heart thumped. He held his breath. He heard a loud knock on the door. His legs felt like wobbly fence posts as he made his way across the room. He opened the door.

"Mr. Minton, I have here a warrant allowing us to search your premises. We will begin immediately. Please find a seat and remain there."

"What the hell's the meaning of this? I have my rights."

The officer held the warrant up for Paul to see. "You may have rights but this paper gives us the okay to do this. Step aside!"

Paul obeyed, trying to smile at the deputies who rapidly moved past him. His felt his confidence sinking as he sauntered over to the couch and sat down. He wondered why the deputies had returned. They appeared satisfied with their previous visit. Who blew the whistle? Surely not Pendleton.

He waited, feeling disgusted as officer after officer moved from one part of his house to another. One of them came up from the lower level carrying a box. "Mr. Minton, can you tell me what's in this box?"

Paul stared in disbelief. He realized that somehow a shipping box of cigarettes had gotten into the lower level. *Pendleton!*

THOR ARRIVED HOME FROM WORK MENTALLY EXHAUSTED. He draped his coat around a metal hanger and hung it. It fell to the floor. *My Lord, do not make this day any more difficult than it already has been,* he said to himself. Angrily, he took off his boots and hung the coat up again. His day had been a tedious one. Two customers had complained about his work...two in one day.

He walked toward the refrigerator and stopped. The *Ice Lord* stared at a smudge on his tile floor about halfway between the basement door and the front door. He opened a cabinet door and removed a rag. Getting down on his knees, he removed the smudge. Thor stood. He saw another smudge near the basement door. His eyes narrowed. *Has that Minton devil been here again?*

Thor walked over to the basement door. He opened it and snapped on the light. He looked down at the steps. I haven't the energy to go down there, he thought. *What could the devil do to me now? He's already tried to put me in prison. The Lord will not permit it. I am safe. I am not sinning. I am working for you, Lord.*

He walked into his sacred room. The altar had been recently resurfaced. Thor had found a new white knitted doily at a craft show he had visited in Baxter. He had placed it in the center, exactly between the two candle sets. Thor got down on his knees. "Oh, Lord, forgive me for any misdeeds I may have committed against you."

Thor prayed in silence for a few minutes. He got up and blew out the candles. He walked into the kitchen for a glass of water. The world lit up around him. Flashing blue, red and white lights splashed through his windows. The sirens he heard moments ago became silent. He stood in agony, holding his breath, waiting. Then, his heart almost stopped hearing the loud rap on the door.

60

IZZY AND KELLY LED THE TEAM OF SHERIFF'S OFFICERS into Terry Pendleton's driveway. They had just returned from Paul Minton's house where they took him into custody. It was enough that he had been seen driving a white van, plus contraband had been discovered in his house.

Izzy turned her face toward the back seat. "I want you to wait in here, Julie, for now. You'll hear from us immediately if we find Tom."

Kelly was about to pound the door for a second time when it opened. "Mr. Pendleton, I have here a warrant giving us permission to search your house and outbuildings."

Thor smiled. "Search all you wish, deputy. I have nothing to hide."

Two teams swept past Izzy and Kelly, heading in different directions inside. "Let's check the basement," Izzy said. "We've been down in that hole before, huh?"

"Okay, let's do it," Martin said.

Izzy opened the door. She snapped on the light. She slid her hand along the rail as she made her way down the steps. Izzy got to the bottom and shone her flashlight in all directions. "What's that over there, Kelly?"

"Looks like a small storage room."

"Yeah, but do you see what I see?'

"God! Yeah! The door is barred. That wasn't here last time, was it?"

"Heck no." Izzy hurried over to the door and lifted off both bars. "Hey, there's some kind of sealant around the door." She grabbed her flashlight and kicked open the door. She gasped. A crumpled body lay on the floor not moving. Izzy knelt down and felt Tom's pulse and listened to his shallow breathing. "Kelly! Get back up there! Call an ambulance! We've found Hastings!"

Kelly ran up the stairwell. He dashed through the front door and got on the car radio. He looked at Julie, seeing fear in her eyes. "We need an ambulance in New Dresden…right now….Emergency! Ah, one block south of the main intersection."

He placed the phone back in its cradle. "We found your friend. Don't know for sure how he is. You can come along if you wish."

Julie walked behind the deputy into Pendleton's house. She saw Pendleton sitting in a chair next to the table. He had his wrists cuffed behind his back. She looked into his eyes. She saw sorrow that she had never ever seen before. I doubt that man is responsible for whatever happened to Tom, she said to herself. I just feel it.

"You wait right here, Julie. I'll check it out and see how he's doing." The deputy rushed down the stairs.

Julie waited anxiously, looking around, seeing officers examining everything in site, going through all the cabinets. She took a seat close to Thor. "Mr. Pendleton, did you kidnap Tom Hastings?"

His eyes filled with tears. He shook his head slowly.

"Then who did?"

Again he shook his head. He parted his lips slightly. "Minton," he whispered.

She saw Kelly stick his head out through the doorway. "Julie, he seems to be okay, but he's groggy from the lack of oxygen. The ambulance should be here soon. You can go along if you wish. But for now, please stay where you are. It's crowded down in the basement."

It seemed like hours to her, but actually only fifteen minutes had passed since an ambulance had been summoned. Suddenly the front door opened and two men in white jackets entered. They followed Deputy Martin down the stairwell.

Minutes later, the deputy stepped into the room, assisting the stretcher bearers. Julie rushed across the room. She saw Tom's forced smile. "Hi, we missed the ski run," he said hoarsely.

She put her palm over his forehead. "Oh, Tom, you're going to be okay."

61

SHERIFF DAVE JOHNSON'S SMILE BRIGHTENED the atmosphere in his office. Deputy Izzy Felton sat in a chair to his left. She rubbed her chin with the knuckle of one of her fingers and returned his smile. Deputy Martin sat next to her, his expression more reserved. Deputy Jackson and County Prosecutor Jack McCarthy occupied the two chairs to the sheriff's right.

The sheriff sifted through a six-page report that Deputy Izzy had prepared for him. The prosecutor held a copy up to his eyes. "You people did a great job. The murder charges against both Terry Pendleton and Paul Minton look solid to me. Then there's the kidnapping of Hastings by Minton. His fingerprints were all over the handle of the wrench that you guys recovered from the basement floor. Besides that we have a list of six Spanish-speaking witnesses who are willing to testify against Minton regarding the cigarette robberies."

Sheriff Johnson ran a hand through his thinning hair. "Who would think that a smart man like Minton would leave his fingerprints all over the stretcher that he used to transport Hastings? Those types of people seem to grow an ego that makes them think they're unstoppable."

Izzy chuckled. "Yeah, and Pendleton not getting rid of the Bibles. Heck, we got a positive ID from the bookstore in Little Falls. Each of the women separately identified him in a lineup."

Deputy Jackson snickered. "Minton got rid of the contraband real well, but he made one mistake…threatening Terry Pendleton. The *Ice Lord* really stuck it to him…snitching a shipping box from the kitchen table and hiding it in a closet in the lower level.

"The look on Pendleton's face when we brought Hastings out of the basement is something I'll never forget. Earlier he had a murder weapon planted in his closet by Minton…and then a kidnapped person in his basement. Imagine how shocked he was on the second one. And then to have one of his Bibles found where Hastings was kept."

Izzy laughed. "Actually, we should thank the *Ice Lord* for sneaking into Minton's house. They sure had it in for each other, and that really helped us solve the crimes. They both had a serious case of egolapsia, especially Minton."

"Egolapsia!" Deputy Martin exclaimed. "What the heck is that?"

"It's sort of like some politicians get. They cannot foresee ever getting caught. Take Nixon…."

Martin held up his hand. "Nixon! How about some others? Would you like me to make a list?"

"Okay, guys," the sheriff interrupted. "That's enough politics. Let's quit while we're ahead," he said, holding back a laugh.

TOM LAY IN BED IN ROOM 431 AT ST. MARY'S HOSPITAL in Big Lakes. He sat up high on three pillows and watched CNBC on television. He heard footsteps in the corridor—they stopped. Tom's stomach tensed. He knew immediately who they belonged to. Julie stuck her head through the doorway. "Hi, how's the patient today?"

Tom looked into her smiling face. "Market's up."

Julie walked up close to the bed and kissed Tom on the lips. He reached out and grabbed her shoulder.

"Ouch," she said. "Wow, you sure haven't lost your strength."

Tom grinned widely as Julie stepped back. "I should get out of this nest soon, hopefully tomorrow."

"Sure. I can come and pick you up," Julie said.

Tom reached out his hand. "Julie...."

"Yes, what is it Tom?" she said, and walked up next to the bed.

"Let's get married...what I mean is: Will you marry me?"

Julie grasped his hand tighter. She placed the palm of her other hand on Tom's cheek. Her face flushed slightly. "Could I delay my answer for a short time? We need to get you out of the hospital first."

Tom's smile eroded. His facial expression changed to a forced grin. He nodded. The tension in his stomach returned.

TOM MADE THE TURN ONTO ROCKY POINT ROAD. His things were all packed into a suitcase that Julie had brought him during his first day in the hospital. It lay on the back seat. His return was solo because Julie had to leave town. Tom wasn't sure why.

I've sure got a great neighbor, he thought. Pete delivered my vehicle to the hospital. Tom felt rather uncomfortable earlier watching a nurse's expression as he got up off the wheelchair in the parking lot—and right into his SUV.

He felt great, totally recovering from the lack of oxygen. Geez, the doctor said I would've been gone in another couple of hours. I have to thank both Julie and Deputy Izzy. Without their immediate action, I would've....

Tom turned up the short steep hill, a short distance from where his old friend Maynard was murdered. He glanced at the house, nestled on a slope of a hill. Smoke funneled straight up from the chimney. Geez, I've forgotten the name of the culprit who killed him. Oh wait, it was....

He shook his head. I had it right on the tip of my tongue. Oh well, doesn't matter anymore. Tom left the township road and drove down his roadway. Suddenly a bulky bird flew across the roadway.

"Keeya is back," he muttered. Early this year he thought. We're going to have an early spring.

Tom looked for deer as his vehicle approached his house. He realized that the son of Prancer had lost his horns by now—wouldn't be the same if I spotted him now, he thought. He didn't see any of the four-legged creatures, but did spot a flock of large turkeys hastily strolling away from the base of the three spruce trees that were close to his front door. He pressed the button and the garage door went up. Tom drove his vehicle in and turned the key. Home again, he said to himself.

Tom rolled his suitcase down the sloped sidewalk and unlocked the front door. He entered and wished someone would have started his woodstove. Within minutes, he had a flame going. Tom's eyes continually scanned the snow covered bay. Instead of ice and snow, he saw Julie's face. He sighed, shaking his head.

I guess I knew all along that it wasn't going to work out, he said to himself. I need a new start. Someone new. Tom went on the Internet with one of his computers. He remembered seeing an ad on television—eHarmony.

Tom filled out some blanks. Then he looked out through the window and saw the snow. I can't do this right now…much too soon. He pressed *Cancel.*

He stood and walked into the kitchen, opened the refrigerator door and fetched a beer. Tom returned to the computer. Ah, what the heck, I'm gonna do it, he said to himself.

Tom returned to his garage and backed his SUV out onto the driveway. His mail would have filled his post office box by now. Tom slowed passing by Minton's place. A *For Sale* sign identified Big lakes Realty. Geez, that's Jolene's outfit, he said to himself. Two vehicles were parked in the driveway. One of them was a Toyota 4Runner SUV. That's hers—no doubt about it.

He U-turned on Main Street, pulling up to the curb next to the post office. Snowbirds aren't back yet, he thought—lots of curbside parking places. Tom fished out his mail and returned to his vehicle, placing it on the passenger seat. He walked toward Stillman's, waving at Wendy Sanderson who was crossing the street, coming from the bank, angling toward the post office.

"Well, you're back," said Ellie at checkout.

"Yup, and in one piece, too. How are things here?"

"Just fine, but...."

"But what?"

"Have you heard about the robberies?"

Tom stood next to the checkout counter, amused. "Robberies... come on now, I thought we were all done with that. What happened?"

"William's Pub had their safe taken. Someone apparently hid in the building while they locked up for the night. Then Spanky's got broken into. The thieves took the computer and cash register."

Tom shook his head. "Hmmm, no cigarettes this time. Neither place would be carrying them after October 1—not after the recent Minnesota law banning smoking in public places."

Ellis nodded. "No cigarettes, but get this!"

Tom edged forward.

"Someone found the cash register in the ditch of the state highway on the way to Pine Lakes...."

"Yeah, and?"

"There was still some money in it."

Tom scratched his eyebrow. "I'm staying out of this one. Deputy Kelly can't suspect me. I've got an ironclad alibi."

Ellie laughed.

Tom left the supermarket and headed for home. Back in his house, he was pleased that two finches shared his bird feeder with the nuthatches and chickadees. They're back, he said to himself.

He sat down at his computer and brought up his e-mail. eHarmony, the Internet dating site, already had a message for him. Geez, a woman from Rockford, Illinois, has responded to my profile. He enlarged the first photo. Awesome, he thought. He scanned through a series of photographs—the one with the woman perched on a mountain peak in Peru held his attention. I may as well forget her. She would be making international reservations every week.

Suddenly, Tom spotted some movement down on the snow-covered bay. "It's a coyote!" he exclaimed. Look at that tail—that strut—the head held so high—this is rare. It prances right out in the open. This animal is in charge!

Tom looked back at the picture on his computer screen, then the coyote—then back at the picture. Something rare here, he thought. The picture and the coyote both show up at the same time—they blend. The Spirits!—they're trying to tell me something. What?

<u>$16.95 EACH</u>
(plus $3.95 shipping & handling for first book, add $2.00 for each additional book ordered.
Shipping and Handling costs for larger quantites available upon request.

PLEASE INDICATE NUMBER OF COPIES YOU WISH TO ORDER

_______ BLUE DARKNESS
_______ THE TOWERS
_______ DANGER IN THE KEYS
_______ NIGHT OUT IN FARGO
_______ PURGATORY CURVE
_______ GRAY RIDERS
_______ SLEEP SIX
_______ GRAY RIDERS II
_______ ICE LORD

Bill my: ❑ VISA ❑ MasterCard Expires ____________

Card # ____

Signature ____

Daytime Phone Number ______________________________

For credit card orders call 1-888-568-6329

OR SEND THIS ORDER FORM TO:
J&M Printing • PO Box 248 • Gwinner, ND 58040-0248

I am enclosing $_______________ ❑ Check ❑ Money Order
Payable in US funds. No cash accepted.

SHIP TO:

Name ____

Mailing Address _____________________________________

City ____

State/Zip ____

Orders by check allow longer delivery time. Money order and credit card orders will be shipped within 48 hours. This offer is subject to change without notice.

THE HASTINGS SERIES

Blue Darkness
(First in a Series of Hastings Books)
This tale of warm relationships and chilling murders takes place in the lake country of central Minnesota. Normal activities in the small town of New Dresen are disrupted when local resident, ex-CIA agent Maynard Cushing, is murdered. His killer, Robert Ranforth also an ex-CIA agent, had been living anonymously in the community for several years. Stalked and attached at his country home, Tom Hastings employs tools and people to mount a defense and help solve crimes.
Written by Ernest Francis Schanilec (276 pgs.)
ISBN: 1-931916-21-7
$16.95 each in a 6x9" paperback.

The Towers
(Second in a Series of Hastings Books)
Tom Hastings' move to Minneapolis was precipitated by the trauma associated with the murder of one of his neighbors. After renting a high-rise apartment in a building known as The Towers, he's met new friends and retained his relationship with a close friend, Julie, from St. Paul. Hastings is a resident for less than a year when a young lady is found murdered next to a railroad track, a couple of blocks from The Towers. The murderer shares the same elevators, lower-level garage and other areas in the highrise as does Hastings. The building manager and other residents, along with Hastings are caught up in dramatic events that build to a crisis while the local police are baffled. Who is the killer?
Written by Ernest Francis Schanilec. (268 pgs.)
ISBN: 1-931916-23-3
$16.95 each in a 6x9" paperback.

Danger In The Keys
(Third in a Series of Hastings Books)
Tom Hastings is looking forward to a month's vacation in Florida. While driving through Tennessee, he witnesses an automobile leaving the road and plunging down a steep slope. The driv-

er, a young woman, survives the accident. Tom is totally unaware that the young woman was being chased because she had chanced coming into possession of a valuable gem, which had been heisted from a Saudi Arabian prince. After arriving in Key Marie Island in Florida, Tom meets many interesting people, however, some of them are on the island because of the Guni gem, and they will stop at nothing in order to gain possession. Desperate people and their greedy ambitions interrupt Tom's goal of a peaceful vacation. Written by Ernest Francis Schanilec. (210 pgs.) ISBN: 1-931916-28-4
$16.95 each in a 6x9" paperback.

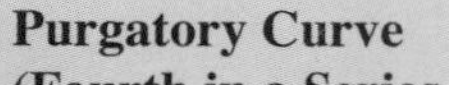

Purgatory Curve
(Fourth in a Series of Hastings Books)
A loud horn penetrated the silence in New Dresden, Minnesota. Tom Hastings stepped onto the Main Street sidewalk and heard a freight train coming and watched in horror as it crushed a pickup truck that was stalled on the railroad tracks. Moments before the crash, he saw someone jump from the cab. An elderly farmer's body was later recovered from the mangled vehicle. Tom was interviewed by the sheriff the next day and was upset that his story about what he saw wasn't believed. The tragic death of the farmer was surrounded with controversy and mysterious people, including a nephew who taunted Tom after the accident. Or, was it an accident?
Written by Ernest Francis Schanilec. (210 pgs.)
ISBN: 1-931916-29-2
$16.95 each in a 6x9" paperback.

Gray Riders
(Fifth in a Series of Hastings Books)
This is a flashback to Schanilec's Hastings Series mystery novels where Tom Hastings is the main character. Tom's great-grandfather, Thomas, lives on a farm with his family in western Missouri in 1861. The local citizenry react to the Union calvary by organizing and forming an armed group of horsemen who become known as the Gray Riders. The Riders not only defend their families and properties, but also ride with the Confederate Missouri Guard. They participate in three major battles. Written by Ernest Francis Schanilec. (266 pgs.)
ISBN: 1-931916-38-1
$16.95 each in a 6x9" paperback.

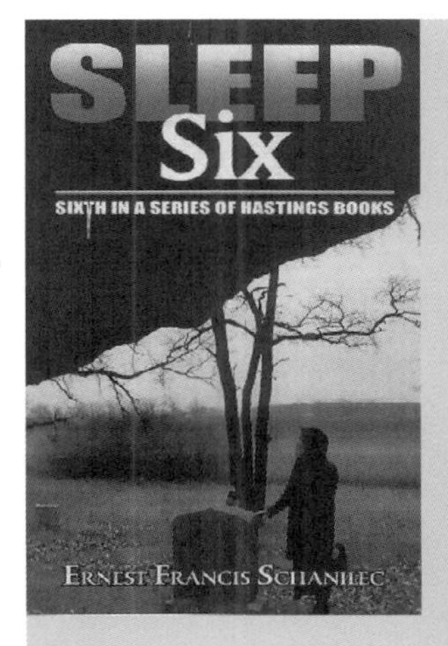

Sleep Six (Sixth in a Series of Hastings Books)
Revenge made Birdie Hec quit her job in Kansas City and move to New Dresden, Minnesota. A discovery after her mother's funeral had rekindled her memory of an abuse incident that had happened when she was six years old. An envelope containing six photographs, four of them with names, revealed some of her mother's abusers. Birdie moved into an apartment complex in New Dresden, using an anonymous name. She befriended three other women, who were all about the same age. While socializing with her new friends, Birdie scouted her potential victims. She plotted the demise of the four men whom she had definitely recognized...
Written by Ernest Francis Schanilec (250 pgs.)
ISBN: 1-931916-40-3
$16.95 each in a 6x9" paperback.

Night Out In Fargo
(Seventh in a Series of Hastings Books)
Tom Hastings property is within view of the senator's lake complex, and once again he is pulled into the world of greed and hard-striking criminals.Hastings is confused, not only because of the suspenseful activities at the senator's complex but also the strange hissing sound in the cornfield next to his property. Armed guards block him from investigating the mystery at the abandoned farmstead. Why are they there, and what are they hiding? Written by Ernest Schanilec.
ISBN: 1-931916-44-6 (280 pages)
$16.95 each in a 6x9" paperback.

Gray Riders II
(Eighth in a Series of Hastings Books)
The Gray Riders are in the saddle again, battling the Union in Western Missouri and protecting the folks of Tarrytown from ruthless jayhawkers. But their biggest threat comes from within - when an albino mountain man named Bone Erloch sets his sights on Sarah, Tom Hasting's pregnant wife. Gray Riders II brings back Grady, Justin Haggard, and all of his saddle mates. There is no shortage of new arrivals to spice up life in Tarrytown. So

saddle up, it's time for a wild ride.
Written by Ernest Schanilec. ISBN: 978-1-931914-50-5 (276 pages)
$16.95 each in a 6x9" paperback.

Ice Lord
(Ninth in a Series of Hastings Books)
Tom finds himself up against a killer who haunts the fishing houses on Border's Lake. Tom spots the first burning house from his back deck, and is forever sucked into a world of vengeance and greed where it will take all his wiles to stay on top of thieving thugs, wisecracking bullies, two women who want his love, and a solemn murderer who believes he is carrying out God's will. The January ice will never feel so chilly again.
Written by Ernest Schanilec.
ISBN: 978-1-931916-56-1 (264 pages)
$16.95 each in a 6x9" paperback.